As
RED
AS
ANY BLOOD

Wisteria Tearoom Mysteries

A Fatal Twist of Lemon
A Sprig of Blossomed Thorn
An Aria of Omens
A Bodkin for the Bride
A Masquerade of Muertos
As Red as Any Blood

Related Stories

"Intermezzo: Spirit Matters"
(a Wisteria Tearoom Interlude)

AS RED AS ANY BLOOD

PATRICE GREENWOOD

Evennight Books/Book View Café
Cedar Crest, New Mexico

This is a work of fiction. All of the characters, organizations, and events portrayed in this novel are either products of the author's imagination or are used fictitiously.

AS RED AS ANY BLOOD

Copyright © 2017 by Patrice Greenwood

An Evennight Book
Published by Book View Café Publishing Cooperative
P.O. Box 1624
Cedar Crest, NM 87008

www.bookviewcafe.com

Cover photo: Pati Nagle
Map illustrations: Chris Krohn and Patrice Greenwood

ISBN: 978-1-61138-704-9

First Edition November 2017

for Chris

Acknowledgments

Thanks yet again to my wonderful publication team for their help with this novel: Doranna Durgin, Sherwood Smith, Sally Gwylan, and Chris Krohn; to my dear friends and patient consultants Ken and Marilyn Dusenberry; and to my colleagues in Book View Café.

And as always, thanks to Mary Alice Higbie and the staff of the St. James Tearoom, who not only inspired the creation of this series, but whose world-class establishment is the closest one can get to visiting the Wisteria Tearoom itself.

The holly bears a berry, as red as any blood,
And Mary bore sweet Jesus Christ to do poor sinners good.

"The Holly and the Ivy," traditional carol

EVEN THOUGH IT WAS A MONDAY, you wouldn't think my tearoom was closed. Mouth-watering aromas wafted from the kitchen, where Julio was getting a head start on the week's baking. Fires in the parlor fireplaces added warmth and the comforting scent of piñon resin to a chilly, overcast day. Kris, the office manager, and my aunt Nat were in the gift shop, loading up the shelves with holiday merchandise. Servers Dee and Rosa bustled around the parlors, adding seasonal touches to the décor, and the stereo played a rotation of classical music and traditional Christmas carols. No doubt we'd get tired of that by the end of December, but today it made the place festive.

It was the day after Thanksgiving weekend, and our last day to prepare for the holidays. I sat in the dining parlor, sipping allspice-and-cranberry scented tea (our own new holiday blend), and watching through the French doors for snow while I did the floral arrangements for the week. Humming along with the music, I filled vases and lidless teapots with red and white roses, sprigs of holly, and trailing tendrils of ivy harvested from the north wall of the house.

After a wonderful Thanksgiving dinner with my buddy Gina's boisterous Italian family, I'd spent Saturday and Sunday putting up three Christmas trees: one by the front door, one in the center of the main parlor, and one in the gift shop to display ornaments for sale. Aunt Nat and Tio Manny had helped. Outdoors, we had a wreath on the door and little lavender balls adorning the bare wisteria vines that twined around the pillars of the *portal*.

1

Despite their prevalence on the rooftops of many Santa Fe businesses, I refused to use fake electric "luminarias," which I'd always abhorred. *Luminarias* were little bonfires, not paper bags. Instead we had twinkle lights around the front windows, and I planned to put out real *farolitos* (the traditional candle-and-paper-bag decorations that had inspired the electric "luminarias") on Christmas Eve.

A tap-tap on the open parlor door made me look up. Julio stood there, smiling, with a small plate in his hand. At one temple a curl of his dark hair had escaped the hairnet he wore under his red baker's cap, giving him a rakish look.

"Hi, Ellen. Need a break?" he said.

"That depends. Are those biscochitos?"

"Yep."

"Then I do."

His smile widened as he joined me at the table. I pushed a bowl of ivy cuttings aside to make room for the plate, and reached for a cookie as he set it down.

"Wait a minute." I stopped, my hand over the plate. "Is this a bribe?"

He gave a soft laugh. "Kinda."

I picked up my teacup and sipped, leaning back as I gazed at him. "What do you want?"

"Wednesday off?"

"Oh, Julio! Why not last week?"

"I'm moving. Didn't have the new place last week."

"Moving?"

A little flutter of alarm began beneath my breastbone. Certainly Julio had a right to move, but if his life was changing, it might affect his work. Specifically, he might start thinking about changing jobs. That terrified me.

"Adam too?" I asked tentatively.

"No, ah…he's got a partner, and they're getting pretty serious. They want to live together."

"He asked you to move out? Oh, Julio!"

"No, no. Actually I wanted to move. It's good timing, really." He nodded to affirm this, then cleared his throat. "I just need one day to move the big furniture. I'll be back Thursday morning, promise. I'll prep all the fancy stuff for Wednesday tomorrow, and Hanh can handle the scones and cookies."

I picked up a crescent-shaped biscochito, stifling a sigh, and bit a third of it off. The cinnamon-sugar crusted cookie melted in my mouth, leaving a whisper of anise behind. "Not like these."

Julio's eyes crinkled as he grinned.

I paused, cookie halfway to my mouth. "She made these?"

He nodded. I took another bite, paying critical attention now. Texture, flavor, aroma—all excellent, leaving me wanting more. The biscochito was perfect.

"All right. Better now than later in the month."

"Thanks, Boss!"

He stood and strolled out, looking so pleased that I couldn't be annoyed about the inconvenience. He had chosen well; Wednesday would probably be slow—or at least not as hectic as the rest of the week. And Julio would be here on Tuesday to make sure everything was going smoothly with the December menu.

I ate the last of the biscochito, wondering for the zillionth time if I had enough staff for the busy holiday season. With our new junior chef, Hanh Mai (or Mai Hanh, properly—but confusing to us Westerners), working full-time and Ramon part-time in the kitchen, we were probably all right. Up front in the tearoom, we now had four servers including the new hire, Dale Whittier, one of Kris's Goth friends. Nat could help in a pinch, and so could I.

Breathe, I told myself. We'll be fine.

My phone rang and I grabbed it, hoping the caller was Tony. It wasn't. I loved Gina, but I had to wait an extra ring before answering, to make sure she wouldn't hear the disappointment in my voice.

"Hi, Gina."

"Have you seen the news?"

"You know my TV's in storage."

"Yeah, but you might have seen this online. Debbie Fisher."

"Debbie Fisher?"

"Yeah, from our class. She's been murdered."

We watched the coverage—lead story on the six o'clock news—on a big screen in the lobby bar at the Inn at Loretto. Gina had picked me up, and I'd left my office manager, Kris, in charge of locking up the tearoom after everyone was gone for the day. Now, seated in a tall, wing-backed chair that should have been comfortable but wasn't, I cradled a large glass of Merlot in my hands as I listened to the details of Debbie's murder. Only fragments of the newscaster's report reached my brain, which was busy with memories of the girl Gina and I had gone to high school with.

"Found in her home…lived alone…stabbed multiple times… robbery was not a motive…any information…"

The photo on the screen had been taken recently, I supposed. It was recognizably Debbie, with the sly smile that had always been her trademark, but older. She wore a tailored business jacket, and her hair was shorter than I remembered, with pale highlights brightening what had been mousy brown in high school. The shot they showed of her home was of a fancy townhouse, so she must have been doing well financially. She looked good, except for a couple of lines on her forehead. And the fact that she was dead.

"Had you seen her lately?" I asked Gina when the reporter switched to another story.

Gina took a swallow of wine and shook her head. "Not since graduation."

"Me neither."

We hadn't been close. We'd hung out a bit in mid school—slumber parties, Girl Scout meetings—but by high school our interests had diverged. Debbie had gone the popularity route: she became a cheerleader, dated jocks, was runner-up for homecoming queen. I had gone the artsy music-and-theater route. We'd lost touch, and I found myself feeling guiltily relieved about that.

"Do her parents still live here? We should write to them."

"Her dad does," Gina said. "And her sister, but she's married, and I think she changed her name. Her mom died, I guess. Anyway the story I heard earlier just mentioned her dad. Let's see what the other stations have."

Gina got up to ask the bartender to change the channel. I took a deep swallow of wine. It was already going to my head, since I hadn't eaten, but I didn't care.

Poor Debbie. No one deserved to be murdered in their own home. This was a sad start to the busiest, jolliest time of year.

At least I didn't find the body.

I hadn't been near Debbie in years, and she hadn't been near the tearoom. This one had nothing to do with me.

Well, almost.

Gina came back in possession of the remote, and surfed until she found another story about Debbie. This time it wasn't the anchor, but a field reporter live from outside Debbie's townhouse, shivering in the evening chill, with obligatory squad cars and flashing lights in the background. Not much new detail, except for the fact that Debbie had worked at a local bank. Must not have been mine, because I'd never seen her there.

It was dusk, but the lights from the police cars lit up the background enough for me to see a man in a dark motorcycle jacket, shoulders hunched against the cold wind, walking past the yellow tape toward the door. I took a deep breath.

"Is that who I think it is?" Gina asked.

"Probably."

"Lucky him."

"It's his job." I took another swig of wine, figuring I knew what Tony Aragón would be doing for the next few days.

The story ended, and Gina looked for another, but no luck. The news had moved on to politics, weather, and sports. Gina returned the remote to the bar and came back. "Want to get something to eat?"

I looked at the dregs in my glass. "I should."

"Luminaria OK?"

The hotel's restaurant was pricey, but it had the advantage of being right there. The food was excellent, too.

"Sure."

It being Monday, and the day after a holiday weekend, we had no trouble getting a table at Luminaria. Too cold to sit outside, but there was only one other party in the place: a group of five dressed for business, quietly chatting over beer and appetizers at a table in the middle of the restaurant. Our waiter showed us past empty tables with lonely candles flickering in their frosted glasses to a booth along the wall. We slid in side by side and ordered more wine.

"So who would want to kill Debbie?" Gina asked.

I shrugged. "Half the cheerleading squad?"

Gina's dark eyes narrowed. "Or Mary Cunningham. She *hated* Debbie."

"Yeah."

I hadn't thought about it in years, but Debbie had been dating Steve Sawyer, the homecoming king, when Mary was his queen. I didn't quite remember why Mary and not Debbie had been queen. It had been a big scandal at the time, by high school standards. The two girls had hated each other's guts.

"Whatever happened to Mary?" I asked.

"Moved to Salt Lake and joined the Mormons. Last I heard she had four kids."

"Oh."

The waiter took our order, then brought our wine and a bread basket, and left us to our ruminations. We talked over every classmate we could think of who'd had the slightest grudge against Debbie. None of it seemed grounds for murder, but then—nothing really was. Nothing in the life of a normal high school kid, anyway.

And none of them were still in Santa Fe. Gina and I were among only a handful who'd stayed, or returned after college. Gina ticked them off on her fingers.

"Michael Guzman, nerd extraordinaire. No interest in girls in school. Now at the Santa Fe Institute."

"Still no interest in girls?" I asked.

"I don't know. Sarah Porter, jockette. Definite interest in girls, but not in Debbie. Currently working for the Forest Service."

I took a blue corn mini-muffin from the bread basket, hoping to mitigate the effects of the wine.

"Careful, those disintegrate," Gina commented.

"I know. But they're good."

I put the muffin on my bread plate, added a smear of butter to the plate, and gingerly broke (you couldn't say cut) the muffin with my knife. I buttered a piece as well as possible without destroying it further, and ate it.

"Erica Wegman," Gina continued as she swirled her wine in the glass. "Valedictorian. Turned up her nose at Debbie, but I don't think she hated her. Probably thought she wasn't important enough to hate."

"Where's Erica now?"

"Waiting tables at the Compound."

"Oh! I had no idea."

The Compound was one of the most expensive restaurants in Santa Fe, far above my budget. Anyone waiting tables there was probably making good money, but it was rather a step down for Erica.

"Didn't she get a full scholarship to Yale?" I asked.

"Harvard."

"I thought she would have been a doctor by now."

"Yeah." Gina pulled a pencil-thin bread stick from the basket and bit off the tip. "Danny Snow. Had one date with Debbie, then dumped her for Gloria Dixon. They got married two years ago."

"I never heard!"

Gina nodded sagely. "They've got a kid. Danny owns an auto repair shop out on Cerrillos Road."

"He was always good with his hands."

Gina gave me a raised eyebrow.

"No," I said, glowering at her. "I mean he got A's in shop and all that. And he was the best drummer in marching band."

"Right." Gina sipped her wine.

"What about Gloria? Did she know Debbie?"

"I don't think so. She was into math and chemistry. I think she was working as a nurse at St. Vincent's until she had the kid."

"She didn't go back to work?"

"Nah. Danny makes good money." Gina finished her bread stick and peered into the basket, then extracted a sourdough roll.

"Dickie Hernandez," she continued as she tore the roll apart. "Skated through school with a C average. Sells insurance now."

"Did he even know Debbie?"

"No idea."

"You know, it probably wasn't someone from our class," I said. "More likely it was someone Debbie knows—knew—now, not back in high school."

"Yeah, you're right. But it's fun to play the game."

"You sure have kept up with folks," I remarked, picking up another muffin crumb.

Gina shrugged. "I send out a chatty Christmas letter. People send back notes, sometimes after New Year's. I guess they feel guilty for not having enough news to fill a sheet of paper."

I nodded, acknowledging that feeling. To be honest, I'd never thought people would be interested in a sheet of paper filled with what I had done all year.

Not until this year, anyway. This year had been pretty interesting. Twelve months ago I had been unpacking boxes and learning all I could about tea and about running a business. My life had changed profoundly since then.

I hadn't even thought about holiday cards yet. Ay yi yi.

"How's Tony?" Gina asked.

I shot her a look. "You just saw him on TV."

"I assume you know more than what I saw."

I hunched a shoulder and drank more wine. I'd had one conversation with Tony in the past week, and it hadn't exactly been comfortable. We'd gone out for coffee after almost a month of not seeing each other. I was nervous, and Tony was distant. He'd been really, *really* angry with me for what he saw as my interference in his investigation of Gabriel Rhodes' death. But I'd had no choice, as I saw it. I'd kept him from arresting an innocent person.

I was wrong, he'd said into his coffee cup, and I'd thanked him.

But so were you. I can't have you go around me like that. It could cost me my job.

I knew it was true. I'd apologized, and while he said he was working on forgiving me, I felt as though our relationship had taken a big step backward.

"You didn't bring him to Thanksgiving," Gina said softly.

"He had dinner with his own family."

"They didn't ask you?"

"Gina…"

"OK, sorry. None of my business."

Our entrées arrived. I didn't have much appetite, and picked at my salmon while Gina attacked her steak.

My mind followed Tony into that stylish townhouse. I didn't want to think about what he was seeing in there. Even though I hadn't seen Debbie in years, even though we'd never been close, I felt threatened by her death. As though my comfortable world had suddenly become less safe.

Safety was an illusion, I knew. Disaster could change your life forever in an eyeblink. Not just murder; there were plenty of other catastrophes that could strike without warning.

I stared blindly at my plate, thinking how grateful I was for all that I had, knowing that it was all so fragile.

"That photo of the biscochitos is a hit," Gina said. "It's getting the best response of any of your ads."

"That's great," I said, reaching for my water glass.

"You were totally right about that. Would you mind sharing the name of your photographer? We might want to use him for some future work."

"Owen Hughes. I'll give you his card."

"Thanks. More wine?" She picked up the bottle.

I shook my head. "I think I've had enough."

"OK."

Gina filled her own glass. Wine never got to her. Growing up in a big, loud, happy Italian family, she'd learned to drink it like water.

Margaritas, on the other hand, were her weak spot. Italian DNA seemed not to bestow any resistance to tequila.

She chattered on about our ad campaign, occasionally tossing me an easy question. My answers were brief, almost Tony-like. I wasn't in the mood, but I did appreciate her sticking with a safe topic.

When she'd finished her steak, the waiter came and gave us an inquiring look. I indicated I was done as well, and declined the opportunity to peruse the dessert menu. If there was one thing I had plenty of in my life, it was sweets.

"Want to come in for a biscochito?" I asked Gina when she pulled up behind my house.

"No, thanks. Early to rise and all that." She caught me in an awkward, front seat hug, and smooched my cheek. "Sleep well, sugar."

"You, too. Don't watch the late news."

She laughed. I got out of the car, hugging my coat to myself against the cold wind. Gina waited until I was inside and had turned on the hall light before backing out.

I was loved, I reminded myself. I had Gina and Nat and Manny.

And Tony, though I wasn't as confident about that.

And Captain Dusenberry. Even if he couldn't offer hugs, I believed that he cared about me.

Wanting comfort, I turned on more lights and walked through the parlors. Everything was ready for the morning. The trees glistened, the floral arrangements gave the alcoves a bit of holiday cheer, and the twinkle lights in the front windows brought back childhood memories of wonder and magic. Watching them gently change colors, I felt better. I left them on, turning off the overhead lights before going upstairs.

It was late, but just in case Tony had decided to email, I turned on my computer. I made a cup of peppermint tea while it booted, and sat at my desk sipping gingerly while I brought up my email.

Nothing from Tony, but there was a message from a vaguely familiar address. I opened it.

Hey, Sis -

Got a spare bedroom? I'm coming home for Christmas.

- Joe

I HADN'T SEEN MY BROTHER SINCE OUR FATHER'S FUNERAL. We'd talked, of course—quite a lot in the months right after Dad died—but I'd been so busy since the tearoom opened that our communications had fallen off a bit. He had meant to come out for Nat's wedding, but wound up staying in New York to deal with an emergency at work. He was a financial consultant at a huge bank on Wall Street.

I hit "reply" and typed:

> You know that I don't. You were going to stay with Nat, remember?

I deleted that and tried again.

> How wonderful! I don't have a guest room, but Nat does. Have you told her you're coming?

Better. I hit "send" and shut down the computer, then retreated to my suite and indulged in a hot, rose-scented bath before bed.

As I soaked, I tried to figure out why I'd been irritated by Joe's message. I loved him. I hadn't seen him for almost three years. He was three years older than me, and had been kindly tolerant of his tag-along kid sister until he left for college. Before Dad died, he had come home every Christmas and Thanksgiving, and usually a couple more times during the year. I'd always been glad to see him. Why wasn't I glad about it now?

The timing, possibly. Now that I was running a restaurant, the holiday season would be busy and probably stressful for me.

Or maybe my annoyance was left over from his having missed our aunt's wedding. His last-minute cancellation had been a disappointment.

Neither of those felt like the true reason. I scrubbed at my heels with my foot brush, thinking about the last time I'd seen Joe. He'd looked well, although he wasn't quite his cheerful self. He'd brought a case of Irish whiskey—Dad's favorite—for the memorial, "to give him a proper send-off."

Maybe that was it. Maybe Joe was reminding me of that time.

I found myself increasing the salinity of my bath water with a few tears. I let them go, scrubbing a little harder at my feet. If sad memories were what bothered me about hearing from Joe, then I was glad he was coming home. We needed to make some new and better ones.

Next morning, December 1, we were off and running with the holiday season. Bookings were unusually high for a Tuesday, especially around midday and at four o'clock, the traditional teatime. People were out shopping in earnest now, and wanted a festive meal.

Kris and I had decided on an experiment: since the dining parlor was often empty unless unless it was booked for a private party, we offered cream tea there for those who just wanted a quick bite and a cuppa. My table could seat up to a dozen, and as the day got busy it looked to be working well as community seating. I glanced in a couple of times and saw small parties chatting together across the table.

The gift shop was bustling all morning. Usually the servers just kept an eye on it as they waited on the alcoves, but by eleven thirty it was clear that this wouldn't do for December, and I stationed myself there for the day. Many people came in just to shop, and others who walked in, hoping to be seated for afternoon tea without a reservation, assuaged disappointment by splurging on merchandise. We were selling lots of packaged tea, and the biscochitos were flying out of the small pastry case by the register.

Just before noon, the jingle of the bells hanging on the front door was followed by a strident and familiar voice that made me wince despite myself.

"Oh, good," pronounced the Bird Woman heartily. "About time this joint decked the halls! What do you think of this tree, Shirley? Great ornaments, but I can't find the price tags."

I stepped into the hall, to find the Bird Woman standing by the tree there, with several of her friends huddled around her like chicks around a diminutive hen. Though the day was milder than Monday had been, with the sun flirting between puffy clouds and only a light, cool breeze, the Bird Woman was bundled in an enormous, tiger-striped, fake-fur coat and matching hat of improbable plushness.

"Hello, Mrs. Olavssen," I said brightly. "Merry Christmas!"

She smiled, her face crinkling. "Merry Christmas back atcha, dearie! How much is this?"

She held up an ornament of a Victorian snow fairy. I gently removed it from her hand and restored it to the tree.

"They're for sale in the shop, if you'd like to look."

She waved a dismissive hand, then took off her hat. "We'll check it out after tea. I'm starving. Is our table ready?"

"Right this way," I said, ushering them into the main parlor.

They had reserved Iris, one of the larger alcoves, which had both a window and shared access to the fireplace. I kept an eye on the Bird Woman as we passed the tree in the middle of the parlor, but though her bright eyes took in the ornaments there, she didn't pluck any. Instead she peeled off the tiger coat, revealing a velour jumpsuit of an eye-popping red, with a necklace of multicolored tiny Christmas lights that actually lit up, blinking much like the lights in my windows. I collected the tiger coat and hat along with the other ladies' coats, promised they would have tea at once, and hurried out to the hall.

Dale was coming toward me, looking snappy in a dark green vest, pale gray dress shirt, and silver brocade tie, brown curls brushing his forehead. Since he was the tearoom's first male server, he'd had the honor of establishing the wardrobe style for that role, to complement the lavender dresses and lace-trimmed aprons of the other servers. We had discussed more formal attire—he had argued for a morning coat—and decided that, with the possible exception of special occasions, a vest and tie were appropriate for someone who would spend much of his day fetching and carrying.

The main parlor alcoves were Dale's responsibility that day. He had only dealt with the Bird Woman once before.

"Mrs. Olavssen's party is here," I told him, hanging the tiger monstrosity on a hook. "You can handle her?"

Dale, nodded as he relieved me of some of the coats. "I just flirt with her. She loves it."

"Whatever works. Go ahead and pour for them, I'll finish this."

He nodded and made an about-face, heading for the butler's pantry where their first pot of tea should be waiting. I finished hanging the coats and went back to the gift shop.

Having the Bird Woman in the tearoom always made me nervous. I never knew what she would do. Consequently, I was a bit distracted over the next two hours, and had to fight an impulse to pop across the hall every few minutes to see what she was up to. Once, I actually gave in, but Dale came out of the main parlor as I reached the door of the gift shop, and gave me a grin and a thumbs up before hustling down the hall. Trusting that he had things in hand, I returned to my station.

Apart from one burst of feminine laughter shortly after Dale took in their food, and later on a chorus of "Deck the Halls" (only slightly off key) sung along with the house stereo system, the Bird Woman's party behaved themselves. They departed in good spirits, with Dale fetching their coats and ushering them out of the parlor in time to prepare Iris for the next reservation. I admit I was impressed with the way he handled them.

With her retinue following, the Bird Woman wandered into the gift shop, fondled every item of holiday merchandise on display, and made her way to the register with a selected armful of them. "You gonna have any tours this month?" she asked as she handed me her credit card.

"Tours?"

"You know, with the ghost lady."

"Oh—Willow Lane? No, that was just for October."

"Too bad. You could call it the Tea Ghost of Christmas Past. Right?" she said, looking at her friends, who obligingly laughed.

I managed a smile. "That's a thought. Maybe next year."

Just as I handed the Bird Woman her receipt, Rosa came in with a fresh tray of biscochitos for the pastry case.

"Ooo, give me a dozen of those," said the Bird Woman. "Those bisco-jobbers. They're great! Here, I got cash."

She whipped out a twenty-dollar bill. I traded a look with Rosa, who slid the tray into the case and started filling a little carry-out box with cookies while I rang up the sale. I stuck a tiny red bow on the box and handed it to the Bird Woman along with her change.

"Thanks, dearie! See you next week," she chirped as she headed for the front door.

Next week?

After seeing her party out, I checked the reservations log. Sure enough, the Bird Woman had a reservation for the following Tuesday.

And the Thursday a week after that. And again, two days before Christmas.

I closed my eyes, reminding myself that she was one of my best and most faithful customers. I was grateful—*grateful*—for the Bird Woman.

After two thirty, things calmed down a bit, and I asked Rosa to watch the gift shop while I went up to my office to call Nat. On my way, I looked in at the kitchen.

Julio was still there, prepping savories for the next day. Hanh was at the industrial mixer and didn't look up, her narrow face fixed in serious concentration, her long, black hair confined by a hairnet. She was petite, but that did not preclude her being formidable. I didn't know her well yet, and I was a little intimidated by her.

Because of the noise the mixer made, I didn't bother trying to talk to them. I just traded smiles with Julio and with Mick, the dishwasher, then headed upstairs.

I glanced into Kris's office. She was wearing her headset, talking on the phone and typing on her computer as she took a reservation. I went into my own office and sighed as I sat in my desk chair. I hadn't realized how much my feet were hurting. I longed for a cup of tea, but didn't have time to go across to my suite and make it.

Nat answered my call on the third ring. "Hi, sweetie! How's it going?"

"Great. Busy. I think I need more coverage in the gift shop. Could you come in some afternoons this month, do you think?"

"Yes, I'd be glad to help. Shall I come today?"

"Tomorrow's fine, if you're free. Thank you! You're a lifesaver."

She chuckled. "I figure I owe you at least six months' help for all you did for the wedding."

I made a dismissive noise. "You helped me *create* this place. I couldn't have done it without you."

"I only nudged a little. You want to come over for dinner tonight?"

"I'd *love* to. Yes. Thanks!"

"See you when you get here. No rush."

After we hung up, I brought up the reservations log on my computer. Wednesday was almost completely booked except for the dining parlor, and even that was taken at four o'clock. I called Ramon and asked him to come in for the whole day, to make up for Julio's absence. Fortunately, he was willing. After hanging up, I took a deep breath.

Don't panic.

A small stack of lilac message slips sat in my "in" box. I glanced through them, hoping for one from Tony, but of course there wasn't one. He was busy with his investigation, no doubt.

One of the messages was from Willow. "She has your trans-lation" was scrawled across the bottom in Kris's hasty handwriting. That could only mean the translation I had asked her to make of the note I had found—a note from Captain Dusenberry—hidden in Maria Hidalgo's diary. I instantly wanted to call Willow, but it would have to wait until after we closed.

Bracing myself, I went back downstairs. Julio caught me on my way to the gift shop, wearing his jacket instead of his apron and cap, a slip of paper in his hand. He handed the latter to me.

"Sorry," he said. "Hanh will need this for tomorrow. We've been busier than we expected."

"No lie," I said, glancing over his list. Butter, cinnamon, anise. I could pick it up on my way to Nat's after work.

"You might want to increase our regular order for the rest of the month," I said.

"Already have. We were just caught off guard today. The gift shop has been selling more pastries than we thought it would."

"Well, that's going to continue. Tell Hanh the customers all love the biscochitos. They're taking them home by the dozen."

Julio smiled, pleased. "I'll tell her. See you Thursday."

"Good luck with the move. Don't strain your back."

"I won't."

He headed for the back door while I ducked into the butler's pantry, intending to grab a cup of tea. Rosa and Dale were in there, both busy with teapots and kettles. There really wasn't room for more than two people to work in the pantry, so I backed out and went to the gift shop, where I found three customers patiently waiting by the register.

From then on, I was constantly busy. The ornaments were selling almost as fast as the biscochitos, and I wound up calling Kris and asking her to bring more down from the storage area behind her desk. I was hanging fairies on the tree when Dale came in carrying a teacup and saucer.

"Thought you might need this," he said, setting it on the podium beside the register.

"Bless you!" I said, abandoning the fairies and pouncing on the cup. A long sip of Assam did much to restore me.

He smiled. "Should we stop seating people in the dining parlor?"

I glanced at the clock, and saw that it was almost five thirty. "Yes. How many are in there now?"

"Just four. Two couples."

I nodded. "Thank you for being on the ball."

"My pleasure, ma'am." With a formal little bow, he left, heading across to the main parlor.

Ma'am?

Feeling old all of a sudden, I drank the tea he'd brought me. I was glad I was that I'd hired him, but I still wasn't used to being called "ma'am." Maybe he was just being respectful.

A customer came out of Dahlia and asked about buying some of the holiday tea blend. I hid my cup in the podium and put on my best Miss Manners smile.

Between taking care of the last few customers, closing out the register, locking up, and shopping for the extra groceries, it was six thirty by the time I reached Aunt Nat's house. The sky was already dark, stars twinkling coldly over the hills and the aroma of piñon smoke filling the night air as I got out of my car, informing me that many of the neighborhood's fireplaces were in use.

Nat's porch light glowed golden beneath the *portal*. Manny greeted me at the door, beer in hand, wearing a sheepskin vest over a red plaid flannel shirt and jeans. He grinned, giving me a hug.

"Here she is," he called over his shoulder, then looked at the large bag I was carrying and added, "*Hija*, what did you bring?"

"It's supplies for the tearoom. Do you have room in the fridge for a few pounds of butter?"

"Ay! Not in the fridge, but I can put them in the chest freezer."

"That'll do," I said wearily.

He relieved me of the bag. "Go on in and grab a beer. You look like you could use one."

"I could, thanks."

He went through a door while I continued to the kitchen. Aunt Nat looked up from the stove, where steaming pots were emitting delicious smells.

"We were starting to worry!"

"Sorry," I said, shedding my coat. "It was crazy busy all day, and I had to stop for supplies."

"No trouble," she said. "It's just green chile stew. Go ahead and sit down, you look exhausted."

"I am."

I opened the fridge, grabbed a beer, and took it over to the table, which was already set for three. With a sigh, I took the middle place and was so devoid of manners as to kick off my shoes before opening my beer.

Nat brought a basket holding a colorful kitchen towel to the table, then went back to the stove. I snagged a warm flour tortilla from the basket, carefully wrapping the towel over the rest, and nibbled it while I watched Nat.

"How was your Thanksgiving?" she asked.

"Fine. The Fiorello clan was there in force. I've never seen so many cannoli in one place. How about yours?"

"It was lovely. We went to Manny's Aunt Dolores's—you remember her from the wedding?"

"Was she the very petite and very intimidating lady in the pillbox hat?"

"That's the one. She's actually a cream puff, she just doesn't take any guff. She's got a great old sprawling adobe up in Española, and she put out this amazing spread. I've never had red and green chile sauce with turkey before."

"The green's the best," Manny said, joining me at the table. He reached for the tortilla basket. "Had a busy day, *hija*?"

I took a swig of my beer. "You could say that. You?"

Manny's company distributed produce all over Santa Fe. He was one of my suppliers, in fact. I made a mental note to warn him we'd be needing additional lemons.

He grinned. "Oh, yeah. December is always nuts."

"Well, one down, thirty to go." I raised my beer, and he clinked his bottle against mine.

"It's not so bad after Christmas," he said.

"Twenty-four to go, then."

It was going to be a long month.

Nat brought two steaming bowls to the table and set them before me and Manny. She shushed me when I started to ask if I could help.

"It's just stew," she repeated, and went back to the stove. She ladled her own serving into a bowl and brought it to the table. "Thank goodness we all made it through the day!"

Amused, I raised my bottle. "What makes you say that?" Nat was retired, and her days were usually pretty relaxed, when I wasn't imposing on her for help with the tearoom.

"Oh, just my bridge club. We met today, and they decided they want a Christmas party. Guess who got nominated to organize it."

"At the last minute?" Manny chuckled. "You gotta learn to say no, *Cuchura*."

"You want to have it at the tearoom?" I asked. "If so, we'd better schedule it now."

"No, no, dear. They're too big. I'll put something lunchy together at La Fonda or someplace."

"Pfft," Manny said. "La Fonda probably booked up months

ago."

"Well, someplace," Nat said. "It doesn't have to be trendy, as long as the food is good."

"They'll want booze?" I asked.

"Most definitely. Speaking of which, have you heard anything about your license?"

I shook my head. "Still waiting."

"It takes forever," Manny commented.

Nat picked up her spoon, and we all dug in. The stew was delicious, with fall-apart-tender chicken, chunks of potato, and green chile that made a warm glow in my belly. I mopped my bowl with what was left of my tortilla and considered asking for seconds. Deciding to wait a couple of minutes and see if I was really still hungry, I drank some water and leaned back in my chair.

"I got an email from Joe. He's coming for Christmas," I said. "Did he call you?"

"No," Nat said. "I haven't checked my email."

"Do you have room to put him up?"

"Of course. There's Sam's room." My cousin Sam, her son by her first husband, had flown the nest over a decade ago, but Nat still called his old bedroom "Sam's room."

"Sam and Betty aren't coming down this year," Nat added. "She's pregnant."

"Again?"

"Well, it's been two years since Charlotte was born."

"Two years isn't enough," Manny commented. "Too close together, they fight like cats and dogs."

Nat gave him a look. "Your sister's kids were only a year apart."

"That's how I know." He gave her a wink and reached for another tortilla.

"Well, we should all go out to dinner or something when Joe gets here," I said.

"Yes," Nat nodded. "He'll want to go to the Compound or Geronimo. I'll see if I can talk him down. And we'll have Christmas dinner here, of course."

Her mentioning the Compound reminded me of the previous evening. I drank some more beer, killing my bottle.

"Did you hear about Debbie Fisher?" I asked.

Nat gave me a sidelong look. "The name sounds familiar," she said slowly.

"It was on the news last night," Manny said. "Murdered in her house."

"Oh, yes." Nat looked at me. "You didn't know her, did you?"

"Sort of," I said. "We were in the same class. I hadn't seen much of her since mid school."

"Oh, dear! And such a terrible way to die. I'm sorry, Ellen. Even if you didn't know her, it must be disconcerting."

Understatement, I thought, but let it pass.

"Is Tony investigating?" Nat asked.

"I think so. I haven't talked to him."

She gave me a long look, then smiled and turned to Manny with a question about his day. I lifted my beer, then remembered it was empty. I was sorely tempted to get another, but knew that if I did I'd regret it.

Sipping water, I listened to them chat. Manny could always wring a funny story out of even the most annoying circumstance. As he chuckled over a series of miscommunications that would have had me tearing my hair, I wondered if that skill could be taught. If so, I'd pay money for lessons.

Wednesday morning at five o'clock, I was startled out of my bed by a hammering at the back door. Heart racing, I threw on a sweatshirt and pants, jumped into my slippers, and hurried down the stairs. The doorbell rang twice before I reached the bottom, and the hammering resumed, only stopping when I got close enough to see through the lights surrounding the door.

It was Hanh. I unlocked the door and she stepped in, a gust of cold air coming with her. She was a good six inches shorter than me, her figure slight even in her down jacket.

She looked up at me with the faintest hint of reproach in her eyes. "Sorry. I don't have a key."

"No, *I'm* sorry," I said. "Julio and I forgot to get you one."

Key for Hanh, I told myself blearily as I followed her through the side hall to the kitchen. She'd been working for two weeks, and had proved herself reliable. It was time she had a key.

Yawning, I watched her hang up her jacket and put on her apron. She bundled her long hair into a hairnet, then went to the fridge.

"There's more butter?" she asked.

"Yes. It was in a freezer for a couple of hours last night, but it should be all right."

She took out a pound, squeezed it, and nodded. "It just needs to sit out a little."

"Would you like some tea? Or there's Julio's coffee."

"No thank you. I had tea with breakfast."

She started taking out equipment and ingredients for baking. I left her to work, and trudged back upstairs. Now that I was up, I could get a head start on the day.

Or I could get another hour's sleep.

I decided to lie down for a few minutes and think about it. I kicked off my slippers and slid between the coverlet and the blanket.

Next thing I knew, I heard footsteps coming up the stairs. At first I wondered if Hanh had a question, then I realized it was Kris's tread I was hearing. I rolled over to look at the clock on my nightstand.

7:57.

With a small yip of chagrin, I scrambled out of bed and into the bathroom. Washed face, brushed hair, slapped on some makeup, came out and found a dress that went with my most comfortable shoes. My feet protested at getting into these, being still a bit sore from the previous day.

I put the kettle on and went across the hall to greet Kris. She had the bank bag on her desk, and was balancing the previous day's receipts. She wore a clinging dress of black wool and knee-high black boots. Still no jewelry other than the jet mourning beads.

"Hi," I said. "Want some tea?"

She nodded and kept typing numbers into her computer. I went downstairs and made a pot of lapsang souchong, and drank a cup before carrying the rest to the office and pouring a cup for Kris. With a second cup beside me on my desk, I was able to face the messages.

Willow's was on top. I didn't want to call her before ten, so I set it aside. The next two were from people who wanted to sell me insurance and auto detailing. I dropped them in the paper-to-recycle bin.

A message from Gina was next, reminding me that she wanted Owen Hughes's card. I was digging for it in my desk when Kris walked in with a handful of more lavender slips.

"Johnson's Dairy is on hold for you. He says they don't have enough cream to fill our order."

"Argh. All right."

She put the messages in my in-box and went back to her office. I picked up the phone and talked to Bill Johnson, owner of the small, local dairy from which we bought the raw cream we used to make clotted cream. They would not have enough to fill the order that Julio had sent for the next week. I explained that our business was up this month, and we'd need additional cream every week. I talked Bill into supplying us with two-thirds of our request, and pulled up my suppliers list to find someone who could sell us the rest. It would be more expensive, but we didn't have much choice. We used cream in the scones, too—and we were starting to get extra orders for those.

I decided to skip Hooper's; their organic cream was wonderful but just too expensive for us. Half an hour and three phone calls later, I had a page of notes on a ledger pad and a verbal agreement from a dairy in Albuquerque to supply the rest of the cream we'd need for December. I felt like I'd been through a battle.

More tea.

I carried my cup to the credenza, and found that Kris had left out the little jar of preserved sour cherries that I had given her for her birthday. Presuming this to be an invitation, I dropped two cherries and a little of the jam into the bottom of my cup and poured tea over them. Normally it was Russian Caravan that I liked to drink Russian style, but the cherries also went beautifully with straight lapsang souchong, their sweet-sourness cutting the smoky flavor of the tea. I took a long sip and sighed, enjoying the tingle of tannin on my palate.

Kris joined me, refilling her own cup. "What did Tony want?"

"Tony?"

"Didn't you see the message? It was in—"

I was halfway to my desk. Putting down my cup, I grabbed the lavender slips from my "in" box and leafed through them until I found one with Tony's name. It was a one-word message: "Call."

He almost never called the business line. I looked up at Kris, watching me from the doorway with a wry smile.

"I'll be in my suite for a few minutes," I said with dignity, picking up my cup and saucer and walking across the hall.

Once behind the closed door, I hurried into the bedroom and grabbed my cell phone. Sure enough, Tony had tried that first, and sent me a text as well. I dialed his number and sipped tea while it rang.

"Shoot," I said as it clicked over to voicemail. I left a brief message, then drained my tea and munched the cherries while I went back to my office, taking my cell with me.

During the next hour, I found Owen's card for Gina, returned two phone calls, and texted Tony three times. To keep from texting him even more, I shut my cell in my desk and went downstairs to check on Hanh.

Ramon was at the kitchen work table cutting out scones, while Hanh stood at the mixer.

"Good morning," I said to Ramon. "Thanks for coming in early."

He nodded, then glanced toward Hanh. I hadn't seen them working together much before now, and Julio had always been there. Ramon was Julio's cousin; he was comfortable with that, but seemed uncertain working with Hanh.

To acknowledge her authority, I went over to Hanh and told her about the cream order, even though it wouldn't affect her that day. She listened politely, then nodded.

"Do you have everything you need for today?" I asked.

Another nod.

"We've been getting orders for scones as well as the biscochitos, so keep an eye on it. You might have to make some extra."

Hanh nodded again and glanced toward the mixer. I hadn't told her anything she didn't know. I left, so as not to delay her further.

In the hall, I met Iz and Dale coming through the back door, Dale very gallantly holding it open, which Iz acknowledged with a shy smile and a bob of her head. From the smell of piñon coming from the parlors, I deduced that Rosa had come with Ramon, her brother, and was building the morning's fires.

I checked the time: 10:50. We opened in ten minutes.

Glancing into the butler's pantry, I saw teapots waiting under cozies, and the food trays ready to be loaded for the first reservations of the day. The smell of fresh scones wafted from the kitchen. I heard the back door open and close, and returned to the hall to find Nat hanging up her coat.

"Thanks for coming," I said, submitting to a hug and a smooch.

"Glad to help," Nat said. "And I'm glad you've got the fires going. It's frosty out there!"

"Is it going to snow?" I asked, following her to the gift shop.

"We can hope!"

The gift shop needed more restocking. I darted upstairs, gathered ornaments and packets of loose leaf tea, and grabbed a handful of unassembled take-out boxes while I was there, then hurried down and, with Nat's help, got everything in place by eleven. When I went out to the hall to turn around the sign, I saw two parties waiting on the front *portal*. I unlocked the door and opened it, smiling.

"Come in!"

The day went much like the previous day, sans Bird Woman. Nat held down the gift shop, which freed me up to make sure we didn't run out of anything. This meant going back and forth between kitchen, gift shop, pantry, and upstairs storage. By noon, I was contemplating changing into track shoes.

Dale saw me carrying an empty firewood sling toward the back door and intercepted me. "Let me do that."

"Thank you," I said, and handed the sling over. This gave me a moment to run upstairs and check my cell phone.

Tony had answered my texts: "Need to talk."

I tried calling again, got voicemail again, left a message and a text, then dove back into the fray. As I arrived at the foot of the stairs I heard a great crash from the kitchen.

I hurried through the side hall and found Ramon and Hanh glaring at each other over a sheet of biscochitos that lay on the floor.

"What happened?" I asked.

"Sorry," Ramon said, looking at me. "Potholder slipped, and I touched the hot pan."

"Are you hurt? Hanh, grab some ice, please."

Hanh, who had carefully picked up the tray using a work towel and set it on the counter, now turned to the fridge.

"It's OK," Ramon said as I held his arm under the faucet and turned on the cold water over the red welt that was already rising on his wrist.

Hanh handed me a dishcloth filled with ice. I shut off the water and pressed the ice against Ramon's burn.

"Hold that there for five minutes," I said, pointing him toward the break table.

Ramon, looking sheepish, did as I told him. I turned to Hanh, who was gazing sadly at the cookies on the baking tray. None of them had fallen off, but they had suffered.

"All broken," she said, shaking her head.

"Well, roll the pieces in sugar and we'll put them out as samples."

She brightened, and flashed me a smile. "Good idea!"

She set to work on this task, and I joined Ramon at the break table. "How's that feeling? No, keep the ice on it."

"It's not that bad, really," Ramon said.

"Well, I'm glad, but I can't afford to have you out of commission, so please take care of it. I'll come back in a few minutes and bandage it for you."

"OK. Sorry about the cookies."

"Don't worry about it. Mistakes happen."

I sat with him and asked him about his music to distract him from the mishap. He told me about a concert he was going to play in at the Loretto Chapel later in the month. His excitement about this made me glad, and I asked about buying tickets.

"I'll get you some," he said, smiling. "You want two or four?"

"Just two. Thanks." I'd invite Tony, and use Gina as a fallback.

After bandaging Ramon's wrist, I took a plate of the biscochito fragments to the gift shop. I couldn't even get them under the dome we used for samples of the scones before two customers asked to try them.

Mental note: tell Hanh to save any broken cookies from now on.

Twice more during the afternoon, I tried and failed to connect with Tony. I left messages; he left monosyllables in return. Normally that would not have troubled me, but the echoes of a November without seeing him had left me insecure.

I resorted to addressing myself in Miss Manners tone, advising myself to keep busy in the gift shop and never mind how many times we missed each other. That helped, but by the end of the day I was frazzled and bordering on cranky.

During a brief lull shortly before closing, Nat beckoned me into Hyacinth, which was empty. "Did you get lunch?" she asked.

I blinked. "No, I didn't get a chance."

Come to think of it, I hadn't eaten breakfast, either. Unless you counted the cherries.

"I thought so." Nat pushed me gently into a chair. "You stay right there. I'll bring you a scone and some tea."

"But—"

"Stay!" she commanded, pointing a schoolteacher's finger at me.

I stayed.

Now that I was aware of not having eaten, I realized I had a headache. I closed my eyes and leaned my head back. I wasn't sure I'd survive a month of this.

Usually Julio made sure I had something to eat, if he thought I hadn't taken a lunch break. He often made soup or sandwiches for the staff. Although we'd gotten through the day without him, I would be relieved to have him back on Thursday.

Nat returned with a tray loaded with teapot, cup and saucer, one scone, a quiche tartlet, and two cucumber sandwiches. She put everything on the little table beside me, left the tray on the other chair, and headed back out to the gift shop as the bells on the front door jangled.

"Thank you!" I called after her.

I put two lumps of sugar in my tea and ate one of the sandwiches while I stirred it. I drank half the cup in one swallow, then told myself to slow down.

I was spreading lemon curd on half the scone when I heard Nat's footsteps returning, and her voice saying, "She's in here."

Looking up, I saw Tony standing before me, hands shoved in his pockets and shoulders hunched forward in his motorcycle jacket, his face a weary scowl.

3

"DON'T BE MAD," I said instinctively.

"I'm not mad," Tony said. "Not at you, anyway. I just got sick of playing phone tag."

"Oh. Yeah. It's been hectic." I put down the scone and stood, picking up the tray from the other chair. "Have a seat."

"No, I need to talk to you. Someplace more private."

"Upstairs?"

He nodded. I loaded my food and the tea onto the tray.

"Sorry," I said, "I missed lunch. You want some tea?"

"No, thanks."

We went upstairs, and I carried the tray to the sitting area by the window. Tony paused at the office doorway to look into Kris's space.

"She's gone home," I said, filling my teacup. I took a bite of scone and washed it down with tea while Tony came over and sat in the other comfy chair.

I waited, watching him. He stared at me, then laced his fingers and stared at them.

By now I had learned that this meant he needed to work up to saying whatever was on his mind. I drank more tea, and ate the quiche tartlet. My headache was receding. I filled my cup again, realized I didn't know what kind of tea I was drinking, and took a sip, paying attention this time.

Keemun.

I looked out of the window, something I hadn't done much all day. It was dark. No snow. The streetlamp on the corner cast an icy glow over the bare branches of the trees across the street.

Turning back to Tony, I found him watching me again. "I need your help," he said.

"OK," I said, putting down my teacup.

He stared at his hands a little more. "With the case I'm on. Woman stabbed in her home. Maybe you heard about it?"

"Yes," I said.

"I'm stuck," he said. "So I thought, maybe…'cause you know about tulle and stuff."

"There's tulle involved?"

"No, no. I just thought you…might think of something I missed."

This, coming from Tony, was quite a compliment. He was justly proud of his work.

"You look at things differently," he added. "But you have to keep it to yourself. I could get in trouble if the details of the case come out."

"Of course. I'll be glad to help if I can. Do I have to look at pictures?"

He shook his head. "I'm more interested in your take on who might have killed her."

I opened my mouth to answer, but he got up and started pacing. "She's got no enemies. People at work liked her, friends and family loved her. We've eliminated most of them. It was someone she knew, though. No forced entry. She let the killer in."

"A neighbor?"

"No."

"Someone posing as a delivery person? It's the holidays—"

He stopped pacing, and sat on the arm of his chair. "Good thought, but we've ruled that out."

"You've checked her phone messages, of course."

"We didn't find her phone."

That was odd. I looked at him, and he shrugged.

"We're still processing her apartment. It'll probably turn up."

I refilled my cup. "The news said robbery wasn't the motive."

"Oh, no." Tony gave a short, bitter laugh, and his voice dropped. "No valuables were taken. She was stabbed…a lot."

I met his gaze. "So the killer was angry?"

He nodded. "Real angry."

I thought back to my evening with Gina. "Well, I can think of one possibility, but it's a long shot."

Hope brightened his expression. "Go for it."

I swallowed. "Mary Cunningham. She hated Debbie in high school."

Tony frowned. "High school?"

"Yes. There was a big blowup our senior year."

"Wait—you knew Deborah Fisher?"

"Not well. We were in the same class."

"Crap."

Tony got up and started pacing again. I added a lump of sugar to my tea and stirred. He stopped in front of my chair.

"Why didn't you tell me you knew her?"

"I…didn't have a chance. And you didn't ask. Does being acquainted with her make me a suspect? I haven't seen her since graduation."

He sighed. "Where were you Sunday night?"

"Here. I'd been decorating all day, so I went to bed early."

"No one to verify that, I suppose?"

Oh, ugh. Being a murder suspect sucked, especially when Tony was the investigator.

I took a deep breath, drawing on what little store of patience I had. "Nat and Manny were here during the day. We walked over to the Palace for dinner, then they headed home."

Tony took out his pocket notebook. "What time?"

I thought back. "We got to the Palace around seven thirty, I think. So eight thirty or nine. I was in bed by ten."

"That might cover you. I'll double check the time of death."

"I sent some emails before going to bed, if that helps."

"Who to?" He held his pen poised over the notebook.

"Well…you."

He made a note, but didn't comment. I thought I saw his cheek darken a little.

"And Gina," I said. "Probably a couple of others. I can look them up."

He waved it off. "That's OK. So tell me about this Mary …"

"Mary Cunningham. She and Debbie were, um, not friends.

They both wanted the same guy. You know."

"Who got him?"

"They sort of both did. He was the homecoming king, and Mary was the queen, but his date at the dance was Debbie. I don't quite remember how that happened."

"Where is he now?"

"Steve? No idea. I think he moved away."

Tony scribbled notes.

"And Mary moved away too," I said. "That's why she's a long shot. She went to Salt Lake, and apparently got married."

Tony looked up at me, plainly disappointed. "Yeah, that's a long shot. Were she and Deborah in touch?"

"I can't imagine either of them wanting to stay in touch. But you might ask Gina. She's kept track of people better than I have. In fact..."

I bit my lip. Somehow, what I was about to say felt like betrayal of my one-time class.

Tony watched me, waiting.

I took a swallow of tea. "A handful of our classmates still live in town. Gina's kept tabs on them. One of them might be the killer."

"Yeah," Tony said slowly. "Maybe. But why?"

I shrugged. "That, I don't know."

"None of those people had a grudge against Deborah?"

"Not like Mary. But that was years ago. Maybe this is a new grudge, not an old one."

Tony frowned thoughtfully, then took out his phone and poked at it. "Has Gina's number changed?"

"No."

He tapped the phone and held it up to his ear. I ate my last bite of scone, drank my last swallow of tea, and started putting things back on the tray.

"Hi, Gina, this is Tony Aragón. I'd like to ask you a few questions. OK if I come over?"

I could hear Gina's voice, though I couldn't make out her answer.

"Yeah," Tony said. "Ellen says you know some old classmates of Deborah's who're still in town."

I carried the tray downstairs. The pantry was deserted, as was the kitchen, where the clock showed 6:15. Clean dishes sparkled wetly in the drying rack. Mick must have just left. I unloaded my tray and put it away in the pantry, then went out into the hall just as Tony came down the stairs.

"Thanks," he said. "This might be the break I need."

"I hope it helps."

"Yeah, me too." He dug his hands in his pockets, but instead of leaving, he stood gazing at me.

"It was good to see you," I said, "even if you're working."

He reached up a hand and cupped my cheek. I couldn't help leaning into his touch, closing my eyes. So tired, and I wanted nothing more than to curl up in his arms.

Suddenly those arms were around me, hugging me hard. I hugged back, felt the roughness of Tony's not-recently-shaven cheek against mine, turned my face to accept his kiss.

It had been a long time.

After several hungry kisses, Tony slowed down, then lifted his head. "Now I want to stay," he said in a rough voice.

"Gina's expecting you."

I stared into his dark eyes, feeling rather hungry myself. Tony swallowed, tempting me to kiss his neck where the muscles had moved.

"I could call her back," he said.

"You could."

After a long pause during which I forgot to breathe, he lowered his gaze. "But I shouldn't."

I bit my lip to keep from complaining. My hands wandered featherlight across his shoulders.

"We're past forty-eight hours since the crime," he added. "Our chances drop fast from now on."

I nodded, then stepped back, resting my hands on his chest. "Go catch the bad guy. I'll be here."

His face tightened with emotion that I couldn't interpret. That it was positive, I deduced from the one last kiss he gave me.

"OK, gotta go," he said breathlessly. "Lock me out."

I followed him to the front door, watching through the lights as he strode down the path until the darkness swallowed him. A moment later the roar of his bike pulling away faded into the gentle, nighttime hum of the city. I locked the door, checked that the sign was showing the "Closed" side, then turned and saw Nat coming out of the gift shop with the bank bag in her hands.

"Oh! I didn't realize you were still here," I said.

"I was just closing out the register. We had a *very* good day!" She beamed, offering me the bulging bag.

"Thanks."

I could feel my cheeks burning as I walked with her to the back door. "Maybe you overheard ..."

"Nothing I didn't expect." Nat smiled and put on her coat, then kissed my cheek. "See you tomorrow, sweetie."

"Night."

I saw her out the back door and locked it, repressed an urge to search the parlors for any other staff who might be lurking, and carried the bank bag upstairs.

Julio was late on Thursday, which had never happened before. Fortunately for poor Hanh, who still didn't have a key, I had gone to bed early and was up by the time she arrived. Hearing her car in the driveway, I went down to let her in.

It was almost 7:30 when Julio showed up and turned on his boom box. I happened to be in the kitchen, filling sugar bowls, but decided not to comment on his late arrival. He'd been moving the day before; probably he was exhausted—though you couldn't tell it from the way he started dancing to his salsa music as he got ready to work.

Hanh looked up from the mixer with a long-suffering expression which she instantly dropped, her face assuming a Zen neutrality. I smiled at her. She flicked a glance at me, but maintained the Zen face as she returned to measuring flour.

"Good morning, Julio," I said. "How was the move?"

"Great! It was great. Just a few boxes left, and some clothes. My art stuff."

"Does your new place have more room?"

"Oh, yeah. I have a studio to myself."

"Wonderful!"

I asked no more questions, feeling that it would be nosy, but I couldn't help wondering about his new home. Julio didn't have a car, so I assumed the new place was near enough for him to ride his bicycle to work, but a place that close to the Plaza, with more space than the apartment he'd been sharing with Adam, would be expensive. Probably more than he could afford on his salary, unless he had other resources.

The day was, if possible, busier than Wednesday, but with Julio back I felt a little less frantic. Still, early in the afternoon I asked Kris to run the numbers on what it would cost us to increase Ramon to full-time for the rest of the month and make sure we always had three servers on duty.

She nodded and made a note on a scratch pad. "I think the extra income will cover it. We're on track for this to be our biggest week all year. By the way, tomorrow and Saturday are booked solid."

"Even the dining parlor?"

"Yep. People are taking it as a last resort."

"Wow!" I stepped to the credenza to pour myself some tea. "You want tea?"

"Yes, please." She nudged her cup forward on her desk. "One sugar."

As I came to collect her cup, she added, "I think we should institute a minimum size group to reserve the dining parlor. There's a party of two booked in there on Saturday. Not a cost-effective use of the space."

"Better than if it stands empty."

"But not as good as running eight or ten or twelve people through for cream tea. We could do at least that many in the time it takes to serve afternoon tea to one party."

I returned with our teacups and settled into her guest chair. "We might not have that much demand all the time."

"This month, I think we will. We're starting to get calls asking to make reservations for *cream* tea."

"Whoa."

"Might want to think about putting a couple of heaters out on the front *portal* and seating people there on nice days."

"In *December*?"

Kris shrugged. "They'll be drinking hot tea, right?"

I thought about it briefly. "I think we have as much as we can handle already."

"OK. I'll do a cost estimate just for grins."

I nodded approval of this. Kris hadn't been this proactive in a while. It was good to see her thinking this way.

The phone rang. Kris picked up her headset, glancing at the screen. "It's Willow."

"I'll take it."

I took my teacup into my office and picked up the call. "Willow, hi. Sorry I haven't gotten back to you."

"It's OK. I know you're busy. Is there a time after hours when I could bring you this translation? I'd like to talk about it a bit."

Out of habit, I looked at my calendar. Social engagements? Hah.

"You could come over tonight, if you like."

"It would be late. Unless you want to join me for dinner—six thirtyish?"

"Ah…sure, OK. Where?"

"Osteria? I can pick you up."

"All right. Thanks."

"See you at quarter after six."

Bemused, I hung up and went downstairs to check on the state of the tearoom as we approached the four o'clock rush. Looking in on the dining parlor, I found Dale politely explaining to a trio of young women that the room was needed, and that they'd have ten minutes to finish up their cream tea.

"Oh, and have you met the proprietress?" he said, noticing me in the doorway. "This is Ellen Rosings. She owns the tearoom."

The ladies looked duly impressed, and were all smiles as I said hello and hoped they were enjoying themselves.

"Oh, yes!"

"Very much."

"Be sure to try the biscochitos from the full afternoon tea menu," I said. "There are free samples in the gift shop."

They thanked me, and I left them to finish their tea. Dale followed me out and we both went into the pantry.

"'Proprietress'?" I said.

"Well, yes." He gave me an impish smile. "It sounds quite impressive, don't you think?"

"Hm."

"Thanks for mentioning the biscochito samples," he said. "I've been nudging that party for a while now, and I think that dislodged them. Great idea—I'll remember it."

"Do we need to make some rules about cream tea?"

"Maybe."

I went forward to the gift shop to check on Nat, and found her ringing up purchases for a party of four. Two women about my age stood patiently by the podium: one in a cranberry red dress and matching cocktail hat with a charming net veil, the other in a classic little black dress and a dainty fascinator with a curled pheasant feather.

"Are you here for a four o'clock seating?" I asked, stepping up to check the reservations chart.

"Yes," said the one in red. "The name's Wegman."

I started to check for her reservation, then looked back at her face. Classic features, short, curling blonde hair, and soft brown eyes. "Erica?"

"Yes, that's right," she said.

I peered at her through the net. Yes—I hadn't recognized her at first. "You might not remember me," I said, smiling, "but I was in your class at Santa Fe High. Ellen Rosings."

"Oh!" she said, then gave me a flustered smile. "I'm sorry, I don't..."

"It's all right," I said. "I didn't make much of a mark. You're in Hyacinth, just over here."

I led the two of them to the small alcove off the gift shop, saw them seated, and promised their tea would be served shortly, then headed to the pantry to let Iz know they'd arrived.

Erica Wegman, Valedictorian, now a waiter at the Compound. I was dying to know how she'd wound up there, but it was none of my business. She must not be hurting for money, because her dress and hat were quite stylish. Interesting that she chose to have afternoon tea on her day off, and that she'd dressed for it.

I was tempted to text Gina and tell her, but I would not have put it past her to show up and ask Erica all the nosy questions I didn't dare to. For Erica's sake, I resisted.

"Hyacinth's here," I said as I entered the pantry, where Iz was brewing tea and Dale was ringing up a ticket.

Iz nodded, concentrating on her work. An idea occurred to me, and I darted upstairs to raid my suite for a two cordial glasses of sherry and a little silver tray to serve them on. Armed with these, I went back to Hyacinth, where Erica and her friend sat chatting by the fire.

"Compliments of the house," I said as they looked up at me. "I thought you might like an aperitif."

Erica smiled. "Thank you! And I think I do remember you—were you in the orchestra?"

"Band," I said, setting the sherry on the table between them, "but I was second chair senior year, so I played with the orchestra then."

"I thought so!" she said, smiling triumphantly. She, of course, had been concert mistress of the orchestra both her junior and senior years.

"I'll be right back," said Erica's friend, standing. She gave me a questioning look, to which I responded by gesturing toward the hall.

"On the right, past the stairs," I said.

I watched her go, admiring the way she had twisted her shining black hair into a knot as a perch for the fascinator. My hair would have been disinclined to hold such a formation.

"Have you been working here long?" Erica asked as I turned to go.

I paused. "Well...I'm the owner."

Her eyes widened a little. "I'm sorry, I just assumed—"

"It's all right," I said, smiling. "I work here, too. Don't be surprised if you come in some day and find me waiting tables."

Erica glanced up at me as she sipped her sherry. "That's what I do. Perhaps you've heard."

"Actually, yes. Gina Fiorello told me. I gather you've stayed in touch with her?"

"I see her now and then. She brings clients in, sometimes."

"Ah." I smiled. "Well, I hope we can stay in touch, too, now. I've lost track of everyone but Gina."

"Me too, mostly. Except I saw Debbie Fisher, a few weeks ago." She gave me a wry smile.

"Debbie Fisher?"

Erica nodded. "She was with a date, so we didn't talk."

"You heard about her, right?"

"Yes. Horrible."

"I was trying to remember why she wasn't the homecoming queen," I said.

"I don't recall. I never went to the dances."

I watched her take another sip of sherry. My memory confirmed her words; I'd never seen her at a school dance. Or a football game, for that matter. She'd given the impression that she was above all that.

"You're looking well," I said. "I love your hat."

"Thanks. I got it in Paris. Don't get to wear it that often." She put down the sherry glass and gestured to her outfit. "I like to pamper myself on my days off. The work uniform is pretty bland."

"Well, you look splendid!"

She smiled happily. Iz came in with a teapot, and I stood.

"And I hope we can assist with the pampering today," I said. "Have a lovely tea, and let us know if you need anything more."

"Thank you." As she turned her attention to Iz, I slipped out and went up to Nat, who was momentarily free.

"Are all the four o'clocks seated?" I asked.

"All but one party." She lifted the glass dome over the empty sample plate. "We need more biscochito bits."

I picked up the plate. "I'll see if we have any. Might have to settle for scone bits."

"We should keep the biscochitos out instead. I've sold cookies to about a dozen people today."

I raised my eyebrows. "I'll see what I can do."

Carrying the plate to the kitchen, I found Ramon clearing up the counters and Mick up to his elbows in dishes.

"Are there any extra biscochitos?" I asked.

Ramon shook his head. "Just enough to serve the guests."

That answered that. Hanh and Julio had both left for the day, so I wrote Julio a note about the biscochitos. We always made a few extra scones, so I cut up some of those into samples for the gift shop.

"Ramon, I think I'll need you full time for the rest of the

month," I said. "Can you do it?"

"Except for rehearsals, yeah. Wednesdays at five."

"That's all right. You could come in earlier on Wednesdays if you like."

"OK." He smiled. "Thanks. Extra money for presents."

"Thank *you*. Please start tomorrow, if you can."

I took the scone samples to the gift shop, where Nat was packing biscochitos into a take-out box for a waiting customer. I set the samples on the counter and put the glass dome over them.

"Was she here for tea?" I asked when the customer had gone.

"She was here *yesterday*. She came back today for the cookies."

"Wow."

"You'd better have Julio make more just to sell."

I nodded. "I wrote him a note."

Nat smiled, and hummed along to the Christmas music on the sound system as she stepped over to the tree and moved some of the ornaments around to eliminate bare spaces. "We need more of these, too."

"I'll get some."

Upstairs, I slid behind Kris's desk to the storage room. She was on the phone explaining that we were booked up next Friday and Saturday, but there were a few seatings available on Thursday. I collected a box of ornaments, then waited until she was off the phone.

"I'm taking this down," I said. "There are two more boxes."

"We've got more on order. They should be here Monday."

"OK. Kris, how profitable are the biscochitos that we're selling in the shop?"

She gave me her wide-eyed, are-you-kidding look. "*Muy* profitable. We make seven dollars over cost on the dozen."

"OK, thanks."

I went downstairs feeling heartened. Maybe I'd be able to make an extra payment on the mortgage that month.

By the time we closed, we had sold every biscochito in the place and had people demanding more. I was exhausted and yearning for a glass of wine. Nat invited me to come home with her for dinner.

"Manny's making *rellenos*," she said, grinning as she put on her coat.

"Oh, I wish I could, but I promised to meet Willow."

"Another time then. Oh, and I talked to Joe. He's coming in on the 22nd."

"Does he need to be picked up at the airport?"

"No, he's renting a car."

"Should I make a dinner reservation?"

"Not yet. I'm still negotiating."

"Let me guess—The Compound?"

"Geronimo."

"Yikes."

We parted with hugs and kisses. I saw her out, then said good night to the rest of the staff and closed out the register, by which time it was almost six thirty. I ducked into my suite to freshen my hair and makeup, collected an envelope that I had set aside for Willow, then went downstairs just as her car pulled up in back.

"Thanks," I said as I got in.

"Thanks for coming. I think you'll find this interesting."

She drove around the "racetrack" that circled the federal building, and parked near Osteria d'Assisi, one of the city's several excellent Italian restaurants. It was busy, but Willow had made a reservation so we were seated right away. We ordered a bottle of wine, antipasto for two, and entrées. I chose *picatto di pollo* while Willow opted for *melanzane sorrento*.

"Oh, I need this," I said, when the waiter had poured our first glasses of wine.

"Long day?" Willow asked, brushing back her pale hair before raising her glass.

I nodded, swirling my glass. "And it's going to get worse."

"Merry Christmas."

I took a mouthful of the wine and closed my eyes to savor it. Soft, fruity, with a warm hint of pepper. I swallowed and looked at Willow. "Is December crazy for you?"

She nodded. "After October, it's my busiest month. Lots of tourists in town for the holiday, and they like night tours."

"Except when it's snowing, right?"

"I have been known to lead tours in the snow."

"Wow!"

She sipped her wine. "*Farolitos* on Christmas Eve."

"Canyon Road?"

"Rosario Cemetery."

"Oh!"

I'd forgotten about the custom of lighting *farolitos* at the graves of family members, mostly done by Hispanic families, though I'd known of a few Anglos who did it. Memory took me back to high school years, when goofing around in cemeteries was a cool and safely daring thing to do. More than one Christmas Eve had found me in Rosario with a handful of friends, walking between the gravestones, admiring the golden flickering of the *farolitos* in the silent night.

I drank some more wine, then reached into my purse for a small bag I'd brought. "Here's your necklace, and I figured you'd want the Apache tears back."

"Yes, thanks!" Willow said, accepting them. "How was the séance?"

"Interesting. Are you acquainted with Tom, ah ..." I realized belatedly that Kris had never told me Tom's last name.

"Rasmussen? Yes, I know him. Was he the medium?"

"Yes. He brought this letter wheel..."

Willow nodded. "It's very ingenious. I've seen it at work. Did you get good messages?"

"Everyone seemed to think so. I got a message, too, though I didn't ask a question."

Willow sat up straighter. "Oh?"

"From Captain Dusenberry. Except that it was interrupted, so I'm not sure what it means."

"What was it?"

"Attic, and then 'n-e'."

"Attic northeast?"

Duh.

"Maybe that's it," I said. "I was thinking it was supposed to be 'near' or something, but northeast makes sense."

"Besides a location, what do you think it means?" Willow asked.

"Well—I figured he was trying to tell me where to look for

something."

"Something?"

"Yeah. Not very clear, is it."

Willow smiled. "You have no idea what? Is it bigger than a breadbox?"

I shrugged. "No clue. Except I don't think it's letters, because you asked if there were more and he said no. That night when he was blinking the lights?"

"Yes, I remember."

The antipasto arrived. I ate a curl of provolone and a bit of bread to slow down the wine.

"Let me give you this before we get buried in plates," Willow said, taking an envelope from her purse. She handed it across to me and I removed two sheets of paper: one a copy of the photo I had taken of Captain Dusenberry's note to Maria Hidalgo, the other a handwritten translation of the Spanish text.

> *My heart –*
>
> *You were right. Your father did not take kindly to my offer. He made it clear I was no longer welcome in your home.*
>
> *If you have not changed your mind, I will meet you on the Plaza at the concert on Saturday. A carriage will be waiting nearby to carry us to the church.*
>
> *If I do not see you then, I will know that you have decided to abide by your father's wishes. I will not blame you if this is your choice, my love, and in that case I will wish you a happy life henceforward.*
>
> *Know that I will always remain,*
>
> *Your devoted,*
>
> *Samuel*

4

I LOOKED UP AT WILLOW. "Whoa."

She nodded, smiling, and lifted her glass. "Sounds like an elopement to me."

"But it never happened. They both died single."

I looked at the photo of the original note, searching for a date, though I already knew there wasn't one. "He must have written this shortly before he was killed."

"I think you're right."

I met her gaze. Ice blue eyes, and yet they looked warm.

"Do you know more than you're saying?" I asked.

She shifted her gaze to the side. "I know there's more to know. I haven't gone looking."

"Why not?"

"It's rarely a good idea to seek communication with a spirit who doesn't want it."

"Is that why you don't do séances?"

"That's one reason why."

I ate an olive and read the translation again. What had gone wrong? Had Maria's family found out about the elopement, and killed Captain Dusenberry? Or maybe they found out and kept Maria from meeting him, and his death was unrelated.

But it couldn't have been suicide. He was shot in the back.

I frowned. I needed to know when that concert took place, in relation to the captain's murder.

"Notice the use of the word 'church'," Willow said. "In the original, it was '*iglesia*,' but that's not how the local Catholics would

43

have referred to their community church. They called it the *parroquia*."

"Not the cathedral?"

"The cathedral hadn't been built yet. Bishop Lamy began construction in 1869. It was actually built around the *parroquia*, which was then disassembled, except for the chapel of *La Conquistadora,* which they incorporated into the new cathedral."

I held up the letter and tapped it. "So…the captain meant the Protestant church?"

"Probably." Willow speared a marinated mushroom.

"Then Maria was willing to be married outside of her faith. Wow."

"I thought you would find that interesting."

"I do."

The waiter brought our entrees, and I put the note and translation into my purse, removing a smaller envelope that I'd brought along. "Thank you, Willow. I owe you one."

"Happy to help."

I slid the small envelope across the table. Willow gave me an enquiring look.

"You've done me two big favors now. That's just a little thank-you."

Willow peeked into the envelope at the Wisteria Tearoom gift card. "You didn't have to do that!"

"I wanted to. You've been a big help."

She smiled and tucked the envelope into her purse, then raised her glass. "Here's to the star-crossed lovers."

The next morning I was just a bit draggy. Half a bottle of wine was more than my usual consumption. I took a hot shower and made a strong pot of Assam, then joined Kris in her office. She had the bank bag on her desk, its former contents neatly stacked in satisfyingly thick piles as she tallied them up.

"We need to get a key made for Hanh," I told her, seating myself in her guest chair.

She opened her desk drawer. "I got three made yesterday

morning after I went to the bank. One for Hanh, one for Dale, and a spare." She handed two shiny-new keys to me. "I assume you want to do the honors."

"Yes, thanks." I put the keys in my lap and took a swallow of tea. "Ramon says he can work full time this month. I asked him to start today."

"OK." Kris made a note. "Next week is almost sold out. Friday and Saturday have waiting lists. Christmas Eve is sold out, too, and New Year's Eve is filling up."

"Wow."

"And I checked prices on outdoor heaters. Too expensive to buy, and leasing is pretty pricey, too, but it's an option."

"Not this year. We'll think about it for later."

Kris nodded, and paused to sip her tea. "Are we having a Christmas party?"

I blinked. I hadn't even thought of that. Employers were supposed to give their staff something for Christmas, weren't they? A party, or a turkey...

Christmas was on a Friday, and I'd decided we would stay closed on Saturday. Same for New Year's and the day after, a week later.

"I don't know when we'd do it," I said. Just the idea of cramming a party into our schedule made me feel exhausted.

"How about the 20th? Potluck dinner?"

"That's a Sunday, right? I'll think about it." I reached for my teacup, but it was empty. "Anything else?"

Kris held out a handful of message slips. I took them, remembered to pick up the keys from my lap before standing, and retreated to my office with my teacup, which I refilled before starting on the messages.

As usual, I flipped through them first to see if there was one from Tony. Lo and behold, there was! I called him back, and he actually answered.

"Hi," he said. "You busy tonight?"

My heart gave a little happy thump. "I don't have any plans."

"Great. Can I come over? I need your advice on a couple of things. I'll bring pizza."

"Is this about your case?" I asked, trying not to be disappointed.

"Yeah."

"OK. Give me until 6:30 or so."

"Great. See you then."

Click.

Stifling a sigh, I turned to the next message.

The good thing about busy days is that they go by quickly. Between ramping up biscochito production, helping Nat keep the gift shop stocked, and lending a hand wherever else I was needed, I had no time to be bored.

At three o'clock, I decided to box up some cookies by the dozen, to speed things up for the four o'clock rush. This turned out to be a good idea; less waiting for customers in the shop, and the cookies moved even faster.

"Maybe I should have just opened a bakery," I said to Julio as I collected a fresh tray of biscochitos for the pastry case.

"Nah," he said, taking off his apron. "This is more interesting. I'm heading out—see you tomorrow."

"Night," I said.

I paused to watch him clock out and leave by the kitchen's back door. Stepping to the windows over the counter, I saw him get into an unfamiliar car that was waiting there: a black sedan. It was cloudy out, making the evening prematurely dark, and I couldn't see the driver.

Julio's new roommate, maybe?

He hadn't said much about the new place. This seemed to confirm my suspicion that he wasn't living alone.

None of my business, I reminded myself, and carried the cookies up to the shop.

We sold out of biscochitos *again*, even though Julio had made dozens more than on Thursday. I left him a brief note about it after we closed.

"Come to dinner on Sunday," Nat said as I walked her to the back door, bank bag tucked under my arm.

"Oh, I'd like that. Thanks."

"You haven't been out much, this week."

"Have, too! I went out to dinner last night, and I had dinner at your house Tuesday. And I was out Monday night."

"But you were here all during business hours. And you skipped lunch at least twice." She paused at the back door to pull on her gloves. "You know, you haven't taken a vacation since the tearoom opened."

I stared at her, searching for an example to disprove her statement, and realizing that she was right. If the tearoom was open, I was on the premises.

"Maybe in January," I said.

Nat nodded. "Think about that. See you tomorrow."

I locked the door behind her, then checked the kitchen. Everyone had gone.

I left the back porch light on, went upstairs, changed out of my dress into a comfortable sweater and jeans, and pulled my hair back into a ponytail. Thinking I should make a salad to go with the pizza, I surveyed the contents of my little fridge. Unless the salad consisted of celery and pimentos, I was out of luck.

When had I last bought groceries? Tuesday, for the tearoom. For myself? I couldn't remember. There was a package of leftover turkey in the freezer, sent home with me by Gina, and not much else.

The back doorbell rang, and I hurried downstairs. I could see Tony through the lights. He had a pizza box in one hand and a six-pack of Tecate in the other.

"Hi," I said, ushering him in.

He headed straight for the stairs, then straight for my suite. I opened the door and relieved him of the pizza box, which I put on my small dinette table. Tony put the six-pack on the counter and took out a bottle.

"Want a beer?" he said, twisting off the cap.

"Yes, please."

I got out plates and napkins, and stuck the rest of the six-pack in my pitifully empty fridge. We ate our first slices of pizza—pepperoni and green chile—in silence, after which Tony took a swig of beer and let out a sigh.

"That's better. Man, what a week."

"You said it."

Another swig. "We're stuck," he said, holding my gaze. "It's getting cold. Zeke and I are both coming up blank."

It took me a second to realize he was talking about his case. Zeke was the other detective I'd met a few months ago.

I put a slice of pizza on my plate. "How can I help?"

"Can I walk you through the case, in general terms? I can't give you all the details, but maybe you'll think of something we've missed."

"OK, I guess—if you won't get in trouble."

"Just don't discuss it with anyone."

He took out his much-battered pocket notebook and ate more pizza while he flipped through it.

"Deborah Fisher lived alone in a two-bedroom townhouse—you saw it on the news?"

I nodded. "Gina made me watch."

"Deborah failed to show up to work on Monday morning. Late in the day her boss called her landlord, who checked her house and found her in the living room. She'd been stabbed, um a bunch of times."

"A bunch?"

Tony glanced at me. "She bled out, time of death probably around ten p.m. Sunday night."

"Had she taken any drugs?" I asked, faintly hoping she hadn't felt the knife.

"I haven't seen the lab reports yet, but there was no evidence of drugs or alcohol. No glasses, bottles, or cans. No paraphernalia."

"Well, that's a change," I said. "She was a party girl in school."

Tony looked at me thoughtfully, then flipped back through his notes. "Nope, nada. Not even a prescription in the medicine cabinet."

I took a bite of pizza, though my appetite was fading. I chewed it very slowly and thoroughly.

"Defensive wounds on her arms and hands," he continued. "She resisted, but she was no match for her attacker. No sign of forced entry, and the door was unlocked, so she let him in."

"It was a man?"

"We don't know that, but probably. Women tend to be less violent."

"Was the murder weapon there?"

Tony nodded. "Butcher knife from the kitchen. Found in the

sink, washed clean. No prints. Traces of the victim's blood."

"Then it wasn't premeditated," I said.

"Probably not, but again, we don't know."

I sighed. "Suspects?"

"Her dad was home alone, and her sister and brother-in-law alibi each other. Her boss and her closest coworkers are all alibied. So are you, Gina, Mary Cunningham, Sarah Porter, and Danny and Gloria Snow. Michael Guzman, Richard Hernandez, and Erica Wegman have no alibis. Haven't tracked down Steve Sawyer yet, but he doesn't live here any more."

"Erica was here yesterday," I said.

"Oh, yeah?"

"She came to tea with a friend. It was her day off."

"You talk to her?"

"Briefly. She said Debbie came in to the Compound with a date."

"She say when?"

"A few weeks ago, is what she said."

Tony made a note. "What else?"

"I asked if she'd heard about Debbie, and she said she had. I think she said it was horrible. Then her tea arrived, so I left."

"Hm." Tony turned back a couple of pages. "Well, Wegman doesn't have an alibi, but she also doesn't have a motive."

"Maybe Debbie teased her about being a waitress. She did like to rub people's noses in things."

"Annoying, but not really a motive for murder."

I shrugged and drank some beer. "Debbie could be nasty about things like that. But I don't think Erica did it."

"Why?"

"Just the way she acted when we were talking. She seemed—not unemotional, but distant about it. As if it had nothing to do with her."

Tony nodded. "If we rule her out, that leaves Guzman, Hernandez, Sawyer, and the father."

"You don't think her father would have killed her!"

"Why not?"

"Why would he?"

"Maybe he abused her as a kid, and she threatened to expose

him. That's just one possibility."

I swallowed. "That's horrible!"

"People do horrible things. For really crappy reasons."

This was depressing. I ate another bite of pizza, but it no longer tasted wonderful.

"You happen to know anything about Sawyer?" Tony asked.

"No. Did you ask Gina?"

"She's lost touch with him. He moved to Denver five years ago, but he's no longer at that forwarding address."

I shrugged. "Can't help. Sorry."

"OK." He closed his notebook, and finished his beer in one long swig. "I have a favor to ask."

"Yes?"

"The funeral's tomorrow. Can you go?"

"Ay yi yi. We're crazy busy."

"You can't take a couple hours off?"

I rubbed my forehead. Nat's words about my not taking a break needled in my memory. "Well—maybe I can. What time?"

"One o'clock, at St. John's Methodist Church."

"As long as I can be back by three thirty. What do you want me to do?"

"Pay respects to your classmate. Talk to any other classmates who are there. Pretend you don't know me."

"You'll be there?"

He nodded. "Observing. The family won't like it. If you can, talk to them. I'm interested in your read off of them."

"OK, but I'm not good at this."

"Sure you are. Just pretend you're Miss Manners."

I gave him a sharp look, then laughed. He was right; in uncomfortable situations, Miss Manners was my fallback.

He got up and dug another beer out of my fridge. "Seconds?" he said, holding it up.

"I'd better not. I'll be up pretty early tomorrow."

"Yeah, me too." He opened the beer and drank some. "Trying to track down Steve Sawyer. You know how many Steve Sawyers there are in this country?"

"Hundreds, I'd imagine."

"Thousands."

"You could start with the ones in Colorado. That would narrow it down."

"Some."

"Would his picture help? I have my senior yearbook."

Tony's eyes went wide. "Yeah!"

I went into my bedroom and retrieved the yearbook. I hadn't looked at it in years. I moved the pizza box to the kitchenette counter and opened the book on the table. The spine creaked. I turned the pages carefully until I got to the senior class "S"s.

"Here he is."

Wearing a sweater with a horizontal stripe across the shoulders, Steve Sawyer at eighteen grinned out of the yearbook, freckled and jaunty. He looked so young.

Tony took out his phone and leaned over the book to take a photo of the photo.

"There's a picture of the football team, too," I said. "Want that?"

"Sure."

I found the page, which actually had two pictures of the team—one by themselves, and one with the cheerleaders. Steve was in the front row, with Debbie Fisher perched on his knee.

Tony peered at it. "That who I think it is?"

"Yes."

"So they were a thing."

"Very much so. She should have been the homecoming queen but she wasn't. I don't remember why, except that she got in some kind of trouble with the school and they disqualified her from the election."

Tony took a photo of that picture, too. "Thanks. That'll help a lot."

"You could also do a web search on the photo. Kris showed me how."

"Holy—yeah, can we do that now? On your computer?"

"Sure."

I picked up the yearbook and headed for my office. As we crossed the hall, I glanced toward the front window and stopped. Soft, fluffy flakes drifted down from the sky, illuminated by the corner streetlamp.

"It's snowing."

Tony grunted. I wanted to stay and watch the snow, but he was impatient so I went into my office and turned on the computer. Tony sat in my guest chair, drinking his beer, while I scanned Steve's senior photo and saved it, then ran a search on the image. Three hits: two from the high school's website, and one from a social media page. Tony got up and came around to look.

"Bingo!" he said, leaning over my shoulder. It was definitely the right Steve Sawyer. He'd put up the photo as a "throwback Thursday" picture. Other photos showed him with a smiling blonde woman and two freckled kids. I clicked on the "About" link.

"Grand Junction, Colorado. He's married. Coaching football at a middle school."

"Oh, I *love* you!"

I gave a surprised little laugh, then bit my lip. Tony set his beer down and turned my chair around to face him. His gaze was intense.

"I do," he said, and gathered me out of the chair into his arms.

"Tony—" I whispered, in between kisses that tasted of beer.

"Ellen," he breathed hotly against my neck.

I learned that the antique *chaise longue* in my office was well and sturdily built, which was fortunate, because we put it to rather a strenuous test.

5

SATURDAY MORNING, THERE WERE FOUR INCHES OF SNOW on the ground. There had been only two when Tony left. I'd invited him to stay, but he wanted to get an early start, and so did I, and we both knew that would be easier if he went home.

When my alarm went off, I lay in bed smiling briefly, realizing that it hadn't been a dream. Tony had told me he loved me. And I had told him the same, when he gave me a chance to breathe.

It was a little scary, but it also felt wonderful. This was a man who rarely articulated his feelings. Not only had he not backpedaled, he'd reiterated the statement when he left for home, standing on my back *portal* with snowflakes sticking in his hair.

I got up, made tea, and walked to my sitting area by the upstairs front window to gaze out at the snow-hushed city. Somewhere an engine rumbled, possibly a plow clearing the streets. The sky was overcast and calm. I would have loved to crawl back into bed, but it was not to be.

I ate cold pizza for breakfast, then made a grocery list, vowing to shop on Sunday if I didn't have time Saturday. Dressed and fed, I went downstairs to build up the fires, because I wanted the warmth and the comforting aroma of piñon.

Julio and Hanh were hard at work in the kitchen. I greeted them both, and strategized with Julio about biscochitos, approving the large increase in purchasing supplies that would be needed to double our cookie output.

"Let's try to keep a few dozen boxed and ready to sell," I said.

"We'll need more boxes," Julio said.

"I'll have Kris order them, if she hasn't already."

With fires crackling in the hearths and holiday music playing, I felt peaceful and content. As my staff and then customers came in, the house gradually filled up with pleasant voices and merry laughter. The snow inspired everyone with holiday cheer. Before I knew it, the morning had passed and it was time to go to Debbie's funeral. I left Nat in charge of the tearoom, changed into a dark dress, then bundled up in my long wool coat, hat, and scarf, and drove to St. John's.

An organ was playing softly as I entered the church, which was less than half full. Up by the altar, a photo of Debbie stood on a small table near the casket, flanked by several flower arrangements. I took a seat in the pew behind the last occupied one. The church was brightly lit, but felt austere and a little cold. I glanced around, looking for Tony, and spotted him lurking in a side aisle. He didn't meet my gaze. Feeling my cheeks grow warm, I turned my attention to the program I'd been given at the door.

The photo of Debbie was the same one I'd seen on the news. A one-paragraph bio was as sterile as the church we were in. I found it unsatisfying. The only thing it told me that I hadn't already known was that Debbie had earned an MBA from UNM.

Looking over the people before me, I searched for anyone recognizable (not the easiest task viewing them from behind, but I trusted that I'd have a chance to mingle after the service). Those in the front row were sitting quietly, but some of the others were talking. I saw Danny Snow to the right of the center aisle a couple of pews in front of me. He was alone. Gloria must be home with the kid.

Three rows ahead of Danny was a splendid black picture hat with a net veil. At first I thought of Erica, but it was Saturday, and I figured she'd be working. Also, I had trouble picturing her in a hat quite that showy. I mused about whether Sarah Porter, the jockette-turned-forest-ranger, might wear it, then the wearer turned to say something to her neighbor and I realized it was Gina.

That could complicate things. Tony didn't want Debbie's family to know that he knew me, and Gina could potentially blow that. I wondered if I should try to warn her, but that might draw too much attention.

I took out my phone, silenced it, then sent a quick text to Tony:

Careful, Gina's here.

The music ended, the pastor came in, and I hastily put my phone away. The service was as bland as the program. None of the family chose to eulogize Debbie. I wondered about that as I listened to the pastor, who clearly hadn't known Debbie personally. She must not have been a member of the congregation. That meant that someone in the family probably was, and they had decided to have the service here.

I wondered what Debbie's preference would have been. Maybe she wasn't religious. Or maybe she wouldn't care.

I became aware of someone sitting across the aisle to my right who hadn't been there when the service started. I glanced that way and saw a vaguely familiar-looking Hispanic man in a navy suit. High forehead on its way to being a receding hairline, brow lined with a semi-permanent frown of boredom as he flipped through the pages of the hymnal.

Who was he? Someone from my class, I was sure. I hadn't known him well, and felt no interest in changing that. I thought over the handful of people Gina had mentioned, then my memory coughed up a name.

Dickie Hernandez.

Probably every class has at least one nasty little weasel, the sort who shoots spitwads from the back row of the classroom. Dickie was ours.

What had Gina said he was he doing now?

I watched him surreptitiously, wondering why he was there if he was as bored as he looked. Maybe he was just curious, or maybe—like myself—he was trying to make sense of the horrible death of a peer.

Music pulled my attention back to the pastor, who was stepping away from the podium, going over to the front pew to speak privately with the family. I took note of two men, one of them elderly (probably Debbie's father), and one blonde, hatless woman. That would be Heather, Debbie's older sister.

Heather had been a year ahead of me in school. Our paths

hadn't crossed much, even during the time when I'd hung around with Debbie in middle school. Like many older sisters, she'd made sure Debbie remembered who was the eldest. She'd always given the impression that she was too mature to join in our entertainments.

Dressed in a navy suit coat and skirt, Heather looked composed if rather pale. She blinked frequently, and gave the impression she was trying not to breathe, so as not to collapse. I was acquainted with that feeling, and my heart went out to her.

The service was over, and attendees began to rise and make their way forward to talk to the family. I waited, watching, while keeping an eye on Dickie. He sat fidgeting for a few minutes, then stood and walked up to the table near the closed casket.

I picked up my purse and followed at a distance, trying to look casual as I made my way forward. Gina was in the crowd gathered around the family pew. To stay out of her sight line, I joined Dickie at the table. He looked up guiltily from reading the card nestled among a huge vase full of white chrysanthemums. I gave him a neutral, maybe-I-know-you smile. He turned away and joined the cluster of people around the family.

I hung back, waiting for Gina to leave, passing the time by examining three framed photographs that stood on the table along with a poster-sized version of Debbie's recent portrait. The first was a family photo, taken at La Fonda, with Debbie, Heather, and their parents. It looked like it was from several years ago; Debbie's hair was the way she'd worn it in high school. Another, more recent and more formal family portrait was of Debbie, Heather, their father, and the unfamiliar man who was now standing beside Heather. That must be Heather's husband, whom I hadn't met. I checked the program for his name: Justin Davis.

I moved to where I could see Justin over the chrysanthemums. He was tall and slender, with curling brown hair pulled sharply back into a hair tie—too short to call it a ponytail. In the photo, his hair brushed his shoulders and he was smiling. Now he looked much more serious—in fact, his face showed some strain. He hung back a little, paying attention to Heather's conversations, only speaking when spoken to. Whatever Gina said to him evoked a flicker of a smile, but it was gone in an instant.

I bent to examine the third photograph, hoping the chrysanthemums would shield me from Gina's view if she happened to turn around. The photo was of Debbie's college graduation: Debbie in a Lobo red cap and gown, holding her diploma, standing on a bright, sunlit sidewalk on the UNM campus, with her mother and father smiling beside her.

That was all there was on display. No collage of photos, no memorabilia. The austerity didn't jive with my memories of Debbie, but of course, she hadn't planned it. Funerals are for the living. Maybe the circumstances of Debbie's death had made her family want to downplay the whole thing.

Glancing up, I saw Gina heading for the fellowship hall, where refreshments were waiting. Dickie stepped up to Heather, said something to her, then turned to Justin, whose expression had changed. Instead of looking haggard, he now looked on guard, and his slight frown told me he didn't care for Dickie's presence. Maybe Dickie had said something obnoxious. I wouldn't put it past him.

I looked toward where I had seen Tony. He wasn't there, but I spotted him not far away, chatting with a man in a light gray suit.

The crowd around the family had thinned. I went forward, holding out my hand to Debbie's father.

"I'm Ellen Rosings. I was in Debbie's class. I'm so sorry for your loss."

Mr. Fisher's hand was gnarled with arthritis, but his grip was still strong. His eyes looked tired and just a bit watery. He leaned on a modern four-footed cane.

"Thank you," he said. "Thank you for coming."

He dismissed me with a kindly nod, acknowledging that it was Heather I should be talking to. I took a step toward her, but she wasn't looking at me. She was staring at Dickie.

If Justin looked guarded, Heather looked downright hostile. Dickie was still talking to Justin.

"I feel really lucky I had the chance to be with her family for Thanksgiving," he said.

Justin mumbled something I couldn't hear. Dickie's eyes narrowed and he smiled slightly, shooting a sidelong glance at Heather, who said nothing and continued to glare at him.

Miss Manners prompted me to step forward with a reminder that we were *Homo sapiens*, not chimpanzees. I addressed Heather, holding out my hand.

"Heather, you may not remember me. Ellen Rosings. I was in Debbie's class."

She looked at me and blinked, then shook my hand limply. Her skin was cold and clammy.

"Thank you for coming," she said automatically. "Did you know Deborah well?"

"Not that well, but I do remember her. Please accept my condolences."

Heather's mouth tightened and her eyebrows drew together. She gave a single nod and brushed at her cheek, then glanced away.

Dickie seemed to be waiting to get the floor back. As if aware of this, Justin turned toward me, giving Dickie his shoulder.

"I'm Heather's husband, Justin," he said.

I shook his hand. Warm and firm, but he glanced away from making eye contact.

"How do you do?" I said. "You must be a great comfort to Heather."

He didn't answer, and his gaze shifted downward. Heather didn't say anything either. She was looking at her watch, rubbing her wrist.

Awkward silence. I didn't quite understand why it had occurred, but I sure understood what it was, and I decided to break it by doing the family a kindness. I turned to Dickie.

"You're Dickie Hernandez, right? You haven't changed! Shall we go get some coffee?"

I took a step toward him, which was also a step toward the fellowship hall. His gaze went to Heather and Justin behind me, as though he wanted to engage with them again, but I had just made that much more difficult. He yielded with a begrudging smile, moving out of my way. I walked toward the hall, sensing the people waiting behind me moving up to talk to Heather and Justin. Dickie kept pace with me.

"Ellie, right?" he said.

"Ellen."

"Smelly Ellie," he said under his breath.

I shot him an amused glance, refusing the bait. "No, you haven't changed at all."

He gave me a dirty look, then laughed.

The fellowship hall was bright and generic. Two long tables held plates of cookies, pastries, and vegetable crudités. People browsed and chatted. I spotted Gina talking with a woman with short, dark hair in an olive drab shirt and pants, who rang a vague bell for me. Sarah Porter, maybe?

I turned the other way and helped myself to coffee. Dickie followed me.

"What have you been up to since graduation?" I asked him.

He straightened his shoulders. "I'm a senior agent for Benavides and Benavides."

Ah, yes. Insurance. "That's quite impressive," I said. "Congratulations."

"Thanks. How about you?" Dickie asked.

"I opened a tearoom last year," I said.

"Oh, tea! La-de-dah!" He made a limp-wristed gesture.

I gave him a tolerant smile, and left my "free cream tea" cards in my purse. "Did you know Debbie well?" I asked.

"Not in school," he said with a sly smile. "I ran into her a month ago and we started dating."

Dating? Debbie and Dickie? Really?

I gave him a measuring look. "You must have been shocked by her death, then."

"Oh, yeah," he said, not sounding terribly upset. "Pissed me off when I heard. She was a lot of fun."

This did not sound like a grieving lover to me. I stepped to the food tables and picked up a cookie: chocolate-chip, mass-produced.

"Did she decide to start using 'Deborah' recently?" I asked Dickie, who was shadowing me.

"Nah, she hated 'Deborah.' Only her family calls her that."

I took a bite of the cookie. Oversweet.

Dickie moved closer. "Say, you want to go to dinner? Maybe catch a movie?"

I faced him, astonished, and took an involuntary step backward. Lucky for him, I had a mouthful of cookie.

"You're looking pretty good. Not as hot as Debbie, but still pretty good," he added, plainly thinking he was giving me a compliment.

"'Scuse me, Mr. Hernandez?" said Tony, appearing out of nowhere. "Can I talk to you a minute? Got another question for you."

Dickie seemed irritated, but followed Tony away. Relieved, I dropped the rest of the cookie in a wastebasket along with my empty coffee cup, then looked around, taking stock of the room.

Gina and maybe-Sarah were still talking. They'd seated themselves in a couple of folding chairs by the wall. I looked around for Erica, but didn't see her. Not too surprising; she and Debbie had moved in different circles.

Heather and her family came in, so I assumed all the attendees were now in the fellowship hall or had left. Heather's dad seated himself, and Heather brought him some coffee, then drifted away, talking with two other women who were about her age, wearing nice dresses. One of them looked familiar, but only vaguely so. I figured they were classmates of Heather's.

Justin had taken up a station by the drinks table, ladling fruit punch for anyone who asked. I was about to go over and sit with Mr. Fisher, but a small, silver-haired woman beat me to it. Since he had company, I strolled to where Gina was sitting. She looked up at me with a smile.

"Ellen! I didn't think you'd be here. Sarah, you remember Ellen Rosings?"

"I thought it might be you," I told Sarah, shaking hands. "You look well."

"Thanks," Sarah said, flashing a smile. "Please, join us."

I did so, taking a chair on the other side of Gina. "You're working for the Forest Service now?"

She nodded. She was tanned and fit. "Gina's been telling me about your tearoom. It sounds wonderful."

"Would you like to come try it?" I said, taking a cream tea card from my purse. "Free sample."

She flashed a smile as she accepted the card. "The first one's always free, eh? Thanks!"

We chatted a bit. I let Gina lead the conversation while I kept an eye out for Tony. I was hoping he'd avoid us, and that Gina wouldn't see him. I probably wouldn't get a chance to warn Gina that he wanted the family to remain unaware of our connection.

That thought sent me back to the previous night and made a warm glow in my heart.

I spotted Dickie, hovering around Heather and her two friends like a vulture waiting for an opportunity to raid a lion's kill. Heather was doing her best to ignore him; her friends were giving him indignant glances.

Tony was at the punch bowl, talking with Justin. I wondered what his interest there was. Brother-in-law as suspect: maybe Justin wanted Heather to be the only heir to her father's estate?

What a horrid thought. I hated that kind of speculation.

"Well, I'm afraid I have to get back to the tearoom," I said, turning to Gina and Sarah. "I'm glad to have seen you again," I added to Sarah, "though the circumstances are sad."

"I'll come visit," she said, holding up my card.

"Call for a reservation," I advised her. "We're booking up a week in advance right now."

I stopped by Heather's group to say goodbye on my way out. Dickie was still hovering, but I gave him a sharp look and he backed off a little.

"Come by for a cup of tea when you need a break some time," I said to Heather, handing her a cream tea card.

"Oh...thank you," she said, accepting the card without looking at it. She was gazing off to her right, toward the drinks table.

The other ladies looked interested, so I gave them cards, too, then left. Unfortunately, I had attracted Dickie's attention, and he followed me out.

It was snowing again. I walked briskly to my car, but not briskly enough. Dickie caught up with me before I could get in.

"So what do you say?" he asked. "Dinner and a movie tonight?"

"I'm sorry, I have to go back to work," I said coldly, hunting in my purse for my keys.

"When's your night off, then?"

"'Scuse me," said the most welcome voice in the world.

I looked up at Tony, my heart swelling with gratitude, and forced myself to speak formally. "Yes, Detective?"

"I need to ask you another question," he said, holding my gaze. Then he gave Dickie a pointed look, and added, "If you don't mind."

Dickie raised both hands in acquiescence, and headed back toward the church, hugging himself against the cold. I looked at Tony.

"What is it with that guy?" he asked.

"He's the class jerk."

"Yeah, I figured that out right off. You OK?"

"I'm fine, but I have to get back to the tearoom."

"Can I come over tonight?"

"Please do," I said, my pulse increasing.

"Good. Um—what should I bring? I figure you don't want pizza again."

I had to chuckle, gazing up at him. "What *do* you eat at home?"

"I almost never eat at home."

He was serious. I had a flash of vision: Tony in a lonely, empty apartment, drinking beer. Just imagination; I'd never seen his place. But what a sad thought.

"I've got some turkey," I said. "I'll make crêpes."

"Wow." He started to lean closer, then glanced toward the church and stepped back. "See you later."

I got in my car and cranked up the heater. I couldn't help looking after Tony, who was trudging back to the church, hands dug in his pockets.

I decided to stop at Kaune's for some groceries on my way home. Just a few things—some lettuce, salad fixings.

And a bottle of champagne. I was in a champagne mood, for some reason.

The tearoom was hopping when I got back. I dashed upstairs, shoved my groceries in the fridge, dropped my coat, scarf, and hat on my armchair and hurried down to the gift shop.

Nat, who had three people waiting in line at the register, cast me a grateful look. I joined her, getting out a bag and collecting the items she was ringing up for a lady in a stylish plaid coat and a cap adorned with a silver thistle badge.

"And a dozen biscochitos," Nat said to me as I bagged the purchases.

"There are none boxed up?" I asked.

"We ran out of boxes."

She nodded toward a package of food storage bags sitting under the counter beneath the pastry case. I grabbed one and stuffed it with cookies.

When I'd helped Nat catch up, I took an empty cookie tray to the kitchen. Kris was coming down the stairs, wearing her coat and carrying the bank bag.

"I'll be back," she said, hefting the bulging bag. "Just dropping this off."

"But the bank's closed!"

"Night drop. Trust me, you don't want this here over the weekend."

"But—we're *not* closed yet."

"I balanced the registers out at three. We'll do a second batch after closing." She smiled brightly. "Merry Christmas!"

OK, yes, I told myself as we parted ways. *We'll have a holiday party.*

I saw Dee and Dale in the pantry and leaned in on my way to the kitchen. "Everything going OK?"

Dee, who had her hands full making tea, nodded. Dale shot me a grin.

"Aye, aye, Cap'n," he said.

"I'm not the captain around here," I said, and his grin widened.

In the kitchen, Julio, Hanh, and Ramon had set up an assembly line for making biscochitos. Every foot of counter space was filled with trays of cookies in various stages of completion. Julio was at the mixer, Ramon was rolling out dough and cutting, and Hanh was coating baked cookies in cinnamon sugar.

Mick glanced up from his station and gave me a smile and a wave. I smiled back as I offered him my tray to wash.

"Hold on," Julio said. "We'll need that."

I hesitated. "Why?"

"We've used every tray in the place. We'll refill that one."

Hanh beckoned me over to the counter near the mixer. "These are coolest," she said, indicating a tray of finished biscochitos. She picked up a spatula and started loading them onto my tray while I held it. The cookies were still warm, and smelled heavenly. When they were all transferred, Hanh gave the empty tray to Mick.

I hustled back to the gift shop and stayed there helping Nat until five, at which point things finally started to slow down. We were getting walk-ins, and had to turn them away. I finally made a handwritten sign: NO MORE SEATINGS TODAY – PLEASE CALL FOR RESERVATIONS. I hung this on the front door, then went back to the kitchen, where I found Julio wiping down the counters while Mick worked his way through a mountain of dishes and cooking equipment.

"Hanh and Ramon gone?" I asked.

Julio nodded. "I sent them home. They'd been here since before eight."

"So have you!"

He shrugged. "My responsibility."

"Do we need to buy more trays?"

"I think we'd better. Six should do it."

"OK. I'll tell Kris."

"Tell me what?" Kris said, coming in from the side hall.

"Baking trays," I said. "We need a few more."

She looked at Julio. "Write down the specs for me."

Julio paused in his work, picked up a slip of paper from his cubby, and handed it to Kris. "Here you go. Six, please."

"You got it, *compadre*."

"And Ellen," Julio said, handing me a small plate of broken biscochitos, "these are for you. We decided we didn't need to do samples today, so we've just been eating the casualties. I figured you'd want some."

"You figured right," I said. "Thank you!"

My mouth watered at the thought of snarfing biscochitos. Oh, yeah—I'd skipped lunch again.

"I could use a cup of tea with these," I said to Julio. "Care to join me?"

He shook his head. "Thanks, but I've got plans."

"Of course. Have a good weekend."

He smiled, going back to work on the counters. "Oh, I will."

Kris walked upstairs with me. "Got time to talk a bit?"

"Sure. Oh, we need more cookie boxes."

"Already ordered those," she said. "I overnighted them; they'll be here Monday."

"Bless you."

"It got nutty while you were gone."

"This whole week's been nutty. Was there a problem?"

"No—just super busy. I have a couple of thoughts I want to run by you."

"Can it wait while I make tea?" I asked wearily as we arrived upstairs.

Kris smiled, nodding. "Oh, yeah—as long as I get some!"

I smiled. "Of course!"

"When I make it, it's never as good as yours," she commented, going into her office. "Plus, when you're out, I have to go downstairs."

I paused. "We could get an electric kettle for the office side. They're not expensive."

"But where would we put it? On a credenza? Mine's kind of full."

I looked at her credenza, which held the printer we shared and various office supplies, with just enough space on the end for a small tea tray. Kris knew that I liked to keep my credenza clear. My office had more room than hers, though.

"I'll think about it."

I went into my suite and put the kettle on, then measured out some Assam. I nibbled a biscochito while I waited. Actually, I nibbled several. To keep from devouring them all, I put away my hat, coat, and scarf. I thought about changing out of my dress, but left it on in case Nat needed some last-minute help in the gift shop.

I carried the tea and remaining cookies into Kris's office. She was on the phone, taking a reservation. I poured for us both, then settled into her guest chair, permitting myself a sigh of relief, and sipped my tea.

The days were blurring together, I realized. It was a good thing I'd gone to the funeral—the change of scene had been good for me, even if it wasn't exactly pleasant. Nat was right. I should take a vacation. Maybe in the new year.

Kris finished her call and reached for her own cup. "Next week is booked solid. We're working on the week after, and it's filling up fast. Christmas week is almost gone."

"Holy moly!"

"Want to reconsider those heaters?"

"Honestly, I don't think we could handle it without more staff, and this would not be a good time to train."

She acknowledged this with a wry smile. "Yeah, you're probably right. But you might want to do it next year. Or you might expand the house."

"Expand it?"

"Build an addition. Maybe enlarge the gift shop to the south."

I blinked. Adding to the house had never entered my thoughts. "That would be expensive."

"It would pay for itself, though."

Something in me resisted the idea of altering the house. The thought that Captain Dusenberry might not approve occurred to me. I tried to dismiss it—the house had certainly been altered before, and it was no longer his. He didn't *need* a physical house. But the reluctance remained.

"I'll think about it," I said, and nudged the cookie plate toward Kris.

"Oh, I've had some, thanks." She put a hand on her mouse, and the light from her monitor flickered over her face. "I've been thinking about the cream teas. I think we ought to limit them to the dining parlor, Poppy, and Hyacinth."

The latter were the two smallest alcoves, carved out of the gift shop with screens and furniture. For that reason, they were a little less comfortable, being more exposed to noise.

"Or should we remove Poppy and Hyacinth?" I pondered. "Expand the shop?"

"That would simplify things, but we can't do it now," Kris said. "We've got reservations booked in them."

"Let's take a look at it in January. You can calculate which would be a better use of the space."

"Gift shop, hands down," she said. "But the gift shop needs the alcoves to drive sales. I think we could do without Poppy and Hyacinth, but I'd advise against removing Dahlia and Violet."

"Oh, no! Not those."

Never Violet. That alcove would stay as long as the tearoom existed.

"But I'm getting ahead of myself," Kris said, and sipped her tea. "Limiting cream teas to the dining parlor, Poppy, and Hyacinth. I also think we should give them a time limit. Actually, set seating times would be the easiest for the servers. They've been complaining about the cream teas disrupting their service to the people having afternoon tea. Have they told you?"

"No," I said. "But I haven't really had time to talk with them much this week."

"Maybe a staff meeting would be a good idea now and then."

"Yes." I nodded. "Well, let's go ahead and limit the cream tea, then. It shouldn't take more than half an hour," I said. "We could seat for cream tea on the hour and the half hour, to make it easier on the servers."

"Good. And cockroach at twenty-five and fifty-five."

"I beg your pardon!"

Kris glanced at me. "Sorry. Just an expression."

I drew myself up. "There are no roaches in this tearoom!"

"I just mean we shoo the guests out five minutes before the hour or the half hour. To give the servers time to reset. Is five minutes enough?"

"For a cream tea? Yes, it should be."

"OK, then."

I ate a cookie, settling my ruffled feathers.

"I think we should raise the price for cream tea, too," Kris said.

"Five dollars isn't enough? They're just having tea and a scone."

"It's not the food, it's the seat they're paying for. They can have tea and scones at home if they want. To have it here, in your elegant Victorian parlors, with Dale and the ladies waiting on them, they need to pay for the space. If we don't want to take a loss on cream tea as opposed to seating guests for afternoon tea, then they need to pay ten dollars for a half-hour seating."

"Twenty-five minutes," I said.

"OK, twenty-five minutes. And one pot of tea—not bottom-less."

"Kris, you're wonderful at protecting the bottom line—"

"Bottomless tea encourages them to stay too long."

"—but there's also hospitality. I want people to feel welcome here."

She raised an eyebrow. "I don't think we have a problem with that."

I sipped my tea. She was right, of course. I was just resisting the idea of change. But the fact was, we were changing whether we liked it or not. The past week had demonstrated that.

"All right," I said. "We'll try it for this month."

She nodded. "One more thing. No cream tea reservations in the dining parlor at four o'clock. If it doesn't get booked in advance for four, we can open it up to walk-ins for cream tea."

"It won't stand empty?"

"Not this month. Guarantee you."

I thought of all the people I had turned away downstairs that afternoon, and realized she was right. "OK. Let's start next week."

"We've got a few reservations booked the old way, but this will be the policy from now on," Kris said. "I'll put a notice on the website."

"Thank you. You're a gem."

She smiled, looking at her screen. "And, we're closed. I'll go close out the register and do the deposit."

"You could do it Monday," I said as we both stood.

"Better to do it now. I'll go by the night drop on my way home."

We went downstairs, and passed Dee and Iz carrying trays of used china to the kitchen. Nat was tidying up the gift shop. I checked that the front door was locked and the sign turned to CLOSED while Kris started balancing the register.

"Whew!" Nat said, closing the empty pastry case and picking up a tray holding a mere half dozen cookies. "What a day!"

"Was it too much?"

She gave me a tired smile. "On a regular basis it would be. For this month, I can handle it."

I hugged her. "Thank you."

We took the cookies to the kitchen and put them on a smaller plate, giving the tray to Mick, who was just getting to the end of the dishes. I held onto the plate of cookies, intending to share them with Tony.

"Remember dinner tomorrow night," Nat said as I followed her to the side hall.

"I remember. Oh—would you mind if I invited Tony? He might be too busy, but—"

"Of course you can invite him! We'd be glad to see him."

"Thanks. I'll let you know."

"Speaking of Tony..." she added, as the sound of a motorcycle coming up the driveway reached us. I glanced at the clock: 6:23. So much for making crêpes.

I went with Nat to the back door to say good night, and stayed to greet Tony. He came up with his helmet under his arm, took one look at the cookies, and helped himself.

"We're still shutting down," I said, holding the door open for him. "Mind waiting a bit?"

"Mnh," he said, then swallowed. "There's more beer, right?"

"Right."

I let him into my suite and left the cookies there, saw the rest of my staff out and wished them a good weekend, and went back upstairs. Tony was sitting by the front window, drinking a beer and watching the traffic below.

"Busy day," he said as I joined him.

"Yes. I'm afraid I haven't started the crêpes. It'll take about half an hour—or should I just make turkey sandwiches?"

"Sandwich is fine with me."

"OK. Be right out."

"Hey."

He caught my wrist as I got up to leave, and pulled me gently toward him. I'm not sure quite how, but I ended up in his lap. One long kiss later he looked up at me with a soft smile.

"That's better."

I hummed as I made our supper. I'd bought sourdough, so I grilled the turkey with some onions, added Swiss cheese, and then grilled the sandwiches. Wishing I had some chips to put beside them, I sliced up an apple instead and used it to garnish the plates, then helped myself to one of Tony's beers and joined him by the window.

"Did you learn anything useful at the funeral?" I asked.

"Some," he said. "How about you?"

"Dickie told me he was dating Debbie. Did you already know

that?"

"Yeah. He's real proud of it."

I drank some beer. "Did you know he had Thanksgiving dinner with her family?"

"No. He tell you that?"

"Not exactly. He was baiting Heather with it when I came up to talk to her after the service. She seemed pretty displeased. So did her husband."

Tony nodded. "What else?"

I ate a bite of sandwich, thinking over the funeral and the reception. "Dickie wasn't mourning. He didn't seem particularly bothered by her death."

"Yeah, I got that feeling too, especially when he started hitting on you."

I smiled. "Thank you for rescuing me, by the way."

"My job. To serve and protect."

I looked out the window. The snow had stopped a while ago, and the cars on the street made wet swooshing noises as they passed. Saturday night, pretty busy. People going out to dinner and socializing.

"Anything else?" Tony asked.

I frowned, thinking. "There's some kind of tension in the family. I think it's more than just grief, but I can't put my finger on it. Maybe something happened at Thanksgiving."

Tony sighed and put down his empty bottle. "Oh, good. I get to talk to Dickie some more."

"Lucky you."

"What about the forest ranger? I saw you talking with her and Gina."

"Sarah? I like her. We were just catching up. Didn't you say she had an alibi?"

"Yeah, she does. It's a little shaky, but poking holes in it would take some work."

"I don't know why she'd kill Debbie. They weren't friends in school, hadn't seen each other lately, or so she said. And she seemed perfectly relaxed to me."

"Mm." Tony ate a bite of sandwich, then sighed. "Might not get an indictment on this one."

"I'm sorry I wasn't more help."

"No, you did good. Thanks."

"Did you find out about Steve Sawyer?"

"Yeah. He was at a school basketball game. Alibied out the wazoo."

"So you're down to..."

"Michael Guzman, Dickie Hernandez, and Erica Wegman out of your classsmates in town. It's unlikely someone made a special trip back to town to do it, and we've pretty-much eliminated family and co-workers. It could still be someone we don't know about."

"But you said she knew the killer."

"Right."

"I'd be surprised if she kept up with Michael. He was a complete nerd in school."

"From what I've seen," Tony said dryly, "that's still true. His alibi, such as it is, consists of the scientific journals he was reading at home and a long text exchange he had with a colleague."

"On the phone? He could have done that anywhere."

"Right. That's why he's still on the list."

"Hm." I ate another bite, musing. "Debbie was a partier in school. Maybe she and Dickie had some party buddies we don't know about."

"I'll ask him, but I think they mostly hung out in bars or at her place."

"What's his home like?"

"Not as nice as hers. Apartment on the south side."

I finished my beer. "Dickie sells insurance. Could there have been a life insurance policy on Debbie?"

Tony raised his eyebrows. "That's a thought."

I ate the last of my sandwich while he took out his notebook and wrote in it. "Thanks," he said, putting it away.

I smiled. "You want some dessert? There are more biscochitos, or—"

He took my empty plate from my hands and put it on the low table, then pulled me close. "Rather have you."

I smiled, sliding into his arms, enjoying the bliss of pure physical pleasure. A tiny part of my brain expressed concern at the fact that these sensations were basically shutting down my thought processes.

My hind-brain told that part of me to shut up.

Tony's phone rang.

"Dammit," he whispered.

Tempted to tell him to ignore it, I held my tongue. I knew he had to check it, so I waited while he looked at the screen.

His eyes went wide. "Oh, shit!"

He stood and strode to the coat rack where he'd hung his jacket.

"What is it?" I asked, following him.

He grabbed his helmet off the floor and shot me a frowning look on his way to the stairs.

"Erica Wegman's been murdered."

6

I DIDN'T SLEEP WELL THAT NIGHT. Tony had promised to keep me posted, but I knew he'd be busy working the new crime scene. He'd probably be up all night. I slept fitfully, waiting for a call or text that I knew probably wouldn't come.

When my bedroom curtains began to glow faintly with morning light, I gave up and took a long, hot shower, then dressed in comfy sweats. For breakfast I ate the strawberries I'd picked up at Kaune's, intending to make a dessert with them for Tony.

This was my weekend, Sunday and Monday, but I couldn't settle in to rest. I ended up at my desk, surfing the websites of the local news stations for stories about Erica. It was apparently too soon. There was nothing.

Why Erica?

All I could think of was that she'd talked to Debbie recently. Debbie and a date—presumably Dickie—had dined at the Compound. What could they have discussed that would get Erica killed?

I tried to think about the situation the way Tony would. In a moment of cynicism, I noted that both the women in the equation were now dead.

Could Dickie the class creep have turned into Dickie the stalker-murderer?

The question of "why" became, in Dickie's case, "why not?" He'd always done annoying things just for the hell of it.

Murder was rather a step up from annoying, but my aversion to Dickie was based on the instinctive knowledge that on some level there must be some kind of anger driving his behavior. It might not take much to fan that anger into fury.

Maybe he had murdered Debbie because she was more successful than he was. She was a Vice President of Something or Other at her bank. He was an insurance agent. "Senior," but still an agent.

Erica might a waiter now, but she'd been the valedictorian of our class.

Could Dickie be murdering successful female classmates merely out of vengeful spite?

People do horrible things. For really crappy reasons.

Great. And I'd told Dickie that I'd opened a tearoom.

I went downstairs and checked all the doors. Then all the windows. Everything was locked tight.

Maybe I should get an alarm.

Since I was there, I collected the vases from the alcoves and carried them to the dining parlor, then removed the fading roses from them and pulled off the petals for potpourri. On Monday, more roses would be delivered and I'd make up fresh arrangements. The holly would be good for another week, at least. I could cut more ivy in the garden.

Maybe I'd wait on that until there was someone else around.

As I extracted a rose from a teapot, my hand brushed against a holly leaf and I yelped. They were sharp; it had drawn a bead of blood. I sucked on it, feeling sorry for myself for multiple reasons.

Maybe it was time for a tea break.

In the pantry, I mused as I made a pot of Keemun. Erica had come to tea on…was it Thursday? I wished now that I had paid more attention to her friend. I couldn't recall that Erica had introduced us, so I didn't even know her name.

Why had Erica wound up waiting tables? I'd been too polite to ask her. Now I wished I'd been rude.

I went to the gift shop and brought up the reservations list, hoping to find a notation on the reservation, but it was just Erica's name. Maybe Nat would know? I'd have to ask her.

Giving up, I returned to the dining parlor to clean up my floral mess, and took the Keemun upstairs, along with a grocery bag full of rose petals to dry for potpourri. No messages, so I curled up in a comfy chair by the front window, with a book in my lap and my phone beside me, nibbling biscochitos and sipping my tea from a mug because it was the weekend.

I knew when Erica's murder hit the news, because both my cell and the office phone began to ring. Kris must have forgotten to put the system on mute when she left the day before. I grabbed the cell, hoping it was Tony, but it was Gina's number on the screen.

"Hi, Gina."

"Have you heard—"

"About Erica? Yeah."

"Tony told you."

"He was here when he got the call."

"He tell you any details?"

"No. Have you heard any?"

"Just a teaser on the news. Stabbed in her apartment, same as Debbie."

My gut went cold. I had a fine selection of professional kitchen knives downstairs.

"Poor Erica," I said softly.

"This means it's probably someone from our class, you know," Gina said.

"Maybe."

"And now we're all targets."

Gina was a successful businesswoman, too. I poured myself more tea, and added a lump of sugar.

"Did you talk to Dickie at the funeral?" I asked her.

"No, but I see him now and then around town. I talked to him a few months ago at Del Charro. He hasn't changed."

"No."

Gina was silent for a few seconds. I could almost hear the wheels spinning in her brain.

"You don't think it's Dickie, do you?" she asked.

"I don't know, but if he shows up at your door, don't let him in."

"No problem. I wouldn't anyway."

I leaned my head back, trying to shake off the dread that was stealing over me. I hated the idea that I had to fear my classmates. Even Dickie. He was a jerk, yeah—but I shouldn't have to worry about being murdered by him. It wasn't fair.

"Anyone else you want to warn me about?" Gina asked.

I froze. I didn't have Tony's permission to talk about the case.

"I would just be wary of all our classmates, right now," I said. "I know that's a pain."

"I don't think Sarah would have done this."

"I don't think so either, but I don't know that she didn't."

"Ugh. We should think about something else. You want to go shopping? Get out of the house?"

What I wanted was to talk to Tony. Other than that...

"Thanks, but I think I just need to rest. It was a really busy week."

"You shouldn't be alone, honey."

"I'm going over to Nat and Manny's for dinner later."

"Hmm. Sure you don't want company?"

The office phone rang again. I glanced that way.

"I'm all right. Hey, Gina?"

"Yeah?"

"Did Erica tell you why she was waiting tables at the Compound?"

"Not really. I gather something went wrong at medical school, and she took a leave of absence or something. She wasn't hot to talk about it, so I didn't bug her for details."

"And now we'll never know."

"Guess not."

I took a swallow of tea and looked out the window. Bits of blue sky showed through drifting clouds. It was beautiful; it should have raised my spirits.

"Well, call me if you change your mind. I need to get a couple of presents, so I'll be out."

"Be careful, Gina."

"You too. Text me when you get home from dinner."

"OK. Text me when you're home from shopping."

"We'll have a text fest."

"Boy howdy."

The office phone rang again as I hung up. I went into Kris's office to turn on the mute, and decided to listen to the messages. One of them was a reservation request. Two were hang-ups.

I frowned at the phone. I didn't like hang-ups.

Caller ID showed a number I wasn't familiar with for both those calls. Local exchange, but these days that could be a cell phone calling from anywhere. I entered the reservation request into the system, flagged it so Kris would see it, then deleted the messages and went back to my tea and my book.

I had read only a few sentences when my cell rang again. This time it was Tony.

"Hi," I said. "How's it going?"

"Not great. Listen, Ellen, don't go out by yourself, and don't let any visitors in."

I winced. The worry in his voice confirmed my fears. I'd been hoping he'd tell me they were silly.

"I assume my family are exempt from that."

"Yeah, sure."

"For how long?" I asked.

"I don't know. Until I get a handle on this."

I bit my lip. That could be days.

"Nat asked me over for dinner," I said.

Silence.

"She said I could invite you," I added. " Want to escort me?"

"Don't have time."

"You have to eat, right?"

More silence.

"You'll think better when you're fed," I said gently.

"Yeah, OK. But it'll have to be quick. I can't hang out."

"That's fine. I should go to bed early."

We agreed on a time for him to come by, then Tony hung up. I tried to read some more, but I couldn't relax, so I got up and started a load of laundry, then tidied my kitchen and made a grocery list.

Except…who knew when I'd be able to go buy groceries?

I could call Gina, but I hated to impose on her. Maybe I could have some groceries delivered.

It was less than an hour since Tony had advised me not to leave the house alone, and I was already going nuts.

I pondered how to distract myself while I transferred my laundry to the dryer, then I realized I had the perfect task: I could look for whatever it was that Captain Dusenberry wanted me to find. If Willow was right, it was somewhere in the northeast corner of the house, upstairs.

What was I looking for? I had no idea, except that it wasn't more letters.

I stood under the chandelier and faced the northeast corner, toward Kris's office, looking at the walls and the places where they joined the ceiling, trying to imagine where the best spot for hiding an indeterminate something might be. The letters from Maria Hidalgo to the captain had been under the floorboards in a corner of the dining parlor.

The pitched roof sloped to the front and back of the building. Dormer windows thrust out above the front and back downstairs doors, creating a nice vaulted space over the center hallway, but the ceilings to either side were sloping. This had once been the attic of the house, used for storage and maybe for servants' bedrooms.

I went into Kris's office, and went to the back wall and the storage space behind it. Full of holiday merchandise, at the moment. I fetched a flashlight and peered at what I could see of the floor, which wasn't much. I gave it a few experimental taps in a couple of spots, but the boards seemed solidly placed and unlikely to move.

Well, phooey.

This was the northeast corner of the house. The ceiling sloped down to the east wall, which was only about three feet high where they joined. Again, I tapped and poked at what I could reach of that seam, but didn't find any anomalies.

I spent another half hour hunting and tapping, with no success. By then I was getting frustrated, so I decided to do something else. I caught up on all the housework I'd been neglecting in my suite, and even changed the sheets on my bed. Ran two more loads of laundry. Made menu plans for the week, and revised my grocery list.

Of course, the way things had been going my menu plans might never be used. I looked at them again, switched a few things around to minimize the number of perishable ingredients, and decided to stop fiddling with it.

At four o'clock I made myself tea and sat with my book in the upstairs sitting area, looking out of the window at a gray and bustling Santa Fe. Almost midwinter: the nights were long, and the sun was tracking well to the south, which meant it didn't blast directly in but slanted at a gentler angle, falling on the north wall of the hall and the doorway to the offices. I watched the traffic on the street below, both pedestrian and vehicular, thinking of holiday celebrations.

I had not done any shopping for presents. That would now be a problem, too—if I intended to honor Tony's advice that I not go out alone. Gina would shop with me, but Gina had a busy life as well.

Maybe next Sunday. Still two weeks before Christmas. That would work, right?

I made a list of people I wanted to buy gifts for, and gift ideas where I had them. Just the thought of shopping for that many presents in one day made me feel tired.

And I could not think of what to give Tony.

Maybe I shouldn't give him anything. Chances were he wasn't planning to get me something, and if I gave him a present, he might be embarrassed.

I was pretty sure I was overthinking this. I put away my list and sipped the last of my tea as I watched the early evening sunlight go golden, then got ready to go to Nat's. I decided to take some biscochitos along, so I was already downstairs when Tony pulled up to the back of the house.

Shrugging into my coat, I hurried to the door and opened it before he could ring. "Thanks!" I said, heading for my car.

Tony was quiet on the drive to Nat's. I glanced sidelong at him, wondering if I should leave him to his silent musing. He noticed and looked back at me.

"What?"

"Same killer?" I asked.

"Probably. There are differences."

"Oh?"

"This victim was stabbed fewer times."

"So…not as angry this time?"

"That could be it."

I turned into Nat's neighborhood. The smell of piñon smoke began to tease.

"Any leads?"

"Nothing new, except that we have one less suspect." Tony said grimly.

"Are you looking at Dickie Hernandez?"

"Yes."

I nodded, then made the turn onto Nat's street, and drove slowly up her gravel drive. Golden light from the porch light spilled out in a welcoming arc. I got out and noted that Tony stood watching by the car until I had reached the door.

Nat let us in, all smiles. "Come in, come in! Tony, I'm glad you could make it!"

She gave him a big smooch on the cheek, which startled me almost as much as it startled him, then led us into the dining room. I took a deep breath, smelling corn, green chile, and piñon, and sighed happily.

"I brought some biscochitos," I said, offering Nat a wrapped plate. "If you're sick of them, I figure Manny will eat them."

"I am *not* sick of them, thank you very much! Come sit down, dinner's almost ready."

Manny was in the living room, adding wood to a freshly built fire. He gave me a nod and kept working. Nat shepherded me and Tony to the table and fetched us drinks. Tony opted for coffee instead of beer, by which I inferred he expected to have a long night.

"Joe called," Nat said over her shoulder from the kitchen. "He changed his flight. Now he's coming in on the twenty-first, and he'll settle for the Compound."

"Great," I said.

"Who's Joe?" Tony asked.

"My brother," I said. "He's coming for Christmas."

"Have I met him?"

"No. He lives in New York."

"You should meet him, Tony," Nat said. "I bet you two would hit it off."

I had my doubts about that, but I held my tongue. Maybe I was wrong. Maybe Joe wouldn't set off all Tony's anti-Anglo, anti-money buttons. But I wasn't going to hold my breath.

Nat brought two steaming plates to the table and set them in front of me and Tony. "Careful, they're hot."

"Smells fantastic," Tony said.

"Go ahead and start. We'll be right there."

We waited. Nat went back to the kitchen. Manny came in, beer in hand, and joined us at the table.

"Hey, *jefe*," he said to Tony. "How's it going?"

Tony glanced at him. "I'm not the *jefe*."

"Bad day, eh?"

"Not a great one." Tony drank some coffee.

Nat returned with plates for herself and Manny. "Well, thank you for joining us," she said. "It's lovely to have both of you here."

I wondered if I should tell Nat about the new murder, and how I might now be a target. I decided it wasn't a good topic for the dinner table.

"You should join us for Christmas dinner, Tony," Nat said. "You could meet Joe."

Tony looked at me. I smiled.

"That would be great," I said.

"I spend Christmas at my mom's," Tony said.

"Does your family have dinner on Christmas Eve, or Christmas Day?" Nat asked.

"Christmas Eve. We go to mass."

"Perfect! We have dinner on Christmas Day, about midday. Please join us."

I was beginning to feel like the woman tied to the railroad tracks in those corny old black and white movies. I could hear the train coming, and I knew it wouldn't end well, but there wasn't a thing I could do about it.

"I'll see," Tony said.

"He might have to work, Nat," I said.

"On Christmas?" she said, her voice filled with indignation.

"We'll see," Tony said, and took a huge bite of *relleno*.

Manny changed the subject to snow and roads and the busy demands of holiday business. I was deeply grateful to him. I answered his questions and otherwise kept quiet and ate my dinner. Tony said less than I did, but when Nat offered dessert, he politely accepted.

Nat brought us dishes of flan topped with fresh whipped cream. Tony took one bite and looked at her.

"You made this?"

Nat nodded, smiling. "Family favorite."

"It's really good." He took another bite "Mm. Now I know why Ellen's such a great cook."

"Oh, I didn't teach her to cook. Her mother did."

For some reason, this gave me a pang of grief. Memories of my mom in the kitchen, getting flour everywhere as the two of us made cookies. I swallowed, looking down at my flan.

"Was her mother your sister?" I heard Tony ask in a gentle voice.

"No, I married Geneva's brother," Nat said. "But she and I became best buddies."

I swallowed hard, then took a deep breath and looked up. Tony was watching me with soft eyes and a slight frown of concern. I mustered a smile for him and took a sip of water.

Soon afterward, Tony and I said good night and left, after Nat firmly told us we could not wash the dishes.

"Will you need me tomorrow?" she asked.

"No, no. Enjoy your day, and I'll see you Tuesday," I said. "Thanks for the wonderful dinner."

"OK, sweetie. Try to get some rest."

She gave me a mischievous smile with that, and glanced at Tony. I pretended not to see.

Manny saw us to the door and demanded a hug, which I gladly gave. He turned to Tony with an open hand, and gave him a hand-on-the-shoulder handshake. As I dug my keys out of my purse, he said something in Spanish to Tony that I didn't quite catch. I looked up, but the moment had passed.

Tony escorted me to the driver door of my Camry, then went around to his side. I drove slowly getting out of the neighborhood in the dark; there were no markings on the gravel roads.

"That was really good," Tony said. "Your aunt's a great cook."

"Yeah," I said, nodding. "Thanks for being willing to come. I needed to get out."

Tony sighed. "Well, you were right. I needed the break, and the food. This one's making me crazy."

"Tony—I have to tell you something about Dickie."

"What?"

I took a moment to collect my thoughts as I made the turn onto the paved road back toward town. "He was dating Debbie. Did you know that?"

"Yeah. You told me."

"Erica came to tea last Thursday, alone. She told me she waited on Debbie and a date at the Compound. I assume it was Dickie."

"Damn."

I glanced over at Tony.

"Wish I had known that a couple of days ago," he said.

"If I had known it would be important, I would have mentioned it."

I heard him sigh. "Yeah."

We didn't talk any more until we reached my house. I shut off the engine and turned to face him.

"I'm sorry—"

"No, don't be. You couldn't have known."

His face was shadowed, but a light from somewhere gleamed a reflection in his eyes. I bit my lip, wanting to be more helpful, and not knowing how.

"It's cold," he said. "Let's get you inside."

He walked me to the back door and waited while I unlocked it. "Want to come in for a minute?" I asked.

"Yes, and I can't. Got to get back." He leaned closed to kiss my cheek. "Lock everything."

"I did that earlier. Even checked all the windows."

"Check them again, then get a good night's sleep. I'll try to call tomorrow."

"OK."

He kissed me, long and intently, then backed away. "Night," he said.

"Good night."

He stepped out of reach and waited. I closed and locked the door, then watched him get on his motorcycle and drive away. When his red tail light had disappeared around the corner, I checked all the downstairs locks again, then went up.

Restlessness made me step to the front window, though I knew Tony would probably have taken a different street to get wherever he was going. I watched the traffic, which was dwindling now. Most of the stores and many of the restaurants would be closed by this time on a Sunday, though as the month progressed, some would lengthen their hours.

I felt like I was living in two different Decembers, being stretched thin between them: one full of holiday traditions, family gatherings, and memories; another completely taken up with running the tearoom, taking care of customers, and watching the books.

There was a third December happening, too—one I didn't like thinking about—where people I knew were being murdered by someone I probably also knew, who was angry for reasons I didn't comprehend. That December frightened me. I wanted it to go away. I wanted it to leave me and my friends—and Tony—alone.

Monday took place in the all-business December, and it went quickly. Julio and his staff were on top of the increased volume we needed. By the end of the day they had all the important set-up for the week completed, and had twenty dozen biscochitos boxed and ready to sell. Despite the extra work, Julio seemed to be in a good mood, and Hanh and Ramon followed his lead.

Kris got us caught up on all matters financial while juggling the reservations line all day. I had a fairly relaxing day doing the flowers and restocking the gift shop. The more I thought about it, and the more time I spent trying to find room to display additional merchandise, the more I agreed with Kris that Hyacinth and Poppy should go and the shop should expand into that space. It meant the fireplace would not be enjoyed by seated customers, but who was to say that the shoppers wouldn't enjoy it? I certainly would, as the chimney would warm up my bedroom.

Tony called at around eight in the evening. He didn't have anything new to tell me, and he sounded so tired that I begged him to go to bed and get some sleep. He promised to call again, and I promised to check all the locks again.

Tuesday began with a rush on the gift shop. All the extra biscochitos were gone by noon. We were booked solid, and I divided my time between helping in the shop and helping in the kitchen. Everything went smoothly until just after one o'clock, when the jingle of the front door bells was followed by a cacophony of female voices. I stepped into the hall and beheld the Bird Woman at the head of a large gaggle, all wearing white hats that looked like a cross between a nun's headdress and a mob cap.

Caught off guard, I blurted out, "What's this?"

The Bird Woman stopped in front of me, and since she came up to my chin, peered up into my face with her bright eyes. "We're the eight maids a-milking!"

7

In a moment of terror, I looked toward the door, expecting to see a live cow. Instead, I noticed that each of the ladies carried a two-foot high stuffed plush toy cow, standing upright (which was odd), with Holstein black and white fake fur.

"Mrs. Olavssen, hello!" Dale said behind me. "Welcome, ladies! Right this way. Let's hang up your coats here."

I shot Dale a grateful look as he shepherded the gaggle toward the dining parlor. He winked back at me. The milkmaids were considerably younger than the Bird Woman, which surprised me. The toy cows troubled me a bit, but I didn't have time to worry about them. More customers were at the door, waiting to be seated.

The next hour passed smoothly, and I gradually relaxed. It was quiet enough, once the guests were all seated, that Nat and I could take turns grabbing a cup of tea upstairs. I let Nat go first while I watched the gift shop and boxed biscochitos. Two of the boxes sold before Nat returned.

"Your turn," she said. "Kris wants you to look in."

"OK. Say, Nat, do you remember when Erica Wegman came in last week?"

"Your classmate? In the red dress?"

"That's the one. She had a friend with her, and I didn't catch her name. Did you, by any chance?"

Nat shook her head slowly. "Sorry."

"Well, thanks anyway."

I headed upstairs and stepped into Kris's office. Since she was on the phone, I went past her desk to fetch more fairy ornaments from the storage space.

"We've had a request to host a company holiday party on a day we're closed," Kris said, when I came out.

"What day?"

"The 20th."

"That's *our* holiday party."

Kris gave me a sharp glance, then a beaming smile. She looked back at her monitor and resumed her "professional" demeanor. "They're offering a lot, for the last-minute inconvenience."

"What company?"

"Benavides and Benavides."

I froze. That was Dickie's company.

"Tell them we're sorry, we have no availability for such an event this month."

Or ever.

"OK. Thanks."

I poured myself a cup of tea and sat by the window, wondering whether I should tell Tony about that request. I decided to wait until I saw him; it didn't seem urgent enough for me to interrupt his work.

It made me uncomfortable, though. I finished my tea, and before going downstairs, looked in on Kris again.

"Kris, do we have any reservations this month from a Richard Hernandez?"

"I'll check."

I waited while she searched the reservations system, and was relieved when she shook her head. "I have an Emily Hernandez on the twenty-first, is all. Party of three."

Dickie had no sisters, and he wasn't married. "OK, thanks," I said, and went downstairs.

Halfway down I heard an odd thumping. I paused, listening, and caught something that sounded like a groan.

Leaving the box of ornaments on the landing, I dashed down the stairs and hurried to the dining parlor. From the open doorway, I beheld an astonishing sight.

The tea things and china had been moved to the sideboards, along with the tablecloth and centerpiece. On the bare table were the eight toy Holstein cows, one in front of each seated "milkmaid." All the cows were jumping up and down and shouting "Moo! Mooooo!"

Not mooing. *Shouting* "moo."

I stood rooted, staring in horrified fascination. Dale stepped up beside me, took one look, and backed away, collapsing against the nearby wall in a fit of silent laughter. I shot him a dirty look, drew myself up, smiled, and stepped into the room.

"My, my," was all I could say. It was an inane remark, but it served to get the Bird Woman's attention. She grinned at me.

The cows were winding down. Apparently their performance was limited to a couple of minutes, because one by one they stopped jumping and fell silent. One of them tipped over on its final jump and was swiftly righted by its attendant milkmaid.

"Well, I've never seen anything like that before," I said.

The ladies all laughed, delighted. The Bird Woman gave me a smile that folded her face into a hundred wrinkles, but it was so innocently gleeful that I couldn't stay annoyed.

"Pretty good, huh?" she said. "I found them online."

"Amazing," I agreed. "Would you ladies like more tea?"

Several of them said they would, but my hopes of curtailing the cow activity were foiled by the Bird Woman, who said, "One more round first!"

The ladies took hold of their cows, each pressing some hidden switch that set the thing to jumping and mooing again. They ramped up gradually, their moos getting louder and longer until I decided I owed my other customers an explanation.

I stepped out, and found Dale still lurking in the hall. "The ladies would like more tea," I told him with frosty dignity. "Please take them some of the holiday blend."

Dale nodded, his eyes dancing, and fled to the butler's pantry. Armed with a plate of biscochitos, I went into the main parlor and visited each alcove there, explaining that the party in the dining parlor was being especially jolly, but there was no cause for alarm, and would you like an extra biscochito? The cookies and the explanation were both accepted with good grace, and after a few minutes, peace descended on the tearoom once more.

I peeked into the dining parlor and saw Dale retrieving teacups from the sideboard. The cows were gone from the table, most of them parked around the walls. The Bird Woman had hers in her lap. Feeling safer, I fetched my box of fairy ornaments from the stairs and went back to the gift shop.

Nat was chuckling behind the podium. I set the box before her and she opened it, handing me fairies to hang on the tree.

"I gather you looked into the dining parlor," I said, searching for a bare branch.

Nat nodded. "So did some of the customers. One of them asked if we could sell her a cow."

Absolutely not.

I hid in the gift shop until the Bird Woman and her maids a-milking left. By then it was almost closing time. I headed back to the kitchen to see if they needed any help, and found Dale hovering in the butler's pantry, looking anxious. He stood up straight when I looked in.

"Ellen, I want to apologize," he said formally.

I blinked. "For what?"

"For laughing, instead of reining in the milkmaids."

"Oh! Don't worry about that. Your reaction was normal."

"But I left you to deal with it, and they were my responsibility."

I chuckled. "You handle Mrs. Olavssen so beautifully most of the time, I think one lapse can be forgiven."

He relaxed into a small smile at that. "She's a hoot."

"She is that."

Dee brought in a tray of clean china from the kitchen and gave Dale a quizzical look. He immediately offered to help her put it away. I went on to the kitchen.

It was after six when I made it up to my suite and looked at my menu plans for the day.

Quiche. Yeah, right.

I called my favorite Thai place and ordered enough food for two, then phoned Tony. He answered, luckily.

"Dinner's on me, but you have to pick it up and bring it over."

He was silent for a moment. I had never spoken to him that peremptorily before, but he had essentially placed me under house arrest, so I felt justified.

"Please," I added.

I heard him sigh. "OK."

I gave him the details, then went up to my suite to set my small, round table with a tablecloth and a candle. When that was done I went down, said good night to Mick and Dee, who were just leaving, and made the rounds checking all the locks. By the time I was finished, I heard Tony's motorcycle out back, and went to meet him.

I relieved him of the carryout bags, set them down, and welcomed him with a hug, then locked the back door and invited him to hang his jacket and helmet on the hooks in the hall before going up. He seemed slightly less dejected, so I ventured a query on the way up the stairs.

"Better today?"

"A little. Some progress."

"Oh, good," I said, but didn't press him for details. I wanted him to relax and enjoy his dinner.

"This stuff was expensive," he remarked as we unpacked green curry and Pad Thai. The aromas of fresh cilantro and savory curry filled my kitchenette and made my mouth water.

"Let me reimburse you," I said, reaching for my purse.

"Nah, that's all right."

"But I said it was on me!"

Tony carried the boxes to the table. "If I hate it, you can pay me back."

"Don't you like Thai? I should have asked."

"Not sure I've ever had Thai."

"Oh. Well, this will be an adventure, then."

I nearly dropped a serving spoon as his arms wrapped around me from behind.

"I like the sound of that," he said, his warm breath tickling my ear. I squirmed around to face him, and we shared a most satisfying kiss. "You gonna hit me with that?" he asked, glancing at the spoon in my hand.

"No. But we should use it before your dinner gets cold."

We opened the last two beers of the pack he'd brought earlier and took our seats at the table. "Here's to solving the case!" I said, raising my bottle.

Tony grimaced, but clinked bottles with me. I offered him the Pad Thai.

While we served ourselves, I entertained him with a description of the Bird Woman's cadre of milkmaids and their jumping cows. His eyes got a little wide, but he didn't comment. Instead, I was glad to see, he tucked into the curry and Pad Thai without any hesitation.

"This is really good," he said. "I would've just got burgers."

I squeezed a lime wedge over my serving of Pad Thai. "Life's too short to subsist entirely on junk food."

Tony chuckled.

"So, you made progress today," I said. "Can you tell me about it?"

"Not much to tell. I took Dickie's picture over to the Compound and showed it around. Nobody recognized him."

"Oh." I took a bite of curry, thinking. "Maybe the people who were there the night he came weren't there today?"

"This was the third time I went," Tony said. "Nobody ID'd him, or any of the other suspects in the spread, and I've talked to all the managers and hostesses now."

"Suspects in the spread?"

"Photo line-up. I showed them pictures of Dickie, Michael Guzman, Steve Sawyer, and Daniel Snow. And a couple of ringers, just to fill it out. Nobody recognized any of them."

"Shoot."

"Yeah."

"May I see the photos?"

"They're in my jacket."

"Later, then." I twirled some noodles on my fork. "What about Debbie's photo? Did you show them that?"

"Yeah. Nobody recognized her, either."

"That's odd."

"A lot of people go through a restaurant in an evening."

"True." I had learned that one first hand. If I were asked to recall a single customer—from a week ago, perhaps—I'd be hard put to do it, even if shown a photo. Unless the customer had done something remarkable, they'd just be part of the blur.

I mused about Tony's case while I ate a chunk of bell pepper in curry sauce. There was a lot that he hadn't told me. Maybe some of it was confidential, but I wondered if more detail would give me inspiration.

"Do you have pictures of Debbie and Erica's apartments?" I asked.

Tony glanced up at me. "You don't want to see those."

"I don't mean the—the messy parts. Are there pictures of other things, like what was in the kitchen and the bathroom?"

Tony chewed a bite of food and swallowed. "Some, yeah."

"Could I see them?"

He thought about that, frowning. "If you swear not to discuss them with anyone."

"I will."

"Not even Gina. Or Nat."

"OK."

I watched him help himself to more Pad Thai. If I had done nothing else good that day, at least I had introduced Tony to a new cuisine.

I took a sip of beer. "Do you know who at the Compound usually worked at the same time Erica did?"

"I asked," Tony said. "Their schedules are all over the place. Unless Erica mentioned a date ..."

I shook my head.

"Then there's no telling. There are a few waiters I haven't talked to yet, but I have a feeling that's a dead end."

I regarded him thoughtfully. "Do you often trust your feelings?"

"Yeah. They're usually right."

I wondered what Willow would have to say about that. Not that it mattered. I was pretty sure Tony considered Willow a kook.

We finished our meal, and Tony went downstairs to fetch his photos while I cleared the table. I moved the candle to the little table between my two armchairs, and set a plate of biscochitos beside it, then started a pot of coffee.

I kept remembering Erica in her wonderful red dress and hat. How beautiful she'd looked. And how brilliant she had been. What a shame.

"Tony," I said as he returned, "Did you know that Erica was a genius?"

He gave me a skeptical look. "She was a waitress."

"She was our valedictorian. She won a scholarship to Harvard. Something went wrong there—I'm not sure what. But the job at the Compound was only temporary—I'm sure of that. She would have gone on to better things."

"Hm." He pulled his notebook out of his jacket pocket and made a note.

"Have you talked to her family?" I asked.

"No. They've been notified, but they don't live in town. Her mom's in LA, and her dad is out of the picture. He divorced her mom and married a blackjack dealer in Vegas. Hasn't been heard from in a while."

"Oh. Well, it might be worth following up with them."

"Maybe." He fished in his jacket again, coming up with a handful of photos. "Here's the lineup."

Tony laid six head shots of men on my café table, in two rows. Dickie was number 5. I recognized number 2 as Steve Sawyer and number 4 as Justin Davis. Two others, number 3 and number 6, looked familiar. I peered at each of them.

"Oh! That's Michael!" I picked up picture number 3 for a closer look. "Wow, he's lost some hair. I didn't recognize him at first."

I put the picture down and tapped number 6 with a fingertip. "Who's this, then?"

"That's one of the ringers."

"But he looks familiar."

I picked up the photo: an Anglo man, about twenty-five, with medium brown hair, brown eyes, square jaw, slightly heavy-set. His expression was disgruntled, but as I suspected the photo was a mug shot, that wasn't surprising.

"Not from our class," I said slowly. "And he's not one of my customers. We don't get that many men, and I'd remember if I'd seen him in the tearoom. But I *did* see him, fairly recently."

Tony took the photo from me and looked at the back, where there was a printed label that I couldn't read from that angle. "Around town maybe?"

"Maybe." I picked up my beer, which I hadn't quite finished, from the kitchenette counter and took a swallow. "What did he do?"

"DWI a couple of years ago. He got caught in a checkpoint. Paid his fine and did some community service. Other than that he's clean."

"Hm." I sat at the table, looking at the rest of the pictures and thinking over the last couple of weeks. I hadn't seen any of the others recently, except for Dickie.

"Oh! The funeral!" I reached for the photo and Tony gave it to me. "Yes, that's it. He was at Debbie's funeral."

"Really?" Tony stepped up behind my chair to look at the photo. "I don't remember him."

"He left early. I saw him during the service, but I don't think he stayed for refreshments."

Tony frowned as I gave him the photo. "He's not from your class?"

"Not that I remember. Do you have his age?"

He looked at the label on the back again. "Looks like 29."

"OK, he would've graduated before me, then." I stood, put my empty beer bottle on the counter, and checked the coffeemaker. "Want some coffee?"

"Sure," Tony said.

I poured us mugs—black for Tony, cream for me—and carried them over to the comfy chairs by the still-warm chimney. Tony joined me, taking a deep pull from his mug.

"So what was our mystery guy doing at the funeral?" he

asked.

"Good question," I said. "Maybe he was in Heather's class."

Tony rubbed his chin and picked up a biscochito. "Do you remember any more about him?"

I thought about it. "He was sitting in the same pew as Daniel. I think I saw him go up and talk to Heather afterward. Then he went up the side aisle—I remember being surprised that you weren't there, because you'd been standing there before."

"I moved closer to the altar after the service, to watch facial expressions."

I nodded. "Yes, I think he left by the front doors. Do you have the guest book?"

"Yeah. Heather didn't want to give it to us, but we pried it out of her."

"Poor Heather." Something was niggling at me, but I couldn't figure out what. "You interviewed her, right?" I asked, figuring it was a dumb question.

"Yeah," he said, shifting a pillow behind himself. "She and her husband were at home the night Debbie was killed."

"And Mr. Fisher was at his home, alone."

"Kind of alone. He's got an apartment in a gated community. Eats dinner in the restaurant there every night."

"And he had dinner there that night?"

Tony nodded. "Then walked home. The gate guards confirmed that they hadn't seen his car go out."

I picked up a biscochito. "He could have left some other way."

"Yeah, but that's leaning toward improbable. Plus, we have no motive for him to kill his own daughter."

I tilted my head as I chewed a bite of cookie, searching memories. I might have met Debbie's father a couple of times before the funeral, but couldn't recall anything remarkable. Debbie's mother had been sassy, like Debbie herself.

"How did Debbie's mom die?" I asked.

"Heart attack. Four years ago. Heather's still messed up about it. Kept bringing it up during her interview."

I nodded. "You don't get over losing your mom in just a couple of years."

Tony froze. "Sorry. I forgot."

I shrugged a shoulder and tried to smile. "It's OK. You probably feel the same about your dad."

The wince was small, but it was there. I hadn't meant to hurt him.

"Now *I'm* sorry," I said softly.

Tony shook his head. "Forget it. Everybody has wounds."

We sat in silence for a couple of minutes. I could hear distant traffic sounds from the street.

"About Christmas," Tony began, then stopped.

"Yes?"

"It was nice of your aunt to invite me."

I waited, but he'd stalled. He sat frowning at the floor.

"It's OK if you can't be there," I said.

"No, that's not…I mean…" He rubbed his face, then sat up straighter and turned to me. "My mom wants me to invite you to our dinner. Christmas Eve," he said in a rush.

"Oh!"

"You don't have to come."

"I'd love to come. May I bring anything?"

Tony shook his head. "There's always too much food. She'll have Angela cooking all week."

"OK. Then what can I bring for a hostess gift?"

"We're not expecting you to bring presents."

Tony's flat tone rang a small alarm bell in my head. He was uncomfortable with the subject.

"All right," I said. "But a hostess gift is just a little thank-you. Would your mother like an ornament, do you think?"

"She's got boxes and boxes of ornaments. Too many for one tree. I know 'cause I just pulled them out of storage."

"I see. Well, does she like tea? I could bring a package of our holiday blend."

"She drinks coffee, mostly."

I bit my lip. With Tony in this mood, I might as well stop

making suggestions.

"Well, I'll think of something," I said. "Chocolate, if all else fails. Or is she allergic to chocolate?"

That pulled a reluctant smile out of him. "She loves chocolate."

"Great. I'll bring her some."

He nodded, but didn't say anything. He still seemed uncomfortable.

"Would you rather I didn't come?" I asked gently.

"No, no! My mom wants you to come. They all do."

I turned in my chair to look straight at him. "Do you? Honestly? Because I'm getting the feeling you don't."

He sighed. "It's just...you don't know my family. It might be weird."

"I would like to get to know them better," I offered.

"*Abuela* speaks Spanish most of the time. I don't want you to feel left out."

"I can understand Spanish fairly well, though I'm rough speaking it."

"See, and she'll talk about you in Spanish, right in front of you. Your feelings might get hurt."

"I'm willing to risk it. But if it would make you uncomfortable, I'll decline the invitation."

"No, I..."

I waited, watching him. He looked dismayed. Glancing away from my gaze, he looked at his watch.

"I have to go. Back to work."

He stood and shrugged into his jacket. I watched him gather up the head shots.

"What about the pictures of Debbie's apartment?" I asked. "And Erica's?"

"I'll print those out for you," he said, zipping the jacket closed. "I'll bring them over tomorrow."

"OK."

I accompanied him downstairs to lock the back door after him. He retrieved his helmet and turned to me as he put on his gloves.

"Thanks for dinner," he said.

"Thank *you,* you paid for it."

"Worth it. Now I know what Thai is like."

"Want to try something else tomorrow?" I asked. "Since I'm not going out by myself. And this time I *will* pay."

"Um, I'll have to see. Depends how much I get done."

"OK. Let's touch base in the afternoon."

"Yeah."

He stood staring at me. If it hadn't been a work night, I would have asked him to stay, but the thought of explaining (or not explaining) his early morning presence to Hanh made me blush.

"Thanks for the help," he said at last.

"I hope it *is* helpful."

"It is. Very."

"I'm glad, then."

He leaned very close, and gave me a long, slow kiss, tasting sweetly of anise. "Lock everything," he murmured into my ear.

"I will. Be careful."

"I'm always careful."

He smiled, but it was a cop smile. I watched him go out into the cold night, wondering which of the many threads of the case he intended to pursue next.

As it turned out, we didn't see each other again until Friday. Tony wound up buried in work for a couple of days, so I ate leftover Thai on Wednesday and went out with Gina for dinner on Thursday. While this could have been disappointing, the days were so busy that I had no time to mope.

"Nonna Fiorello wants me to tell you you're invited for Christmas," Gina said over sushi.

I sipped my jasmine tea. "Give her my thanks, but I'm booked up already."

"Good. You've got better things to do than go stag to a family party."

Again.

Not that I'd mind—I loved Gina's grandmother, and I'd enjoyed celebrating Thanksgiving with them. But, yeah. Being a solo guest at a holiday dinner was a little sad.

"Joe's coming," I said. "Did I tell you?"

"No! He still single?"

I shot her a suspicious look. "I don't think he's your type."

She shrugged, grinning. "I've had a crush on him ever since fifth grade. Don't tell me you didn't know."

"If I did, I must have blanked it from my memory."

Gina helped herself to a piece of dragon roll. "Maybe we could all walk up Canyon Road on Christmas Eve."

"Um...maybe. We'll see. It would have to be late."

"Oh, yeah, definitely. Too crowded early in the evening." With a nimble deployment of chopsticks, she pulled a paper-thin slice of pickled ginger from the heap on a side plate. This made me think of food photography. I opened my purse.

"Here's that business card you wanted. The photographer." I handed her Owen's card.

"Thanks!" She stashed the card in her own bag. "Say, is Tony making progress with his case?"

"Last I heard he was."

"Because I'm getting a little tired of feeling paranoid, you know?"

"Tell me about it."

"It's Dickie, isn't it?"

Startled, I looked up at her, dropping my California roll. "What makes you say that?"

"Because of all our old classmates, he's the one who most deserves to be in jail."

I was glad that the sushi place had music playing. This was a conversation I hoped wouldn't be overheard. I adjusted my chopsticks and retrieved my roll. "Well..."

"And because he was being a jerk to Heather at the funeral."

"Did you hear him say something to her?"

"No, but I could tell by her face he was doing his usual

thing."

"When was this?"

"After the service."

I ate my roll, musing. Had Tony talked to Heather about Dickie? I'd have to ask him.

Friday morning, I was in the gift shop shortly before we opened when I heard a tapping at the front door. I went out to the hall and saw Angela Aragón, Tony's sister, bundled against the cold in a pink parka and matching knit hat, waving at me through the lights.

"Angela! I didn't see your name on the reservations list," I said as I opened the door for her.

"Oh, I'm not here for tea," she said, wiping her boots on the doormat. "I'm on my way to class. I just wanted to talk to you if you have a minute."

"Sure. Come on in. Do you have time for one cup of tea?"

She checked her watch. "I have about fifteen minutes."

"That'll do. Poppy's open."

I led her to the smallest alcove, took her coat, and fetched tea, china, and a few biscochitos. Nat gave me a nod as I passed through the gift shop with my tray.

"I'll open up when it's time," she said.

"Thanks!"

I joined Angela, who was already seated in one of two poppy red wing chairs. She smoothed her dark brown hair in a self-conscious gesture, and her eyes held a hint of worry that reminded me of Tony.

"This is nice of you," she said. "I didn't mean to be any trouble."

"It's no trouble," I said, handing her a filled teacup. "I've been meaning to invite you to tea, actually, but this month has been a little crazy."

She nodded. "Me, too. Finals in a couple of weeks."

"Would you like to come in January some time? We'll have afternoon tea and a good, long chat."

"That sounds wonderful! Yes, I'd love to, maybe before the semester starts."

"Good. We'll compare calendars." I added milk to my tea. "What did you want to talk about?"

"Oh—I just wanted to check that Tony had asked you to Christmas dinner."

"Yes, he did. Did he not tell you?"

"He said he had, but Mama wanted to be sure. Sometimes…"

"Sometimes he forgets, I'm sure. He's often so busy."

"Yes." She smiled a little wistfully and sipped her tea. I did the same.

So I wasn't the only one who had to work to communicate with Tony. Dutch comfort, but I'd take it.

"Tony said your mother will have you cooking for a week," I said. "Is there anything I could help with?"

"Oh!" Angela laughed, dismissing it with a wave of her hand. "He was exaggerating. We make tamales, that's probably what he's thinking of. But it only takes a couple of days."

"One of these years I'll learn how," I said.

"You've never made tamales?"

I shook my head. "Don't tell. I don't want to lose my native New Mexican status."

"Well…I could ask Mama if she wants extra help…"

"Actually, I think I should learn at a quieter time of year," I said. "There's enough going on this month already."

Angela nodded, looking relieved, and I knew I'd given the right answer. I offered her the biscochitos.

"Mmm," she said after trying one. "These are better than mine!"

"Julio and Hanh get all the credit. You remember Julio?"

She nodded. "He made the skulls we decorated."

I took a swallow of tea, distracted by thoughts of the kitchen and the ever-present to-do list. With an effort, I banished them and smiled at Angela.

"Tony didn't say what time I should come over on Christmas Eve."

"Oh—we have dinner kind of late that night," she said. "Seven thirty."

"Perfect. We close at six, and that will give me time to freshen up."

"Mama will ask you to join us at midnight mass. Don't feel like you have to."

"Thank you," I said. "I'll have to see—my brother will be here from out of town. We usually have presents and all on Christmas morning."

Angela nodded and took another biscochito.

"Tony said I shouldn't bring any gifts," I added, "but I'd like to bring your mother a hostess gift. Would she like some of these?" I gestured at the biscochitos.

Angela, her mouth full of cookie, nodded enthusiastically. She drank some tea and swallowed. "If you don't mind, I'll tell Mama you're bringing them. Then I won't have to make any."

"That's fine, if you're sure I won't be interfering with her plans."

"Oh, no! She'll love them. She went on about your food for weeks after you treated us to tea."

"Is that why she invited me for Christmas? Because I asked you all to tea? That wasn't necessary."

"No, that isn't why."

I gave Angela an inquiring look, but refrained from prompting. I didn't want to pry.

"Tony talks about you, you know," she said.

"He does?"

She nodded. "And he's never talked about his—about dating, much."

"I see." I took a sip of tea, telling my silly, fluttering heart to calm down.

"So Mama's been wanting to invite you," Angela said. "But Tony's shy about it."

"Why?" I asked before I could stop myself.

"Well, you live here." Angela gestured to the Victorian décor around us. "Mama's apartment is pretty small. She's got the same curtains she had in the nineties."

"That's not important," I said.

"It is to Tony, I think."

"Oh."

I bit my lip. Sooner or later, Tony and I were going to have to discuss this. We'd been dancing around the subject of money—specifically what I'd inherited and invested in the tearoom—ever since we'd met.

Yes, I was fortunate; more so financially than he. I had never been so aware of it before getting to know Tony. I tried not to rub his face in it, but it was always there. I knew that cops didn't make a lot of money, although as a detective I assumed his salary was better than a beat cop's. And I was pretty sure he was helping to support his grandmother.

It was pointless to try to explain to him how much of my worth was at risk, and how easily I could lose it all. So far I'd done well with the tearoom, but the mortgage was always there, looming over my shoulder. Yet, to Tony, I must seem fabulously wealthy.

I realized Angela was watching me. Again, I shook off distraction and gave her my attention. "How many biscochitos should I bring?"

She gave me a shy grin. "I usually make six dozen. Mama takes some to work."

"I'll bring six dozen, then, unless you'd like more?"

"That's plenty. Mama will be thrilled."

A thought flicked through my brain: the cost of butter, cinnamon, anise…and the time it took to bake.

"I'm looking forward to seeing your mother and grandmother again," I said.

Angela nodded. "*Abuela* really wants to see you. She's the one who said we should invite you."

"Is she? I'm flattered."

Angela smiled to herself, as if at a sweet memory, but didn't share it. She lifted her cup to drink the last bit of tea.

I picked up the pot, offering to fill her cup, but she shook her head. "I have to get going. Thanks for the tea!"

"Thanks for the clarification. Please tell your mother—and *Abuela*—that I'm looking forward to Christmas."

We stood, and I fetched Angela's coat and hat from the hall. Coming back, I paused to pick up a paper bag from the pastry counter. While Angela put on her coat, I slipped the remaining biscochitos into the bag.

"Here. Have your mother try them. If she doesn't like them I'll think of something else."

Angela grinned. "She'll like them. Thanks, Ellen."

She caught me in a quick hug, then hurried out the front door. I watched her go, feeling pleased and a little nervous, then returned to clear our tea things from Poppy.

"Such a sweet girl," Nat said, coming in to help me.

"Yes."

"She'd be a good sister."

I straightened up and fixed Nat with a Class A Stink-eye. She grinned and went back to the gift shop. I carried my tea tray to the kitchen, handed it over to Mick, and then went upstairs, where I tried very hard not to think about the Aragóns. *Any* of them.

Work ran late, with Kris wanting to plan a staff meeting as well as our holiday party. It took us a while to shoehorn the meeting into our schedule. Mondays were starting to look almost like regular business days now, with Julio, Hanh, and Ramon churning out biscochitos all day in the kitchen, and Kris at her desk until late. We decided on a one-hour meeting on Tuesday morning at nine, and Kris composed an announcement message letting everyone know that they'd be paid for their time.

Once we'd dealt with all the urgent matters, Kris balanced out the register and left for home, a bulging bank bag tucked under her arm inside her coat. "See you tomorrow," she said with a fleeting smile.

I followed her downstairs for my now-nightly ritual of checking all the locks after the staff was gone. As I stepped into the kitchen, I was surprised to see Julio just hanging up his apron. Everyone else—even Mick—had left.

"You're here late! Is everything all right?" I asked.

"Yeah. I just wanted to get a little ahead on tomorrow," Julio said. "I'll be coming in a bit late, if that's all right."

"Sure."

"Hanh will be here on time. I'll try to be in by nine."

"OK."

Curiosity made me speculate. Maybe Julio had a hot date, and intended to sleep in. I told my curiosity to mind its manners.

"How's the new place?" I asked.

"Oh, I love it!" Julio said, flashing a smile as he shrugged into his jacket. "It's great. Really great."

"I'm glad. Careful going home," I said, following him to the back door.

He nodded. *"Mañana."*

I watched through the lights as he unlocked his bicycle and rode down the driveway. When he was out of sight, I locked the back door and made the rounds, checking that the fires were banked as well as checking the locks. It wasn't until I looked at the time (after seven) and went up to consult my menu plan that I heard from Tony.

My cell phone started ringing as I entered my suite. I caught it up and made myself wait until the third ring before answering.

"Hi," I said, trying to sound nonchalant.

"What's for dinner?" Tony asked.

I looked at the menu plan. Shrimp etouffee.

My menu plan definitely needed a reality check.

"You know, green chile cheeseburgers sound really good right now," I said.

"You got it. Be there in half an hour."

I set the table, then poured myself a virtuous glass of water and sat down with a notepad and pencil to finish my gift list. I already had my family's names, Gina, my staff, and Tony. I added Willow, then stared at the list, unable to think of a gift for any of them. My brain was full of fairy ornaments and biscochitos.

Nat was right. I needed to get out more.

I sent Gina a text asking about going shopping on Sunday afternoon. Maybe she'd drop a hint about what she wanted.

Other than a date with my brother.

And I had no idea at all what to get for Joe. We had fallen out of touch the past few years. Single malt, maybe?

I sighed. Liquor was an easy out. I could do better than that.

The back doorbell rescued me. Setting the list aside, I went down to let Tony in.

"Starting to snow," he said, handing me a white paper bag from which familiar, enticing aromas rose. I could see that the shoulders of his leather jacket were speckled with moisture.

I spotted the red and blue logo on the bag. "Blake's! Bless you!"

"Only the best for you," Tony said, setting a sixpack down on a chair. He hung his helmet and coat up on hooks, extracted a slightly crumpled manila envelope from his coat, grabbed the six-pack, and headed for the stairs.

I locked the door and followed him up, noting with amusement that he didn't wait for me to lead. Maybe he was hungry. I certainly was.

Tony opened a couple of beers while I unpacked the food. Not only were there two double-decker green chile cheeseburgers, there were two bags of fries. A feast.

There is a certain delight in eating high quality junk food. Blake's Lotaburger had been around for decades—since before I was born—and despite not being the Holy Grail of green chile cheeseburgers (that distinction belonged to the Owl Cafe in San Antonio, New Mexico), they were everyone's go-to, at least in Santa Fe. The slow, sensuous burn of green chile, mitigated by the tang of cheese and a perfectly grilled burger—salty fries on the side—was comfort food at its finest.

When we had taken the edge off our hunger, I asked Tony how his day had gone. He shrugged.

"Chasing dead ends, mostly. I talked to Heather about the mystery guy."

"Oh?"

"You were right, he's from Heather's class. She told me he took her on a couple of dates in school, but that was all."

"Hm." I ate a fry. "When did she meet her husband? Jared?"

"Justin. College, apparently." Tony took a bite of his burger, chewed it, and washed it down with beer. "I called Erica's folks," he added.

"Oh?"

"Her mom started crying. Left a voicemail for her dad."

"Oh."

"Like I said, dead ends. That's a lot of what I do, really. Oh—I brought you pictures of Debbie's apartment."

He retrieved the manila envelope from my bookcase, opened it, and offered me a handful of pages from a color printer. I looked through them slowly while I ate my cheeseburger.

Debbie's apartment had been decorated in a minimalist, modern style that I found rather austere. Lots of neutral gray and white tones, not much color, except for a pair of blood red cushions on a black leather couch.

The kitchen was more of the same: brushed steel everywhere. I peered at a photo of the open refrigerator. There wasn't much inside: a pizza box, some cans of seltzer, diet soda, milk, creamer, eggs, broccoli, a wilting bunch of spinach.

I shuffled through all the kitchen photos. "Does Debbie's place have a wine cellar?"

"No."

"Pantry cupboard?"

"No."

"Huh. Then either she's really changed, or she's pregnant."

8

TONY FROZE, BURGER IN HAND, staring at me. Dread that I'd said something horrible overcame me.

"W-was pregnant, I mean," I said.

Tony put down his burger. "What makes you think that?"

I shrugged. "No booze anywhere in her apartment. Leftover pizza, but no beer. Debbie was always a party girl. I think you said she didn't have any drugs, either."

"Yeah. No drugs or alcohol in the apartment."

"Well, that would be a big change for her," I said. "Not so much the drugs, but the alcohol."

He watched me in silence. Realization dawned, and I put my burger down.

"You knew."

"Yeah. OMI came back with that right away."

"OMI?"

"Office of the Medical Investigator, down in Albuquerque. They do all the autopsies for the state."

"Oh." I toyed with a fry. "You didn't tell me."

"Babe, I'm not supposed to be telling you anything."

"But I'm right."

"Yeah, you're right."

Trying not to feel miffed, I picked up my beer. "The no alcohol is strange. She was kind of infamous, in school," I said, and a memory clicked into place. "Oh, my God, that was it! That's why she was disqualified from being homecoming queen!"

"Wait—what?" Tony said.

"She got caught with a fifth of vodka in her locker! It was a huge scandal. Kids were betting on whether she'd get kicked out of school without graduating. The school let her stay in the end, but they took away the homecoming crown."

Tony gave a nod, but didn't say anything. I looked at the printed photos on the table before me. Picked up the one of the open fridge. "Spinach and broccoli," I remarked. "Both high in folic acid. She was pregnant."

Tony got up and paced a little. He ended up by the chimney, leaned an arm on it, then stepped back in surprise.

"That's warm!"

"From the fires downstairs," I said. "They're down to coals now. It's safe."

He came back to the table, slid into his seat and folded his hands in front of him, meeting my gaze. "Debbie was stabbed thirty-one times. All but five were in the lower abdomen."

"Oh my God!" I covered my gaping mouth, breathing through my nose. Poor Debbie!

Tony stood, picked up our plates, and carried them to the kitchenette. I was grateful; food was the last thing I wanted to think about.

So Debbie's killer was also—maybe primarily—trying to kill her unborn child. As Tony returned to his seat, I looked up at him.

"W-what about Erica?" I asked unsteadily.

"She was stabbed fewer times. Nineteen. Mostly around the neck and upper chest."

"Different," I managed to say.

Tony nodded. "Not as angry. Not as personal. And she probably wasn't pregnant, but I'll verify that. We're thinking it was the same killer, though, from the way they held the knife."

My throat was tightening. I took a swig of beer, then regretted it. What I needed was a glass of water. I managed to swallow, then got up and fetched water for both of us.

"Thanks," Tony said as I handed him a glass. "You OK?"

"Not really." I drank some water, then sank back into my chair at the table.

"Should I go?"

"No—no, please stay." I picked up my glass, but my hand shook, slopping water on the printed photos. I put the glass down and brushed the water off of the already-wrinkling pages.

"Don't worry about that," Tony said, catching one of my hands. "Ellen. Stop."

I stopped, looking up at him. There was deep sadness in his dark eyes.

"I shouldn't have told you this," he said.

"I-I won't tell anyone," I offered.

"I'm not worried about that. I mean I shouldn't have put this on you."

"I wanted to help."

His hand tightened on mine. "Well, you have helped. A lot. But you shouldn't have to deal with this crap. I'm sorry."

I took a deep breath and swallowed, then pulled at my hand. Tony released it. I picked up my glass with both hands and drank some more water.

"Was it Dickie?" I asked. "Do you think he—"

"Don't think about it."

I couldn't help thinking about it. I rubbed at my eyes, which were leaking.

Tony got up and came around the table. He lifted me to my feet, then deftly picked me up and carried me into my bedroom, where he sat me on the foot of the bed and wrapped his arms around me.

I sobbed a bit. Tony held me, not saying anything, just letting me finish quietly freaking out. When I was breathing more or less normally, he loosened his hold and kissed my forehead.

"Sorry, Ellen," he murmured. "I won't make you do this any more."

"Oh, no you don't!" I pulled back to look him in the eyes. "You can't shut me out now!"

He smoothed my hair back from my face. "This stuff'll give you nightmares."

"I'm a grown-up. I can manage."

He hugged me again. To be honest, I needed the comfort. The thought of Dickie killing Debbie—because she was carrying his child? And then Erica…why Erica? Could she have been pregnant, too? I couldn't imagine Erica ever, ever going out with Dickie, much less sleeping with him. But then, I wouldn't have imagined her waiting tables, either.

I laid my head on Tony's shoulder and closed my eyes, trying to push away the awful questions. He pressed his cheek against mine—warm and a little rough—and rubbed my back between the shoulder blades with a firm hand.

"You got any Valium?" Tony asked.

"You take Valium?"

"For you, babe. Not for me."

"Oh. No, I don't."

He kept rubbing circles on my back until my shoulder muscles started to relax. I took a deeper breath and let it out in a sigh. Tony leaned back to look at me.

"I need to make a phone call," he said gently. "I'm going to go downstairs for a minute, then I'll be back. OK?"

I nodded.

He slid his hands down my arms to grasp my hands, gave them a squeeze, then let go and left the suite. I lay back on the bed, staring up at the canopy, trying not to think about anything. I listened to Tony's tread on the stairs, then heard the murmur of his voice, too distant to understand what he was saying.

A Christmas carol began running through my head, one that I'd sung in school, and was on our holiday rotation for the tearoom:

> *The holly and the ivy, when they are both full grown,*
>
> *Of all the trees that are in the wood, the holly bears the crown.*
>
> *The rising of the sun and the running of the deer,*
>
> *The playing of the merry organ, sweet singing in the choir.*

I felt detached, drifting. Numb. Reaction to the awful. I knew this place: it was the space at the head of a long, downward-spiraling path I had traveled before. I looked into the mist, but didn't enter.

> *The holly bears a blossom, as white as lily flower...*

I should plant some holly in the garden. Already had plenty of ivy.

Tony's tread on the stairs brought me back to the present. I sat up, not wanting him to think I was a blubbering mess.

Quivering, maybe, but not blubbering. Not at the moment.

I rubbed my hands over my face and made an attempt to smooth my hair. Tony came in, shooting a concerned glance my way. I tried for a courageous smile.

He sat beside me and took my hand in his. "I have to go."

"You could spend the night."

"That sounds great, but I can't."

I nodded understanding, disappointed. Tony put his arm around me and kissed my cheek, and as I turned toward him, he kissed me for real. Then he let me go and stood up.

"You OK coming down to lock me out?"

"I'm fine," I said carefully, smoothing my hair some more.

He waited while I fetched my keys, and we walked down together. I watched him put on his jacket and retrieve his helmet from the row of hooks in the hall. "I'll call you," he said.

I nodded. He meant it, I knew. Probably he'd be too busy, but he really did mean to call.

"Tomorrow night I'll take you out for a real dinner," he said at the door.

"OK."

He put a hand on my cheek. "You going to be OK?"

"Yes."

One kiss, long and slow. Another on the forehead. Then he was gone, striding to his bike. I closed the door, locked it, and watched through the lights until his taillights turned the corner and the sound of his engine was lost in the Friday night traffic.

I would be OK, yes. Maybe no more than that, but for now OK was enough.

Remembering Tony's reaction to the chimney, I decided to double-triple-check the fireplaces. The ones that warmed the chimney in my suite were on the south side of the house, back-to-back fireplaces that were shared by Hyacinth and Poppy on one side and Dahlia and Violet on the other.

The downstairs lights were out except for the twinkle lights around the windows at the front of the house. I left it that way, enjoying the colors in the darkness.

The trees were all unplugged. In the gift shop, the ornaments on the tree and the merchandise on the shelves all glinted faintly in the dark, throwing back the soft colors of the twinkle lights. I checked the coals in both sides of the fireplace, making sure they were raked to the back of the fireboxes, and that the screens were in place.

Might as well check the other fireplaces while I was at it.

I crossed the hall to the main parlor. Here, too, the tree in the middle was dark, while the twinkle lights in the windows made faint, colored gleams on the ornaments and garlands. I examined the fireplace, then opened the door from Rose into the dining parlor to check that side.

No twinkle lights here. The room was pitch dark. I had turned the back light off once Tony was gone, and there was no moon to shine through the sheers over the French doors.

I knew my way around the room, though—didn't need any lights. I stepped to the fireplace, feeling the faint warmth of the coals on my ankles. Reached out a hand to touch the screen.

The piano in the main parlor began to play.

Five descending notes. At first I thought it was a scale, but the next few notes identified the melody and made the hair at the nape of my neck rise.

...the holly bears the crown.

Tony was right. I had nightmares.

They were vague and disturbing, and none of the details stuck in my memory. I tossed in my bed, not wanting to take a sleep aid because it would make me groggy in the morning. By dawn, I was exhausted and fell into a weary sleep. It was the smells of baking—particularly anise—wafting up from downstairs that finally pulled me awake.

Biscochitos.

I dragged myself into the shower. None of the dreams had stayed with me, but the legacy of weariness and a tinge of primal fear were left behind.

I emerged in my bathrobe and stared blankly at my kitchen. I should eat something.

My half-eaten cheeseburger was in the fridge. I'd had the presence of mind to put it away before going to bed. That was when I'd noticed Tony's empty plate on the counter; he must have finished his burger while he was making his phone call. The water-damaged photo printouts were gone, too.

It was sweet, the way he wanted to protect me. Unfortunately, he couldn't protect me from my own imagination.

Cold cheeseburger for breakfast didn't do it for me. I grabbed a yogurt that I'd picked up at Kaune's, ate it without tasting it, and decided to get dressed. I pulled a random, reasonably comfortable dress out of my closet and put it on, made an attempt at hair and makeup, and headed downstairs.

A male voice in the kitchen aroused my curiosity, so instead of making tea right away I went through. Hanh looked up from the counter where she was cutting out cookies, and reached over to turn down the radio on Julio's boombox.

"Good morning," she said, watching me as if awaiting orders.

I offered a smile. "Morning. You don't have any coffee going, do you?"

She shook her head. "There's some genmaicha. Please help yourself."

She nodded toward the end of the counter, where a side-handled pottery teapot sat gently steaming. I took down a mug from the shelf of utility china and filled it, tilting the pot carefully with the unfamiliar handle.

The teapot was massive, two-toned cream and chocolate, and retained the heat nicely. "Is this your pot?" I asked.

Hanh nodded. "I've had it for years."

"And you brought your own tea. You know, you're welcome to use any of our tea."

Hanh smiled, glancing up at me. "You don't have genmaicha."

It was true, we didn't. I sipped, and found the nutty flavor of the traditional rice-blended green—the "People's Tea"—comforting.

"We'll have to change that," I said. "I'd forgotten how much I liked it."

Hanh's smile widened a bit as she worked. That was about as

demonstrative as I'd ever seen her.

"Are you on track for today, or do you need help?" I asked.

"I'm fine. Ramon is coming in." She glanced at the clock, and I followed her gaze. Seven-forty-two.

Almost four hours until we opened. I could relax.

I walked through the parlors, sipping my genmaicha and plugging in the tree lights. In the main parlor, I stopped beside the piano. Doubt wanted me to question whether I'd really heard the instrument playing the night before, or imagined it.

I firmly dismissed that doubt. Yes, I had heard it. I wasn't sure *why*, but I was certain the captain had played the piano for me. Perhaps he just meant to comfort me.

I opened the keyboard cover and played middle G. That was the first note I'd heard, standing in the dining parlor. I played on, descending from G to C.

Of all the trees...

The front doorbell rang. Frowning, I looked up. I was sure that I'd turned the sign around to "CLOSED" the night before, and our hours were on the door.

Another ring. I shut the piano and went to investigate.

Through the lights, I could see a short figure in a white parka outside the door. Beyond, I was surprised to see that the yard was covered in snow—a couple of inches, at least. The figure outside moved to look in through one of the lights and I recognized my neighbor, Katie Hutchins. I hastened to unlock the door.

"Katie! Come in, come in."

Katie's round cheeks were bright with the cold, and she smiled as I pushed the door shut against the chilly breeze that accompanied her.

"Thanks, Ellen! Merry Christmas!"

"Merry Christmas," I said. "How's the B&B doing?"

"Oh, great! We're booked solid through New Year's. Skiing's good this year."

I nodded. "What can I do for you?"

"Well, I was wondering if you might sell me some of your biscochitos. Is that what I'm smelling?"

"Yes."

"A couple of our guests had tea here yesterday and they just raved about them!"

"Ah. Yes, we've been doing quite well with them. Let me see…"

I led Katie into the gift shop and opened the pastry case. Less than a dozen cookies were left in there from the previous day. I put one on a napkin and handed it to Katie.

"See what you think."

She took a bite. "Mmmm!" She closed her eyes, looking blissful as she chewed. "Oh, Ellen, that's wonderful! Could I get two dozen?"

"I'll have to ask the kitchen. They're making them as fast as they can. Have you met my new assistant chef?"

Katie, munching on the rest of her cookie, shook her head.

"Come on back," I said, heading down the hall.

Katie shed her parka and hung it on a hook along with her white stocking cap. Freed from the hat, her silver-gold hair curled around her head.

"You got a perm!" I said. "It looks nice."

"Thanks." She poked at the curls. "Not sure I like it, but I needed a haircut. It kept getting in my way."

We went down the side hall to the kitchen, and met Ramon putting away his coat.

"Ramon, you remember Mrs. Hutchins?"

Ramon nodded. "I think so. Hi."

"Ramon is helping Julio this month," I said, continuing to the kitchen. "And here's our newest chef, Mai Hanh. Hanh, this is Mrs. Hutchins, from the Territorial B&B across the street."

Hanh, her hands covered in flour, gave Katie a little bow. "How do you do?"

"Do we have two dozen biscochitos ready?" I asked.

Hanh gave me a slightly wide-eyed look. "I can check. Might be still warm."

"I can come back in a couple of hours, if that would be better," Katie said.

Hanh nodded, returning. "Still warm. Better to wait."

"Thank you, Hanh," I said. "We'll get out of your way."

Katie and I went back to the gift shop, collecting her coat and hat on the way. I packed up the cookies in the pastry case and put them in a bag along with a handful of the tearoom's business cards.

"Thank you," Katie said as I handed her the bag. "We've been running low on your cards. Do you still have the cream tea ones?"

"We're not giving them out this month. We're booked pretty solid ourselves."

Katie nodded. "Well, Bob or I will come over in a bit to get the rest of the biscochitos," she said, hefting the bag. "Thank you again, and can Kris just send us a bill?"

I promised she would, saw Katie off through the front door, and went upstairs to get my coat so I could shovel the snow from the front walk. I traded my pumps for boots and went out back to fetch the snow shovel from the storage shed behind the kitchen. As I was closing the shed door I heard a car coming up the driveway, and looked up.

It was the black sedan I'd seen Julio getting into a few days before. In the daylight I saw that it was a sleek Mercedes. It pulled up to the back of the house and Julio got out, going in through the kitchen door. The Mercedes used the empty parking spaces to turn around, and as it came back down the driveway, I saw the driver.

Owen Hughes.

9

OWEN GAVE ME A FRIENDLY SMILE AND A WAVE as he drove past. I looked over my shoulder at the Mercedes as he drove away, absorbing the fact that he had, at the very least, formed a friendship with my head chef.

None of my business.

I walked around to the front of the house and shoveled snow, my mind reviewing everything I knew about Julio, and about Owen, and about Julio and Owen in the same context.

Julio had recently moved, and I had wondered about that making it harder for him to bicycle to work. Today, the addition of snow had apparently made him choose not to. He'd caught a ride with Owen instead.

Owen was a Goth, a friend of Kris's, and a brilliant photographer. In fact, his photo of Julio's biscochitos was partly responsible for their success this month.

My mind offered memories of the day Owen had taken that photo, along with many others, back in November. Julio had been there, helping to stage the food for the shoot. I'd enjoyed watching Owen work, and hadn't paid that much attention to Julio, except that I recalled he'd been unusually silent.

Oh.

At the beginning of that afternoon, I'd been late getting back from an errand, and had walked into the kitchen to find Julio and Owen facing each other. They'd never formally met before then, and I'd introduced them. And Julio had made a comment about Owen's long, black hair.

None of my business.

My mantra for the day.

I paused, realizing that I had cleared the path to the sidewalk, and the entire *portal,* of snow, and that I felt much better than I had when I'd first risen that morning. The crisp, cold air and a bit of exercise had done me good.

Time for some tea and reflection.

I put away the shovel and went upstairs, resisting the temptation to pop into the kitchen and say hello to Julio. I would see him during the day; no need to make a point of it. Instead I raided the butler's pantry for some leaf tea, as my stash upstairs was getting low. We had no genmaicha, but we had a nice jasmine green. Iz caught me in the act of filling a small jar from the canister.

"I'm out, upstairs," I said.

Iz nodded. A rare dimple graced her cheek as she loaded a tray with teacups and saucers.

"Did you get much snow up at the pueblo?" I asked.

"About five inches," Iz said. "My mom let me drive the Jeep."

"If you need to leave early, let me know."

"Thanks. I might," she said, glancing toward the window.

Upstairs, I shed my coat and boots and padded around my suite in stocking feet while I made a pot of green tea. I checked my phone in case Tony had called, but there were no messages. When the tea was ready I stepped into my shoes and carried it across to my office, where I checked my email with equally Tony-free results.

I started working my way through the stack of lavender message slips in my in-box, on the theory that anything was better than thinking about last night's conversation with Tony. By the time I heard Kris's tread on the stairs, I was down to half a dozen messages.

"Ugh, the streets are awful!" Kris said as she hung up her coat and scarf. She had on a long black sweater-tunic over black leggings and calf-high boots. A black beaded scarf brightened the outfit as much as one could expect.

"I almost got T-boned by one of those green courtesy cars."

Candy-apple emerald green, I recalled. They were from a local hotel, and were often a menace as they shuttled their guests around town.

"Tea?" I offered.

"Yes. I hope it's lapsang souchong."

"It isn't, but the next pot could be."

"Fair enough."

I told her about Katie's request for biscochitos, and she agreed to draw up a bill. From then on we were off and running, and didn't slow down until five thirty, at which point I decided I needed some alone time. I told Kris she could go home, then carried a fresh cup of tea into my suite, where I sat in my chair and looked out of the window at the snowy yard to the south.

There had been patches of blue sky in the morning, but by late afternoon it had clouded over, and now dark was falling early. The snow in the yard glowed softly blue-gray in the fading daylight. Lights around town were already coming on. The sound of traffic on wet streets reached me faintly. I snuggled into my chair, grateful for the warmth coming from the chimney.

That thought brought back the previous evening. I shoved the memories away, sipping honey-sweetened tea to give myself something better to focus on.

It had been a good day, better than I'd expected. I was proud of myself. Not only had I not mentioned Owen to Julio on any of my several visits to the kitchen, I had also refrained from obsessively checking for messages from Tony.

I glanced at my cell phone, lying on the table, and decided I would wait until after six, when we'd be officially closed, to look at it.

As if mocking me, the phone rang.

I put down my teacup and hastened to the table. Caller ID informed me that it was Gina.

I answered. "Hi, Gina!"

"Hi, yourself. Yes to shopping tomorrow, if it can wait 'til after church."

"Of course. Would you mind picking me up?"

"Not at all. Brunch?"

"Sure."

"Good! I've got some juicy gossip for you."

My thoughts flew to Julio and Owen. I smacked them down. *None of my business!*

"Oh?" I said, trying to sound casual.

"Yes, but you have to wait."

"Tease."

She chortled. "See you tomorrow!"

It was nearly six, so I went across the hall. Kris was gone, her office dark. My in-box held a fresh batch of message slips. I went downstairs to see who was left, and found Nat shutting down the gift shop.

"Want to come over to our place for dinner?" she asked. "Manny's been playing with the smoker."

"Thanks, but I sort of have a date."

"Sort of?"

"Sort of."

Nat made no further comment. I saw her out the back door, then went into the kitchen where I found Dee chatting with her brother while he washed the end-of-day dishes. Julio and the others had gone home; the kitchen was spotless except for Mick's work area.

Dee had taken off her lace apron and had her winter coat slung over her arm. She looked up when I came in.

"Kris said we're going to have a party. Is that right?"

"Yes," I said. "We'll talk about it at the staff meeting on Tuesday."

Dee smiled. "That's great! Thank you, Ellen!"

"Well, it's not going to be super-fancy," I said.

"That doesn't matter. It'll be nice to just hang out with everyone and not be working."

"I agree."

I made the rounds up front, checking locks and fireplaces. Everything was in order. The pastry case was empty; we must have sold out of biscochitos. That was just how it was going to be, apparently. Climbing up the stairs, I began to think about what I should do for dinner, assuming that Tony wasn't going to have time.

That assumption was mistaken. No sooner had I shut down my computer than I heard my cell phone ring. I hurried across the hall to answer it.

"Got a reservation at Il Piatto," Tony said. "Can you be ready in ten?"

"Sure," I said.

"Be right over."

Hallelujah!

I refreshed my hair and makeup, then considered changing into a sexier dress, but decided against it as likely to make me late. Instead I collected my coat and purse and went downstairs to wait for Tony.

He didn't take long. I had scarcely settled into a wing chair when I heard his motorcycle out back. I met him at the door.

The evening air was cold and humid. Low clouds glowed gently with city light. Il Piatto was within walking distance, but it looked like it could easily snow, so I headed for my car and Tony followed.

"Good day?" I said.

Tony gave a nod. "Some progress. Waiting to hear about a couple of things."

Since he didn't seem to be in the mood to talk about his investigation, I told him about my day instead, leaving out the revelation of Julio's acquaintance with Owen. Tony probably didn't care about the details of a day in the tearoom, but he let me talk on. Maybe he liked the sound of my voice.

"This is nice," I said as we walked from the car to the bistro. "Are we celebrating something?"

"Not yet," Tony said. "I just wanted to take you for something better than junk food, and I know you like this place."

"I do indeed. Thank you."

We were given a table in a back room by the window. Tony took the seat facing the door. I looked out at the street, watching pedestrians hurry past in the cold, their breath coming out in wispy clouds. Many of the businesses on the street had put up colored lights, lending the evening a festive air.

I ordered a glass of wine and a plate of mushroom ravioli. Tony got the special: a chunk of braised beef with potatoes and broccolette. We made small talk while I nibbled a virtuous salad and Tony nursed a beer.

Finally I couldn't stand it any more. "So what was your progress?" I asked.

He fixed me with a measuring look. "I wasn't going to talk about work. Don't want you to lose your appetite."

I stabbed an olive. "I'm not *that* fragile."

"Hm. Well, most of what I did today was ask for information. I did have had a chat with your friend Dickie."

I looked up at Tony. My pulse jumped. "You arrested him?"

"No. Just invited him in for a talk." Tony drank a swig of beer. "He wasn't that friendly."

"That doesn't surprise me. Did he say anything useful?"

"Not much." Tony finished his beer and set the empty bottle down. "But he enjoyed the coffee I gave him, and now the lab has his cup."

"DNA sample?"

Tony nodded.

"That means you have something to compare it to."

"Well, yeah." Tony reached for the bottle, then changed course and drank from his water glass. "The OMI took samples during the autopsies. You don't want to know the details."

"No," I agreed.

Our entrees arrived. I set my salad aside and said yes to a sprinkling of fresh-grated cheese on my ravioli. The aromas were reawakening my appetite.

Tony dug into his meat without hesitation. I watched, marveling at his ability to carry on with normal things like eating after spending a day dealing with the kind of awful information he'd been pursuing. I hoped it didn't mean he was growing callous. I didn't think so. He had a cynical side, but he also had a heart.

The ravioli was excellent. I took my time, concentrating on savoring the flavors and textures and not thinking about anything else.

Tony was quiet, for which I was grateful. Gradually I felt steadier. The food was helping; as I regained my equilibrium, I realized I'd been a bit light-headed.

Oh, yeah—I'd forgotten lunch again. I really needed to stop that.

I paused for another swallow of wine. Tony's gaze flicked to me, then returned to his plate.

"About Christmas," I said. "Are you going to join us Christmas day?"

He nodded as he chewed a bite of his meal.

"Good. And I'm joining you Christmas eve. You mentioned midnight mass…"

Tony swallowed. "Yeah. Mom likes to go. *Abuela*, too, if she's feeling up to it. Lately she goes to sleep earlier, though."

"Do you think we'd have time to walk up Canyon Road between dinner and the mass?"

Tony's brows rose a little. "Probably."

"I should have asked if that's something you'd like to do," I added. "I usually do it, but not until eleven or so. It's too crowded before then."

Tony nodded. "That would work. Angela could drive our mom and *Abuela* to mass, and we could meet them there. Oh—unless you don't want to go to mass."

"I'd like to, actually. I've gone before, a few times."

Tony gave me a long look, then a slight smile. "My mom will be thrilled if you go. For all the wrong reasons."

"That's not why I'm considering it."

"I know."

"Would *you* be glad if I went?" I asked, then kicked myself. It was a nosy question, and could be misinterpreted.

Tony dodged it. "I go for my family, not for myself," he said.

I nodded. "Catholics sure do pageantry well, especially at Christmas. And I love the smell of frankincense."

Tony's mouth quirked in a smile. He picked up his empty beer bottle again, then set it down.

"Do you want another?" I asked.

He shook his head. "Gotta get back to work."

"On Saturday night?"

"We're close. I want to nail it down."

"But what can you do right now?"

"Go over the reports. Go back over interviews. Think."

I swallowed disappointment. He'd been generous already, taking the time for a leisurely meal, and a fairly expensive one, for Tony's budget. To demand more would be ungrateful.

It wasn't that he didn't *want* to spend time with me, I knew. It was that he was driven to complete the task. Maybe when that was done, we'd get some time together.

Before the next task came along.

The waiter cleared our plates and offered dessert. I shook my head, knowing the delay would chafe Tony. I didn't need sweets anyway; what I wanted was quality time with him, and the best way to get that was to let him finish his job.

I drove back to the house and demanded a hug. Tony delivered a first class hug-and-kiss combo that left me aching for more, then insisted that I go inside and lock the door before he got on his bike and rode away.

I could think, too, I decided. I went upstairs and took a long, hot bath, then snuggled up in bed with a pen and notepad, determined to wring some more insights out of what I knew about Debbie's murder. The first page on the pad was my gift list. I yawned, then turned to a fresh page.

I was asleep before I made a single note.

A phone was ringing somewhere. Too far away to answer, maybe. I debated the matter while I listened to it.

Probably someone else would get it. It really wasn't worth the effort of getting up.

Oh…I wasn't up.

With a gasp, I wrenched myself out of my doze. Phone still ringing. I stumbled out of bed to the front of my suite. Cell on the table by my chair; I scrabbled at it with sleep-clumsy hands. Time in big bright numbers: 9:19.

Gina calling.

"Hlo?"

"Hi, Ellen. Nonna wants me to ask if you'd like to join us at church. I woke you up, didn't I?"

"Um…"

"Yes, I did. Never mind, then. Go back to bed and I'll see you a little after eleven."

She hung up. No goodbye. Just like Tony.

I slunk back to bed. I was just awake enough to be unable to go back to sleep. I lay on my back, staring up at the canopy. Green brocade. Italian.

Why would Nonna Fiorello invite me to church? Everyone

wanted me to go to church with them lately.

Tony's family made sense. Nonna didn't, unless she was matchmaking. I thought back to Thanksgiving. Most of what I remembered from that night was a lot of food, wine, and laughter—and a long, long table filled with Fiorellos.

Fiorelli?

If Nonna Fiorello wanted to match me with someone in her huge family, that could be a problem. I couldn't remember any single males at that party who had even vaguely attracted me. I was pretty sure I remembered being introduced to a couple, but they had made no impression.

I closed my eyes, trying to remember the faces of the men I'd met. Some of them I knew already: Gina's dad, of course, and her uncle Marco, and her brothers Dan and Paul. But there'd been new ones, cousins I'd never met before. One had glasses. One wore a dark suit that was making him sweat even in November. Their faces drifted up vaguely in my memory as I struggled to forget them and sleep. Names drifted by: Nicolas, Tito, Vincente.

Dickie.

I sat up, heart pounding, indignant.

Dickie had *not* been at the Fiorellos' Thanksgiving.

A slide-thump made me jump. My notepad, falling off the bed. I leaned over to pick it up, then rummaged around in the covers until I found my pen. Stuffing a pillow behind my shoulders, I blinked at the blank page.

OK. Deep breath. Think.

I closed my eyes and inhaled, then looked at the page again. What did I know that was new?

Debbie was definitely pregnant. I wrote it at the top of the page.

The killer knew that. How?

Most obvious possibility: Debbie told him. Why would she do that?

Bragging, maybe. Or letting him know he was the father.

I winced.

To strip the thoughts of their horror, I wrote them down. It helped, a bit. I wondered what other reasons Debbie could have had for revealing her condition.

The killer could have been there when she did the pregnancy

test. I frowned. Unlikely. I didn't remember Tony saying anything about finding a pregnancy test kit. Presumably the evidence people had searched the trash. If there'd been one, Tony wouldn't have needed me to send him down that line of thought.

I wrote it down anyway.

What other reason could Debbie have had for telling her killer she was pregnant?

I thought back to school, and Debbie's personality. She'd had a mean side. It could come out when she was annoyed. That was one of the reasons we'd drifted apart.

So she might have told the killer in order to annoy or torment him.

Who would be tormented by that information? Surely not Dickey, even if he was the father. He'd probably laugh, or say "tough luck," or something like that. Certainly he wouldn't offer to help.

I frowned as I realized that I honestly couldn't imagine him being enraged enough to kill Debbie. Not unless he felt threatened somehow. Could Debbie have tried to blackmail Dickie? Force him to marry her?

God, *why?* She had no reason to do that. Ugh!

All of which made it less likely that he was her killer.

I sighed, chewing the end of my pen. Had Debbie wanted the baby? Yes, or she wouldn't have changed her diet and drinking habits.

Oh. The food in the fridge—all the healthy greens—indicated that she'd known for a while, long enough to clear her house of alcohol. Not likely, then, that the killer was there when she found out she was pregnant. I crossed the "pregnancy test" option off my list.

She knew in advance. So she had deliberately told her killer. And, presumably, she had not expected the killer's reaction.

Which meant that Debbie's murder wasn't premeditated.

But Erica's…was?

Same M.O. (more or less), but a different motive. Less fury.

If the motive for the first murder was spontaneous rage, what was the motive for the second?

It didn't make sense.

I realized I was slouching over my notepad. I shifted the pillow behind my back so I could sit up straighter.

Tony had predicted that Erica wasn't pregnant. Assuming he was right, there was *definitely* a different motive. But what was it?

I was getting a headache.

My bedside clock told me it was almost ten. I needed tea.

Setting the notepad aside, I got up, started a kettle, and pulled on some comfortable clothes. (Pants! Hurrah for the weekend!) The house was chilly, so I turned on the space heater in my suite. I was tempted to make some scrambled eggs and toast, but Gina was picking me up for brunch, so I settled for tea.

I had the day to myself. No staff making noise, no mouth-watering aromas from the kitchen. No strangers in my house.

I refilled my teacup and wandered out to the sitting area by the front window. The sky was bright and pale, and tiny snowflakes were falling past the bare trees. Yesterday's snow hadn't melted. The city lay under a soft, white blanket.

I fetched my teapot and a cozy to keep it warm, then curled up with a lap rug in one of the overstuffed chairs and sat watching the silence. Birds flitted in the tree branches, making me want to put out seed, but I didn't have any. I stayed where I was, just watching. A profound feeling of peace came over me.

This was my church. Trees and birds and quiet snowfall. The sleeping garden and the gray, twining trunks of wisteria vines. Nature. The world outside my window, which was Santa Fe, northern New Mexico, home.

I was one small person. There were many things I wanted to achieve, and many things I felt I ought to do, but for now, just for this moment, I was content to be still and just appreciate my window on the world.

As I often did in moments of peace, I thought back to where I had been a year before. And for the first time, perhaps, the answer was, *here*.

I had bought the house in November and moved in just before Christmas. There had been some remodeling to do, and much packing up and clearing out of my parents' house before it went on the market. But I had spent last Christmas in this house, working to bring my dream into reality.

Never would I have imagined all that had happened since then.

The tearoom had brought so many *people* into my life—brilliant, talented, beautiful people. Also a few annoying people and a couple of terrifying ones, but mostly wonderful, delightful human beings. Julio, Kris, Mick and Dee, Iz, Rosa and Ramon, Dale.

And Vi, Gabriel, Mrs. Carruthers. People who were greatly missed.

People who were amazing and puzzling, like Willow, and Owen Hughes, and Captain Dusenberry.

And Tony.

All in a year's time.

And all those people had gradually filled the terrible hole in my heart made by the loss of my parents. Not completely—probably never completely—but to a great degree.

I no longer woke up crying. I no longer spent days in numb despair. My life was full of vibrant color and music, and a flow of people who came to the place that I had made as a haven of peace and beauty, and who had enjoyed it. I felt deeply grateful.

I lifted the cozy from the teapot to refill my cup, and found the pot was nearly empty. One last cup, then I would get on with my day. I savored it, remembering all I had learned in the last year. I had always loved tea, but I hadn't really studied it before I'd decided to open a tearoom. And still I had so much to learn!

I set the empty cup down and drew a deep breath of content-ment. Closing my eyes, I tried to picture where I'd be a year from now. Here, of course. But would the tearoom be the same? Would it have a new room, a bigger gift shop?

Would I still live here alone?

I could not answer these questions, and was a little afraid to try. Instead I took my tea things back to my suite and washed them, then got ready to go out with Gina.

She arrived at 11:15, banging on the back door a microsecond after ringing the bell. I hurried downstairs, coat over my arm, and opened the door.

"Sorry I woke you earlier," she said, kissing the air beside both of my cheeks. "Nonna insisted."

"What's she up to?" I asked as I pulled on my coat.

"She didn't say. Ready for brunch? I'm starving."

"Me, too!"

We climbed into Gina's car and debated the merits of various restaurants, all of which were likely to be crowded on a Sunday. "Have you tried Counter Culture?" Gina asked.

"No. Is it good?"

"No idea, but it's a little off the beaten track so maybe it won't be a zoo."

"Worth a shot."

She headed for Cerrillos Road and turned off in a neighborhood full of mechanical street names. The small lot that the restaurant shared with its neighbors was packed, so we parked across the street. The sun was playing hide-and-seek with the clouds, and the snow was beginning to melt. We skirted a puddle and entered a low-ceilinged, older building with long tables and a friendly bakery counter right by the door. After studying the rather extensive chalkboarded menu, I settled on *huevos rancheros*, while Gina ordered lemon ricotta pancackes. We carried our coffees to a smaller table by the wall.

"So, what are we shopping for?" Gina asked.

"Presents for everyone but you." I pulled my woefully unfinished gift list out of my pocket and smoothed it on the tabletop.

"What, I don't get a present?" she said indignantly.

"Not one I buy when you're watching."

She leaned forward to peer at my list. "You've got some work to do there."

"Yeah."

I took a pen from my purse, hoping it would inspire me. It didn't help.

"How about you?" I asked. "What are you shopping for?"

"Something for Nonna. She's the hardest person on earth to buy for."

"She loves to cook, right?"

"These days she loves to boss everyone else around in the kitchen."

"Maybe a cute apron that says 'Boss Chef' or something."

"Hm." Gina quirked her mouth. "Don't know how that would go over. But some kind of fun apron isn't a bad idea. Don't bite your pen."

I hastily removed the pen from my mouth. "I need something to give my staff. Not terribly expensive, and something they'd all like."

"Then a Goth coffee mug is out."

"Absolutely."

"What about some kind of little candle holder that takes one of those tea lights?"

"That's not bad," I said, and wrote it down with a question mark.

Distracted by the other names on the list, I mused about what to get them. Gina was always tough, because she rarely hesitated to buy whatever she wanted. I was hoping she'd drop a hint while we were hanging out together.

Nat and Manny: wine, probably. Alcohol was a simple gift, but Nat was always saying she didn't need more stuff, so—wine, or maybe something nice from the cheesemonger up on Marcy Street.

Tony?

I had no clue.

Our food arrived, so I set aside the list. Gina hummed as she poured maple syrup over her pancakes. I took a bite of *huevos*, and my mood was instantly improved by the salty, spicy flavors of home.

"So," Gina said, cradling her coffee cup in both hands. "Want to hear the gossip?"

I glanced up at her, trying to look disapproving, but in fact I did want to hear it. She grinned.

"Heather filed for a divorce."

"Heather, Debbie's sister?"

"Mm-hm."

My brain started whirring while Gina took a bite of her pancakes.

When? Why?

Should I call Tony? No, not on Sunday morning. He might be asleep.

"Where'd you hear that?" I asked.

"From Sarah Porter. Her older sister Judy is best friends with Heather."

I took a swallow of coffee. "Did she mention when Heather filed?"

Gina nodded. "Right after Thanksgiving. Apparently there was a family tiff, and it got worse after the holiday."

"A tiff? That's not grounds for divorce."

"Well," Gina leaned toward me and lowered her voice dramatically, as if it could possibly matter to the strangers around us. "Heather told Judy that Justin was cheating on her."

10

JUSTIN WAS CHEATING ON HEATHER. I drank more coffee while I tried fitting that piece of information into the puzzle of Debbie's murder. It shouldn't matter, but the fact Heather had filed for divorce so soon before the murder made it suspicious.

Could Justin have killed Debbie in retaliation?

No, no, no. That was *too* awful. Also, it didn't make sense. Either Justin wanted to stay married to Heather, in which case killing her sister was a bad idea, or he wanted the divorce, in which case he had no reason to retaliate.

I looked up at Gina. "Who was he cheating with?"

She shrugged. "Judy didn't know. If Heather knows, she didn't tell."

Maybe it didn't fit into the puzzle. Maybe it was coincidence.

I frowned.

"Did Tony mention the divorce to you?" Gina asked, all innocence.

"No."

Maybe Tony knew, and didn't think it was important to the case. Either that, or he didn't know, and I should tell him.

"He does talk to you about the murder investigation, doesn't he?"

She was fishing for more gossip. Oh, the things I could tell her…but I wouldn't. I had no desire to violate Tony's confidence.

"Yes, some," I said, "but he hasn't mentioned Heather's divorce."

Gina looked disappointed, but let the subject drop. I switched to my pathetic shopping list.

133

"I need a present for Tony," I said.

Gina brightened. "Oh, that's easy! We'll just go to Victoria's Secret."

"Gina!"

"What?"

I felt my cheeks getting hot. "That's a little…I mean, I don't think…"

"Too soon? Don't worry, they have G-rated stuff too. Maybe you'll find a treat for yourself."

I knew better than to argue with Gina where shopping was concerned. We headed for the malls, and spent several hours looking for perfect gifts for everyone. I didn't find anything at Victoria's Secret that I thought I could give to Tony without blushing to the tips of my toes, but they had a nice camisole that I got for myself. Gina spent quite a bit there, dashing my hopes that I'd be able to sneak back and get something for her. She bought all the things that interested her, except for a floor-length silk robe that was out of my price range.

For my staff, I decided on tea mug sets—pretty china mugs with infusers and lids—something we didn't carry in the gift shop, and that I hoped they'd enjoy using at home. I'd had a set like that in college, and had loved the lid that kept my tea warm.

For Tony, I found a pair of motorcycle gloves that were lightweight and lined with thermal fabric. Just expensive enough that it would probably be an indulgence for him, but not so expensive that it would seem like charity.

My brother, Joe, proved more difficult to shop for. Anything I saw that might appeal to him, he could probably get in better quality in New York. In desperation, I went into a shop that specialized in local chile products, thinking that New Mexican food might be harder to find in the Big Apple. I was looking at a bewildering array of salsas and sauces when my phone rang.

It was Tony. "*Las Posadas*," he said when I answered.

"Yes?"

"It's tonight. Want to go?"

"Um." I looked at Gina, who was idly browsing the cookbook section. I hadn't been to *Las Posadas* in years, but as a kid I'd enjoyed it. "Sure. Should I meet you?"

"Nah, I'll come to your place, and we can walk."

"OK. I'm not home right now."

"Well, it's Sunday, so I've got dinner at Mama's. Want to come?"

"Not this week, but thank you."

"Yeah, you're right. Save it for Christmas. I'll come by around seven, OK?"

"That sounds good."

"Great."

Gina sidled up as I put away my phone. "That Tony?"

"Yes. We're going to *Las Posadas* tonight."

"You need to hurry home?"

I checked the time: just after five. My feet were hurting, I was tired of holiday music, and the crowds of shoppers were starting to get to me.

"No," I said, "but I think I'm about done."

"Me, too. Let's go get a drink."

"Someplace quiet, please."

"Pranzo?"

"Sure."

We stashed our purchases in the trunk of Gina's car and headed for Sanbusco Center, not far from my house. There had once been a bar upstairs at Pranzo, but that was now a second dining room. We opted for the cozy downstairs bar, where Gina ordered a Dark and Stormy while I opted for a less intoxicating glass of wine, with a side of calamari. I didn't want to be woozy if I was going to be walking around outside with Tony later.

"You get to eat the baby Cthulhus," Gina said as we settled in with our drinks. "Did you know that Sanbusco Center is a registered historic landmark?"

"No."

"It is. Built in 1880, and 'Sanbusco' is a made-up name. It was originally the Santa Fe Business Company."

"Are you dating that real estate agent again?"

"No, a different real estate agent. Ed. He's the best."

I nodded, lazily swirling a mouthful of Montepulciano. I took out my gift list and a pen and crossed off a few names, which made me feel like I had accomplished something.

"I still have to figure out what to get Ed," Gina remarked,

stabbing a piece of calamari with her fork.

"You didn't get him something at Victoria's Secret?"

"We haven't been dating *that* long."

"Ah."

But Tony and I had, apparently, by Gina's standards.

It didn't feel that way to me. It didn't seem long at all, really. It wasn't like we saw each other every day.

Or even every week. November had been pretty lonely.

I deliberately turned my thoughts to happier things. "So the Fiorellos are having a grand Christmas feast?" I asked.

"We always do. Nonna's really disappointed you won't be coming."

I gave her a wary glance. "Why?"

"She likes you."

"I like her, but she just entertained me for Thanksgiving."

"You know Nonna, she's always throwing a party." Gina sipped her drink. "So when does Joe get in?"

"The twenty-first."

"And how long is he staying?"

"I'm not sure. You could ask Nat, he's staying with her."

"He skis, doesn't he?"

"He did. Probably he still does. I don't know what the skiing's like in New York." I squeezed lemon over the calamari and ate a piece.

"Tame, compared to here."

Skiing. Maybe I could get Joe some nice goggles or something. Not gloves. Thermal socks?

"I bet he'll want to go up to Taos," Gina said. "Maybe for a weekend. Does Tony ski?"

"I don't know."

"We could do a little group thing."

"Does Ed ski?" I asked.

"No, he doesn't. I'd have to go stag."

"Tsk."

"Hey, we're not engaged. We're not even up to Victoria's Secret."

Maybe I lacked imagination. I couldn't picture myself switching boyfriends as often and as easily as Gina did. But then, I hadn't dated much in high school, unlike Gina.

The thought rang a distant bell of memory. "Did Debbie date a lot of different guys in school?" I asked. "When she wasn't going with Steve, I mean."

"Yes, and also when she *was* going with him."

"How do you know that?"

"Judy had some things to say about Debbie. Not terribly kind things."

"Oh."

The gossipy aspect of this conversation pinched my sense of courtesy. I could feel Miss Manners watching. But it might be helpful to Tony's investigation, so I didn't change the subject.

"Did Debbie date Dickie in high school?" I asked, spearing the last piece of calamari.

Gina stared at me. "You're joking, right?"

"Well, no. She was dating him before the murder."

"Really? Wow! I would never have expected that." Gina drained her glass and set it down with a satisfied sigh. "I wonder why."

Why, indeed. Dickie hadn't been in love with Debbie, and I suspected she hadn't loved him either. So why was she dating him? Even after learning she was pregnant...

"Another round, ladies?" The waiter asked.

Gina shook her head and reached for her purse. "Nope. One's enough."

"Let me get this," I said. "You drove."

I settled with the waiter and Gina took me home. A light snow had started to fall, so we hurried to the trunk to get my purchases and exchanged a quick hug before Gina got back in the car.

"Love to Nonna," I called, then scurried into the house.

Gina waved as she started the engine and backed out. I locked the door and went upstairs to sort my spoils. I still had a few things to get, but I'd made a good start.

No time for a shower. I changed into warmer clothes and collected parka, hat, scarf, gloves.

Gloves! I heard Tony's bike as I was starting downstairs, and ran back up to hide his gloves, just in case.

"Hi!" I said, slightly out of breath as I opened the door. "Coming in?"

Tony brushed some snow off his bare head. "Nah, we're late. Sorry I didn't get here sooner."

"No problem. You want a hat?"

He shook his head. I stepped out and locked the door, then buried my hands in my pockets as we walked down the driveway to the street. The snow wasn't sticking yet, but everything was wet, and it would get slippery when the temperature dropped some more.

"How's your mom and *Abuela*?" I asked.

"Fine. Angela says hi."

"Hi, back. Is school keeping her busy?"

Tony nodded. We reached Palace Avenue and turned toward the Plaza. Immediately, we were surrounded by other people walking the same way. I heard music up ahead, guitars and violins, and people singing.

"I haven't done this since high school," I said.

"I haven't done it since I was a beat cop."

"You had to work *Las Posadas*?"

Tony's gaze caught on a pair of young guys across the street who were laughing. After a second, he lost interest. "A couple of years, yeah."

"Crowd control. No fun."

"There are worse gigs. At least at this one, there aren't many drunken brawls."

"Unlike Fiesta."

"Don't get me started."

We neared the Plaza and had to slow down. The streets here were completely blocked off to vehicle traffic, and packed full of people, as was the Plaza itself. We weren't going to get that far. People in the Plaza held candles, making pretty spots of glowing light in the gentle snowfall. We stopped a few yards from the west end of the Palace of the Governors, hemmed in by the crowd.

The procession was already in progress. I couldn't see Mary and Joseph or the musicians, but apparently they were at one of the "inns" off to our right and were being turned away by the "devil," because the crowd started booing and jeering.

I glanced at Tony and saw that he was on the alert, looking all around us. We were completely surrounded by people now, and it would have been difficult to get out of the press. The sort of situation in which, back in high school, I would have started mooing.

My memory flashed back to the Bird Woman's jumping cows, and I laughed. Tony gave me a curious look, and I shook my head.

"Moo," I said, raising my voice over the noise of the crowd. "Moo!"

He laughed, shaking his head.

The boos tapered off and the music started up again, getting louder as the procession approached where we stood. Soon we saw a pair of lantern bearers making way. People stepped back to let the musicians through, and they passed before us, singing and playing. Mary and Joseph came after them, escorted by more lantern bearers. They made their way to the Palace, where an angel in glowing white came out to greet them. Mary and Joseph asked for shelter, the angel welcomed them, and the whole procession passed through the Palace's *zaguan* and disappeared, followed by many of the cheering crowd.

I looked at Tony. "Want to go in?" I shouted over the noise.

He shrugged, not looking enthusiastic. "You want cider and cookies?"

Inside the courtyard, there would be hot cider and biscochitos for the crowd, but I didn't feel like waiting in line for it.

"Yes," I yelled. "Let's go to my place and I'll make some."

Tony grinned in approval and took my hand, turning away from the Plaza. Like salmon swimming upstream, we edged through the mass of people heading inward. When we were out of the crowd and able to walk freely, I felt much relieved. The snow was starting to stick, now, and falling a little more enthusiastically.

"I used to love that when I was a kid," I said. "I would have been all over the cider and cookies then, but it seems like too much trouble now."

"Yeah." Tony said, lengthening his stride. "And besides, I bet yours are better."

When we turned from the street onto my unlit driveway, Tony halted me with a gesture and stood listening and watching for a moment, then headed toward the house at a slower pace. I slid my hand into his elbow.

"Thanks for calling," I said. "This was nice."

"Mm."

"Were you working today?"

"Yeah, some. No big news."

"I learned something you might not know."

Tony looked at me sidelong. "Oh, yeah?"

"Let's get inside and I'll tell you."

We went shook the snow off our coats in the hall. The house was dark and chilly. I was tempted to build a fire just for the warmth, but decided it was too much trouble. Instead I led Tony upstairs and lit my candles.

I had picked up some cider at Kaune's, so I put a pot of it on the stove to heat, adding whole allspice and cloves and a couple of cinnamon sticks. I knew for a fact that there were no biscochitos downstairs, but I had a small stash up here, and I brought them out for Tony. I set them on the side table between my two cozy chairs.

"Have a seat. This'll be ready in a few minutes."

Tony sat in the chair nearest the door and took out his phone. I returned to the kitchenette and watched over the cider until it was hot.

Tony glanced up from his phone as I carried two steaming mugs of cider to the chairs. I gave him one, and curled up in my chair with the other. With the first sip I relaxed, grateful to be here and not in the crowded Palace courtyard.

"So what have you got?" Tony asked, picking up a biscochito.

"Oh! Well, it's gossip, but I thought it might be important. You may already know it."

"Know what?"

"Heather's divorcing Justin."

Tony paused, cookie halfway to his mouth. "No, I didn't know that. How do you know?"

"Gina heard it from Heather's best friend's sister."

He blinked. "OK."

"Apparently Justin was cheating on her. She filed after Thanksgiving, but before Debbie's murder."

Tony's gaze went distant, like a chess player's when sorting through a dozen possible moves. I took a biscochito and ate a bite. Tony's cookie was still in his hand, forgotten.

Was Heather's divorce significant? I didn't know. It made

whatever happened at the family Thanksgiving seem more important. And Heather had certainly been angry about that at Debbie's funeral. I remembered her look of fury when Dickie went up to talk to her and Justin.

Tony emerged from his reverie, took a swig of cider, and ate his cookie thoughtfully. I didn't want to break his concentration, so I stayed silent. Finally he turned to me.

"How well do you know Heather?" he asked.

"Not that well. She's two years older."

"Was Heather's best friend at the funeral?"

"Yeah. Judy Porter. Sarah Porter's sister."

"Did you talk to her?"

"To Sarah, not to Judy."

"Hm." He frowned.

"You were talking to Justin at the funeral," I said. "Did he say anything interesting?"

"No," Tony said slowly, "but I'm gonna go back over my notes. I remember thinking it was strange that he wasn't sticking close to Heather."

"Maybe she didn't want him to."

"Yeah."

Tony's eyes narrowed as he gazed into space. "Maybe I'll go talk to him again."

"You might ask him what happened at the Thanksgiving dinner. Dickie was prodding them about that at the funeral. Heather looked furious."

Tony gave me a long look, then nodded. "Yeah. Thanks." He drank the last of his cider and put down the mug.

"There's some more, if you want it," I said.

"Nah. Thanks, that hit the spot."

He stood and stretched, then took one more cookie from the plate. I set my mug beside his and stood as well, stepping toward him.

"Would you like to stay a while?"

He watched me as he chewed and swallowed. "I don't know. You don't have a TV."

"You're right."

"What would we do?"

"We could sit by the front window and watch the street," I said, gesturing toward the hall.

"Hm. Doesn't sound that exciting." He popped the rest of the biscochito into his mouth.

"Well, maybe you could think of something you'd like better."

I slid my arms around his waist and looked up into his dark eyes. He smiled as his arms came up around me.

"Maybe I could."

His kiss tasted of cinnamon sugar and clove. I melted against him, enjoying the heat of his body.

It was a good thing I'd hidden his gloves.

The next few days were completely nuts. I didn't see or hear from Tony except for a couple of brief texts telling me there was nothing new. I hoped he wasn't running out of steam on the case. The murders—Debbie's, especially—were getting cold.

Santa Fe, meanwhile, was bustling with holiday cheer. All day the streets were full of people out shopping for gifts, friends meeting for lunch or drinks, and tourists touring. At night it shifted over to locals dining out and partying, and skiers unwinding in all the hot spots.

On Thursday, a new storm front moved in. That morning I eyed the overcast sky from my upstairs window, hoping the snow would hold off until late in the day. We were booked solid and had multiple orders of biscochitos by the dozen to be picked up. We didn't need traffic problems.

Kris and I spent the morning finalizing plans for the employee party on Sunday. Business had been so good that I decided to treat everyone to a catered meal from El Vaquero, and allow each staff member to bring one guest. It would make the party big—too big for the dining parlor—so we'd serve in the hall and sit in the main parlor. Besides the New Mexican buffet, we'd have soft drinks and iced tea.

"No booze?" Kris said as we conferred at her desk.

"No," I said firmly. "Liability. Not everyone is twenty-one. Plus, I'm spending enough."

She sighed. "OK."

"Could you call the menu in to El Vaquero?"

"Sure. What did you decide for dessert?"

"Flan."

She made a note, and I went back to my office, leaving her to sort out the details. The pile of message slips in my in-box was beginning to resemble a lavender snow drift. I took a handful off the top and skimmed through them, looking for Tony's name.

Three of the messages were from Dickie. Two of those just said "Call me," but the third gave me pause:

Want to talk about Debbie. Call me. Buy you a drink.

How very like him.

I dropped his other two messages into the recycling bin, then put the remaining slips back in my in-box and headed downstairs.

The kitchen was in full biscochito mode. Dee and Rosa were boxing finished cookies while Julio, Hanh, and Ramon shepherded batches through various stages of completion. The ovens were full, and the windows were cracked open to let the warm air—awash with cinnamon sugar and a whiff of anise—escape.

Mick, earbuds in place, was preparing to fire up the dish washing station and attack the already-formidable pile of used cookie-prep equipment. He gave me a smile and a wave, which I returned. Not wanting to interfere with the smooth operation of the cookie machine, I headed for the gift shop, where Nat was wiping down the pastry case.

"Morning, dear," she said cheerily. "This sugar does get everywhere!"

"Morning." I kissed both her cheeks. "You make everything shine."

She chuckled. "No, you can't butter me up enough to hire me to clean, but thanks for trying."

"How's Manny?" I asked as I tidied the display of packaged tea.

"Frazzled. He's putting in a lot of extra hours."

"Aren't we all. Is he coming to the staff party?"

"Yes, and he got a gleam in his eye when I told him about it. Don't be surprised if he sneaks some mariachi music onto the house stereo."

I plugged in the tree and stepped back to inspect it. Plenty of ornaments now. Half of them would be gone by the end of the day.

Dale came in with the firewood sling, heading for the fireplace shared by Violet and Dahlia. I glanced out the front window: no snow yet.

I spent most of the day up front, filling in for whichever server was currently assisting the biscochito machine. Since that was a tedious job, I had them rotate in shifts. Nat and I, and even Kris, took turns as well. After my cookie shift, I returned to the gift shop to help seat the four o'clock round of guests, just as Sarah Porter walked in.

She'd been dressed unremarkably at Debbie's funeral, but today she had on a trim, black pantsuit and a pale green silk blouse, with her hair up in a French twist that made her look a little like Audrey Hepburn circa *Breakfast at Tiffany's,* except with a tan. She looked stunning, and I'd never have guessed she was a forest ranger.

"Sarah! How lovely to see you!"

She smiled shyly. "Thanks. Thought I'd redeem your gift," she said, taking the cream tea card I'd given her from her pocket.

"Of course." I checked the reservations list. Lately Kris was putting the cream teas in the smallest alcoves, right off the gift shop. Sarah was scheduled for Poppy, and I led her over to the pair of red wing chairs set off from the shop by a carved sandalwood screen.

"Your tea will be right out. Is there anything else I can get you?"

She hesitated, then shook her head. I left her to enjoy the fire, and went back to seat more guests. As I led a party of three rather giddy visitors from Wisconsin across the hall, I heard voices out on the front *portal*. After showing the Wisconsinites to their alcove, I returned and peeked through the front door lights.

The sky was still fairly bright, though overcast. The *portal* was crowded with ballerinas.

MOST OF THE BALLERINAS WERE YOUNGISH, but a few were rather mature for the dance stage. All of them wore long, white tulle skirts, white bodices glimmering with sequins, and glittering snowflake tiaras.

"Oh, no," I said under my breath.

I scurried to the gift shop to check the reservations. Sure enough: Olavssen, party of nine. Mercifully, they were booked for the dining parlor, so they wouldn't be *too* much of a spectacle.

Once they were in there.

Though the gift shop's front windows were partly blocked by displays of merchandise, I could see the ballerinas moving around out there. Something niggled at me; I glanced back at the reservations screen.

Party of nine.

Nine ladies dancing.

"Oh, *no!*"

I searched the reservations for the rest of the month, and was relieved to see only one more for the Bird Woman, on the twenty-third. I didn't think she'd be able to round up ten lords, eleven pipers, and twelve drummers all for the same day—much less fit them in the dining parlor. I breathed a little easier, then gathered my courage and went out the front door.

"OK, everybody do that thing where you link arms around each others' waists," called a strident voice I knew too well.

Giggling, the ballerinas formed into a vague line with the Bird Woman in the center, her snowflake attire augmented by a white feather boa. They lined up before the south windows on the *portal*, which was conveniently bare of the café tables and chairs we had out there in better weather. Suppressing a moment's regret that I had put the furniture away, I stepped out and saw Dale standing in the snowy yard with a handful of cell phones, gamely going through them and taking pictures.

Unlike professional ballerinas, the group had not arranged themselves according to height, so their line was a little asymmetrical. As the Bird Woman was the shortest, they made a sort of ragged "V" formation with her in the middle.

A few paces away, standing in awe on the path from the gate, was a party of four women in quite unspectacular winter coats and hats. I stepped toward them, summoning a friendly smile.

"Do come in. This is just a little photo session. What's the name on your reservation?"

I shepherded them inside and tucked them into Dahlia, then went back out in case any more guests were hesitant to pass the snowflakes.

Dale was still taking pictures. I joined him, offering to hold some of the cell phones.

"Thanks," he said softly. "Sorry about this."

"It's fine. Just get them into the dining parlor as soon as you can."

"Aren't you cold? You don't have a coat."

"I'm all right."

Dale, in his usual dark vest and dress shirt, brightened by a cheerful red bow tie, was admittedly better dressed for the cold than I in my knit dress and heels. My feet were half-submerged in snow.

Mental note: wear velvet and boots the next time the Bird Woman is coming to tea.

Fortunately, the ballet costumes were even less suited to the weather, and the snowflakes vetoed the Bird Woman's call for a second set of pictures with a different pose. Dale and I stood by the door distributing cell phones as they trooped in.

The Bird Woman, bringing up the rear, gave me a cheery smile and said, "That's OK—we can do another one after we have our tea."

I smiled and nodded, thinking gratefully of how early it got dark this close to the solstice.

As I watched Dale herd his snowy chicks down the hall to the dining parlor, I mused about the Bird Woman's apparently wide-ranging acquaintance. I had not recognized a single ballerina as having visited the tearoom before. They were all different ages, all different shapes, sizes, and colors. The Bird Woman had her core group of friends, whom she regularly brought to tea, but these were not they.

I wiped my feet and went into the gift shop, where Nat was hanging more ornaments on the tree. "Everyone checked in?"

"Yes," she said. "What should I say about the ballerinas? People are asking."

"Um."

"How about I just say they're a special group?" Nat suggested.

"They are that."

Feeling ruffled, I fetched a cup and saucer from the pantry and snitched some biscochitos from the pastry case, then slipped into Poppy. "Mind if I join you?" I asked as Sarah looked up.

"No, come on in!" She gestured toward the second chair. "This is wonderful," she added, indicating the fireplace and the décor. "I didn't even know this house was here."

"It's not that conspicuous," I said, pouring myself some tea. "The B&B on the corner gets more attention."

"Is that one Victorian too?"

"Yes, this whole street dates back to before the Civil War. Except for the office building next door, of course. Several of the historic buildings are on the National Register."

Sarah nodded. "I guess I never paid that much attention. I just figured all the stuff around the Plaza was old and boring."

I laughed, though it was sad to think of people feeling that way about history. I'd always found it fascinating, but then I was a bookworm.

"Have a biscochito," I offered.

She took one and tried a bite. "Mmm...wow, that's great!"

"I'm glad you came in. I was sorry I didn't get to talk with you at Debbie's funeral."

She nodded, swallowing. "Me, too. Funny how it seems like just yesterday we were in school."

"Yes. I can hardly believe Debbie's gone."

"And now Erica, too."

"So you heard about that."

"It was on the news."

"I'm afraid I don't watch the news much," I said. "Did you know her well?"

"Erica? You kidding?"

"I meant Debbie, actually." I picked up the teapot, offering to fill Sarah's cup.

"Oh." She held out her cup and saucer. "No, Judy asked me to go to the funeral. She's friends with Heather and wanted backup."

"Backup?"

"Just moral support. Heather was pretty upset."

"So I saw."

"She and Debbie didn't really get along that well."

I nodded, adding milk to my tea. "I remember."

Footsteps made me glance up. Through the gap between the sandalwood screen and the wall, I caught a glimpse of Rosa carrying a tea tray into Dahlia. A moment later a chorus of "Oooh" arose from the Wisconsinites.

"I'd better get back." I drank the last of my tea and set down the cup. "Would you like another scone?"

"Oh, no thanks," Sarah said, sitting up. "I should get out of your way—"

"No, no. You've got plenty of time." I stood. "It was nice to chat a bit. I'm glad you came in."

"Me, too. I'll definitely come back. Maybe I'll bring Judy."

I smiled, then stepped out into the gift shop. A moment of dejá vu struck me; the last time I'd chatted with someone from my old class over tea in this room—Erica—she'd turned up dead the next day.

Stop it, Ellen. It's just coincidence. And besides, that was in Hyacinth, not Poppy.

My cynical self reminded me that Hyacinth was right next to Poppy. I looked toward Sarah. Couldn't see her face, just her feet, wearing good sturdy black shoes. Nice enough, but not fancy, and not heels. I supposed no self-respecting forest ranger wore heels. I said a silent prayer for Sarah's safety, then turned away.

Nat was at the register with a customer, two take-out cookie boxes on the counter. I looked in on the main parlor, where all four parties were quietly conversing, happily enjoying their tea. With a measure of trepidation, I continued down the hall and looked in the open door of the dining parlor.

The ballerinas actually looked quite charming all around the dining table in their fluffy white skirts, with the holly and ivy arrangement between them and Dale hovering with a teapot. The Bird Woman was holding court at the far end of the table. Her guests were all beaming beneath their snowflake crowns like kids at a birthday party.

Had none of them *ever* been to tea before?

I went upstairs, musing. Where had she found these women, and why had she brought them here?

"There you are," Kris called as I headed for my desk. She beckoned me into her office, so I changed direction. "Here's the quote for the staff party," she said. "You need to sign off on it and I'll send it back."

I looked over the itemization, winced a little at the bottom line, and signed. We could afford it, I reminded myself. We'd make the cost back in a couple of days, if not one day.

Gracias de Dios por los biscochitos.

"Anything else I need to deal with right away?" I asked as I handed back the page.

Kris shook her head. "We're booked solid for New Year's Eve, now. Sure you want to close early?"

"Positive."

"Maybe stay open 'til three?"

"No. We close at noon."

My staff was working hard enough, and I'd considered not opening at all on New Year's Eve, but I'd been persuaded to open for half a day. We'd stick to that. I wanted to give everyone a good, long break for each holiday.

I stepped into my office and glanced through my messages, then went back downstairs, nervous about what the Bird Woman might be up to. All was peaceful, so I looked in on the kitchen, where the cookie machine was still going strong.

"All good?" I asked Julio, who was armed with a cinnamon-sugar shaker and frowning in concentration.

He looked up, nodded, then put down the shaker and stepped to the back counter. "Here. You can take these up front for samples." He placed a plate heaped with broken cookies in my hands.

"What happened?" I asked.

"Nothing. This is just the ones that broke as we were moving them. We've done twelve dozen since noon, not counting what's in the oven."

"Gross," said Ramon, who was cutting out cookies and putting them on a baking sheet.

I looked at him in dismay, thinking something had gone wrong. He shot me a grin. "A hundred and forty-four. That's a gross."

"Oh!" Relieved, I smiled back. "Well, great work, everyone!"

I sent a smile around the room, then took the broken biscochito bits up to the gift shop. Nat slid half of them into a box, arranged the rest nicely on the plate, and put them under the "SAMPLES" dome.

Glancing at the clock, I was surprised to see it was almost five thirty. Unless biscochitos counted, I'd forgotten lunch again. Maybe I needed one of those wrist computers that told you when to do things.

No—I'd hate that.

I strolled back to the dining parlor. The ballerinas were all singing, now—"Silver Bells"—just softly. They looked happy and peaceful. The Bird Woman's craggy face wore an expression of bliss.

As I stood in the doorway, I noticed one crystal on the chandelier swaying gently back and forth. Smiling, I went quietly away.

I was upstairs in my suite, deciding what to make for dinner, when Tony called my cell. The tearoom was shut down for the day, and snow was falling gently in the darkness outside.

Catching my phone up from the table, I smiled as I answered. "Hi, Tony! Want to come for dinner?"

"I can't."

The tone of his voice stopped me flat. Something was wrong.

"What is it?"

"Babe, you've lost another classmate."

"Oh, no!" I swallowed. Dread that it was Sarah filled my heart. "Wh-who?"

"Dickie."

"Dickie Hernandez?"

"You know another Dickie?"

Stunned, I tried to wrap my brain around the information. I'd been afraid of Dickie, hiding at home, not going out alone—and now he was dead?

"He called me," I said, belated remorse stinging me. "He left a message."

"Oh, yeah? What'd he say?"

"Just that he wanted to talk. I never called him back."

"Too late now," Tony remarked. He didn't sound concerned.

"Was it—the same as the others?" I asked, bracing myself.

"No. Hanged in his apartment. Looks like a suicide, but we're investigating."

"Wow. I-I'm sorry."

"Yeah. So, might be back to square one on the others. Jeez, I wish it was Friday."

"Why? You work on the weekends too."

I shouldn't have said that; it wasn't kind. I felt my cheeks flush, but Tony laughed.

"Yeah, but if it was Friday I'd let myself have a couple of beers."

The thought of him drinking alone made me sad. "Please come for dinner," I said. "I can have it ready whenever you like."

"Thanks, but I really can't. I want to wrap this one up and get back to Debbie."

"Tomorrow, then? I'll drink beer with you."

He laughed again. At least that was something.

"OK, sure. I'll text you or call."

"Good. Thank you for letting me know about Dickie."

"Don't drop your guard."

"No. I won't. See you tomorrow."

"Hey, Ellen?"

"Yes?"

"Thanks."

My heart filled with gratitude as I heard him disconnect. I'd done something right, apparently.

Friday went smoothly. The sun came out and started working on melting the snow. Shoppers were out in droves, too. I was too busy to fret about hearing from Tony, though I had chosen a dress with pockets so I could keep my cell phone with me.

It was after six when it rang. I was helping Rosa clear the dining parlor after the last reservation had left, so I stepped into the hall to take Tony's call.

"Can you meet me at Del Charro?" he said.

"As soon as we're done for the day here. Might be half an hour or so."

"That's OK. Send me a text when you leave, and another when you're parked. I'll come walk you to the bar."

"OK."

I found a parking space on the street not far from Del Charro, just before seven. Tony appeared a couple of minutes after I texted him, and we hurried through the snow and a chill breeze off the mountains, into the noisy warmth of the bar. It being Friday, there was live music. I would have preferred the quieter restaurant, but Tony led me to a minuscule table in the back of the bar with a view of the corner where the singer was strumming his guitar.

Tony plucked the short menu from between the salt and pepper shakers and the sugar bin, and offered it to me. The house specialty was burgers, with a short half page of alternatives. We ordered burgers and beer and sat back to wait for their arrival.

Tony watched me with an expression of suppressed amusement.

"What?" I said finally.

He nodded toward the singer, who was crooning country oldies from the seventies and eighties. "Recognize him?"

I glanced at the singer, then took a closer look. It was Justin Davis, Heather's soon-to-be-ex husband. I looked back at Tony, who grinned.

"I didn't know he was a musician," I said.

"Neither did I."

I listened for a while. To get a gig this close to the Plaza you had to be a real musician, and Justin was. I rather doubted that this was actually his career, though. When I'd first met him, he had come across more like one of the money crowd: bankers, attorneys, realtors, etc. He looked so different here—casually dressed, singing for tips and whatever pittance the bar paid him—that I hadn't recognized him at first.

So why was he here? Blowing off steam? Looking for a change?

I realized that although I'd assumed he had money, I didn't know anything about how he got it. Maybe he *was* a musician and the money was Heather's. I didn't know her financial background either.

I leaned toward Tony. "Is Heather financially independent?"

"You mean is she rich?" Tony said, his expression deadpan.

"OK, yeah. Is she?"

"She doesn't have to work."

The waiter brought our beers and a couple of glasses of water. I drank some of the latter, trying to remember what Heather and Debbie's father had done for a living. Civil engineering? I had a vague recollection that he had built things. His daughters hadn't seemed *rich* in school, but they weren't poor either. If Debbie'd had tons of money, though, she would have flaunted it.

"There was no life insurance policy on Debbie," Tony said. "So that wasn't the motive."

"That would have been Dickie's motive, if anyone's."

Tony nodded. "And the DNA test came back. Dickie isn't the father."

Still deadpan. He was in cop mode. I swallowed, realizing that Tony in cop mode wasn't my favorite person to hang out with.

So why did Debbie die? Because someone was angry that she was pregnant.

And it wasn't Dickie's kid.

I just couldn't picture Dickie so enraged, but maybe he'd had a dark side. Darker than the normal, everyday jerk side.

He'd tried to reach out to me, and I hadn't responded. Had I missed an important conversation? I'd never know, now.

Justin started singing "Wichita Lineman," the yearning tones of the old song appropriate to my mood. I looked around at the crowd in the bar: lot of tourists, quite a few older folks, several younger ones with the distinctive pale-goggle tan of the skier. They'd probably rather hear something more lively. In case Cop Tony was testing me again, I looked carefully for anyone I recognized in the crowd, but didn't spot anyone.

I opened my purse and took out a five dollar bill. When the song ended, I made my way through the close-set tables and put the bill in Justin's tip jar. He looked up at me with an automatic word of thanks, then did a double-take as he recognized me.

"You have a great voice," I said.

"Thanks." He looked guarded, as if wondering why I was here.

"Buy you a drink when you have a break?" I said.

"Sure."

I smiled, then went back to my table. Tony raised an eyebrow at me.

"Nice tip," he said.

"I always tip musicians. I know what it's like to put yourself on the line like that."

Tony frowned slightly, as if thinking that over.

"I invited him to join us for a drink," I added.

Tony glanced toward Justin, then gave a nod. I followed his gaze and saw Justin watching us. He looked away and struck up another tune.

"Why?" Tony asked.

"Because he could probably use one. And because I thought you might want to talk to him."

"Not gonna interview him here."

"Who said 'interview'? Is it against the rules to just talk to people?"

"Of course not."

But Cop Tony would be thinking about every comment, trying to place every word into the context of the murder case. Maybe offering Justin a drink wasn't such a good idea.

Our burgers came, and we ate them while Justin played "Country Roads" and "Rhinestone Cowboy." There was some turnover by then—people leaving and new parties taking their places —and Justin's tip jar got a little more full. He announced he was taking a break, encouraged people to stick around, then got up and headed toward the bathrooms. A few minutes later he came up to our table.

"Hi," he said, standing there looking at us.

"Hi," I said back. "You know Tony Aragón, right?"

"Yeah," Justin said, the guarded look on his face again as his gaze flicked to Tony. "What brought you here?"

"We came to listen to your singing," Tony said.

"Please join us," I said, and scanned the room for our waiter. I didn't see him, but another—a woman in black jeans and a black silk western shirt, unbuttoned as far as possible while retaining decency —gave a nod and headed toward us.

Justin scrounged a third chair from another table. I scooched my chair closer to Tony's to make room.

"What can I get you?" the waiter said, coming up to our table.

Justin ordered a beer. Tony and I were still working on ours, and declined a second round. Justin turned an expectant look toward me.

"How's Heather?" Tony asked.

I shot him a frown.

"I don't know," Justin said evenly. "Haven't talked to her since she kicked me out."

"When was that?"

I kicked Tony's ankle. He drank a swig of beer.

"Right after the funeral," Justin said.

"Why'd she kick you out?"

"Tony!" I turned to Justin. "I'm sorry, I really just wanted to buy you a drink."

A wry smile twisted Justin's lips. "It's OK. I figured I'd get asked about this. Afraid I can't spend a lot of time on it here."

The waiter put his beer down in front of him. Justin picked it up and took a hard pull, his gaze locked on Tony.

"I could talk to you wherever you're crashing," Tony said, taking his notebook from his pocket. "Want to tell me where that is?"

Justin gave him an apartment address. Tony wrote it down.

"I didn't know you were a musician," I said, desperately trying to change the subject. "How long have you been playing here?"

"This is my first night, actually. I've been on hiatus for a while, but I've got bills now."

"Heather cut you off?" Tony asked.

Justin gave him a look. "Yeah."

"And is country music your forté?" I said.

Justin shifted his gaze to me. "Just a side interest. I have an MM from Juilliard."

Holy crap!

"Oh," I said, trying to sound casual. "Do you have a primary instrument? Or are you a vocalist?"

"Woodwinds."

"You must have considered the Opera orchestra, then."

"Yeah. I'm too late for next year, but I'll put in an application for the year after. If I'm still here."

I glanced at Tony and saw him looking a little glazed. At least he no longer resembled a dog that smelled bacon.

"Well, if you need something sooner," I said, taking a card from my purse, "I might be interested in a trio or quartet to play at my restaurant now and then. The Wisteria Tearoom."

Justin's face perked with interest as he took my card. "I've heard good things about that place," he said, one corner of his mouth curving up in a smile I couldn't quite interpret.

"Thanks. I'm afraid I couldn't offer a lot. You probably make more here."

"Be a nice change, though." Justin glanced at his watch, stood, and picked up his beer. "Gotta get back. Thanks for the drink."

He raised the bottle to me and drank, cast a dark look at Tony, then headed back to his corner. Tony watched him go, then looked at me.

"What's an MM?"

"Master of Music," I replied, picking up my own beer.

Justin started singing "Desperado."

"And what's Juilliard?" Tony asked. "Some college, right?"

"A performing arts conservatory in New York. World class."

"Huh." Tony looked at Justin. "What's he doing singing country in a bar?"

"Paying the bills." I ate a couple of fries, though I wasn't really hungry any more.

"Are you really going to hire him?" Tony asked after a minute.

"Probably not. He cheated on his wife."

Tony didn't respond, so I looked up at him. He was watching me with a thoughtful expression.

"I gave him a business card, that's all."

"But your business is where you live," he said.

"Happens to be, yes." I drank some beer. "I didn't tell Justin that. Did you finish with Dickie?"

"Almost. We'll probably wrap it all up over the weekend."

"Are you still thinking it was suicide?"

"Looks that way." Tony ate a fry. "There was a note in his pocket."

"What did it say?"

"Said he was sorry for killing Debbie and Erica."

"Oh!"

Not only a suicide, but a confession to murder? My heart did a little clench-unclench thing. If Dickie was the killer, I was now safe.

I looked toward Justin, then back at Tony. "Why did you just grill Justin, then?"

Tony shrugged. "Habit." He picked up his beer, took a sip, then tipped it back and put the empty bottle down. "Looks like we're almost done with this mess."

I stirred a puddle of ketchup with a fry. "What else did the note say?"

"That's it."

I frowned. "No wisecracks? No sarcasm?"

"People who kill themselves aren't usually in a funny mood."

I drank the last of my beer. Dickie had pretty much always been in a mood to make jokes, especially cruel ones. It didn't seem like him to bypass an opportunity, particularly such a spectacular one.

Could he have been genuinely contrite? If so, what had brought him around to that? I couldn't imagine anything that would.

"Are you sure the note was from him?" I asked.

"It's his handwriting. Had an expert verify it."

"May I see it?"

"I can take a picture of it for you."

"OK."

My brain wouldn't let go of the problem. Did Dickie know that Debbie's baby *wasn't* his? Could he have killed her in a fit of jealousy?

But then why kill Erica? What could possibly be the reason for that? Unless he really had been going after classmates.

I shook my head. The pieces didn't fit together right. Something was missing.

"Can I get you guys some dessert?" Our waiter—the original one—was back, collecting our empty plates. "Chocolate mousse cake?"

Tony looked at me. I shook my head.

"Just the check," he said.

Justin's song ended. He got a round of applause, then struck up "Christmas for Cowboys." I opened my purse and took out my billfold.

"I'm getting this," Tony said.

"You bought dinner last time."

"Yeah, but I invited you. Doesn't Miss Manners say I should pay?"

I met Tony's gaze, then laid a five on the table. "I'm the one who offered Justin a drink."

He sighed. "OK. I get it. You're mad. Why?"

"I'm not mad."

"Then what?"

I stared at the picture of Lincoln on the five. "I don't know. I guess I'm frustrated." I looked up to find Tony watching me. "Are you confident that Dickie killed the others?"

"He confessed."

I didn't have an answer for that. A handwritten note did seem to be a clincher.

Miss Manners approved of handwritten notes. They showed that one really cared.

Tony walked me to my car beneath a sky dark with hanging clouds. No stars tonight. After the warmth and noise of the bar, the cold night was a relief, though it made me huddle into my coat.

"Thank you for dinner," I said as I got out my keys. "And the music. Interesting that Justin was playing here. I would never have guessed."

"Yeah," Tony said. His gaze was intent, as if he was deciding whether to say more.

"My turn tomorrow?" I said.

"If I'm free."

Cop mode. Definitely.

"OK," I said with a smile, and reached to unlock the car. His hand on my upper arm stopped me, and I turned to face him. He stared at me, frowning a little.

"Sure you're not mad?"

"I'm sure. I'm tired, and the beer made me sleepy. Sorry if I sounded cranky."

He shook his head. "Will you be OK driving home?"

"I should." I slid my arms around his waist. "Want to follow me?"

His eyelids drooped as he gazed down at me. A streetlight somewhere cast a steely reflection on his eyes.

"I shouldn't," he said in a low voice.

I gave a little shrug, then kissed him. "OK. Think about tomorrow night, then."

He returned the kiss, rather enthusiastically. "Be thinking about it all day."

He let me go and I got in the car. He stood on the sidewalk watching as I pulled out and drove away. Last I saw of him, in the rearview mirror, he hadn't moved.

I yawned as I turned into my driveway. The house was dark. I must have forgotten to turn on the back porch light, or maybe it was burned out. I'd check it in the morning.

I shut off the car and sat for a minute, thinking over my conversation with Tony. Maybe I should avoid seeing him when he was in cop mode. Except, for one thing, that was a pretty cowardly way to handle a relationship, and for another, he was in cop mode a *lot*.

Just as I picked up my purse to go in, the light in the dining parlor flashed on, then off.

I froze. Two more quick flashes, then the light came on and stayed on.

A dark figure stood on the *portal*, silhouetted against the French doors, half-turned toward the dining parlor.

12

I STARTED THE CAR AND GUNNED IT BACKWARD down the driveway, swinging into the street that I trusted would be empty at this hour. Luckily, it was. I threw the car into drive and punched the accelerator.

My first impulse was to drive to Gina's and seek asylum there, but by the time I reached Palace Avenue I realized it was pretty late for that. Friday night—she probably had a date.

I stayed at the stop sign while I pulled out my phone and called Tony.

"You OK?" he answered immediately.

"N-not really. When I got home there was someone on the back *portal.*"

The last time that had happened, the someone had ended up dead.

"Where are you?"

"In my car. I backed out of the driveway."

"Go a block or two away and park on the street. I'll be right there."

He hung up. I put the phone down and turned right. All the parking spaces were full, so I continued forward to the next intersection, the street that ran in front of my house. I turned onto it and crept along, thinking I might see the stranger getting into a car, but there was no sign of anyone walking around the house as I cruised slowly past.

The twinkle lights in the front windows looked nice.

No parking here, either. I drove on up to Marcy Street, where I finally found a space. I shut off the engine and made sure my doors were locked, then checked all my mirrors and the street in front of me for pedestrians. One couple bundled in heavy coats scurrying for a car; no mysterious loners.

I sat back to listen for Tony's motorcycle. Instead I heard the thumping of my own heart. My phone rang and I answered.

"Where are you?" Tony said.

"Parked on Marcy."

"OK, stay there. I'm going to check out your house."

"Please be careful."

"Don't worry," he said, then hung up.

Please don't kill anyone.

That would not be good, for any of us.

Who was snooping around my house? Dickie would have been my first guess, if he hadn't been dead.

Second guess, and only a very distant possibility, was the baby Goths Ramon had once hung around with. They'd snooped around the place earlier in the year, but Ramon had since become my employee, and I doubted he'd encourage it now.

I tried to recall any details about the figure I'd seen. All I knew for sure was that it wasn't huge. Average height, maybe a little taller. Average build, maybe on the slim side. Who could that be? Or—possibly an easier question—who could it *not* be?

The Bird Woman. Couldn't be her. Too tall.

My brain refused to address the problem. I gave up and turned on the radio for company. Soothing strains of choral music evoked a sigh, then I recognized the tune.

… The rising of the sun, and the running of the deer.

My heart gave an extra-hard thump. Could Captain Dusenberry be messing with my radio?

Based on what Willow had told me about ether, it was possible. But, no. I had turned on the radio myself. Whoever programmed the music for the station had chosen the song. It was just coincidence.

There are no coincidences.

Willow had told me that, too. She'd sounded dead serious at the time.

Maybe the captain had nudged me to turn on the radio, knowing what would be playing?

I shook my head and took a deep breath. Too weird for me. Too weird to think about, at this moment, when Tony was stalking an intruder on my property.

The holly bears a berry, as red as any blood…

No blood, please.

I switched the station, hunting for something different. The choices weren't exciting: commercial, "Jingle Bell Rock," talk show, pop, commercial, oldies, *Feliz Navidad*." I left it there.

My phone rang. I almost dropped it in my anxiety to answer.

"Come on home," Tony said. "Whoever it was is gone."

I closed my eyes and took a deep breath, letting it out in a sigh of relief. Then I started the car, drove around the corner, and turned into my driveway. Tony's bike was parked behind the house, and Tony was waiting by the back door. The dining parlor light was still on.

I parked and joined Tony. "Why didn't you leave the porch light on?" he asked.

"I did. It must have burned out."

He reached up to the light fixture and fiddled with it. The light came on, blinding me. I looked away.

"Oh!"

"Somebody unscrewed it," Tony said.

I stared resentfully at the fixture.

"I found a partial footprint in the snow," Tony said. "Took a picture of it, but it probably doesn't have enough detail to draw any conclusions. Looks like whoever it was came and went by the driveway."

Where the gravel had already absorbed most of the snow. No prints there.

"Thank you," I said. "Want to come in? I'll make cocoa."

I needed something hot and comforting. A warm drink would be nice, too.

"OK," Tony said.

As soon as we were in and I had locked the back door, I plastered myself to Tony. He hugged me and I buried my face in his jacket, which was stiff with cold and smelled of snow.

"Scared?" he said gently.

I lifted my head and nodded, sniffing as I let him go.

"Wait here. I'll check the doors and windows."

I stood by the dining parlor, looking in at the chandelier. No moving crystals, but the light was on.

"Thank you, Captain," I whispered.

Thinking back to the moment that light had flashed on and off, revealing the stranger on the *portal*, I realized that Captain Dusenberry might well have saved my life.

A ghost saved my life.

OK, no excuse for not believing in him. Not any more.

"All clear," Tony said, returning. "You OK?"

I nodded. We went upstairs, where Tony again checked every room before letting me go into my suite.

"Have a seat," I said, trying to sound normal as I took out a saucepan. "This'll just take a couple of minutes."

I poured milk in the pan and turned the heat on low, then added sugar, cocoa powder, a dash of chile powder, and a pat of butter. While it warmed I whisked it all together. The act of cooking was calming; by the time the cocoa was simmering, I had regained my composure.

"Heck of a night," Tony commented. "Glad it's Friday."

"For you. I have to work tomorrow."

"Does that mean I'm going home?"

I looked up at Tony, catching my breath. That was the most blatant hint he'd ever made about staying the night.

"Only if you want to," I said.

He grinned and leaned back in his chair, hands behind his head. My heart melted a little. Cop Tony had gone away, or gone dormant at least, and here was the man I loved so much.

I swallowed and whisked the cocoa a little harder.

It occurred to me to say that he seemed pretty nonchalant considering that someone had been stalking me on my property, but I didn't want to send him back into cop mode. Tony out of cop mode was a rare and precious state, and I didn't want to jeopardize it.

I turned down the heat and whisked the cocoa a little more, then poured it into two mugs and carried them to the sitting area.

"Mmm," Tony said after a cautious sip. "Oh, that's good. Got any of those biscochitos?"

"Not up here. There might be some downstairs."

He shook his head. "This is fine."

I agreed. This was fine. I snuggled into my chair with my mug, taking tiny sips so as not to burn my mouth.

We sat in silence for a few minutes. Maybe we were both thinking about the intruder, but we didn't discuss it. Perhaps Tony wanted to stay out of cop mode as much as I wanted him to.

Instead we sat enjoying each other's presence, enjoying the cocoa and the quiet night. When the mugs were empty I put them in the sink, then came back and held out my hand to Tony.

He smiled and stood. On the way to my bedroom, he paused to lock the door of my suite. A little cop moment.

Then he took my hand again, and slowly brought it up to plant a kiss into my palm. I switched out the lights and softly drew him in.

I was deep in the middle of a complicated dream—about building an addition to the house to enable us to bake more cookies—when the sound of the back door closing woke me.

Tony startled up to a half-sitting position.

"Hanh," I said, rubbing my face.

"What?"

"It's Hanh. Assistant chef. Comes in five minutes early every morning."

To double-check, I looked at my bedside clock: 5:55.

"Oh," Tony said. "I thought you were calling me 'hon'."

"I could. Would you like that, hon?"

Tony stared at me for a second. "No."

"OK." I yawned, and rolled onto my side. Tony's hands, warm and slightly rough, began to caress my back.

It was time to make cookies, but my back was being rubbed. No question of getting up just yet.

Soon my back was being kissed as well as rubbed. After that, my memory got kind of blurry.

Full awareness hit me when the salsa music started. I checked the clock again: 7:46 this time. Julio was here, and probably also Ramon. The servers would be coming in soon.

Guess they'd all see Tony's bike.

Well, no point in worrying over it. I'd pick a dress that would coordinate with red cheeks, and carry on.

I sighed and sat up. Tony startled awake, and I put a hand on his arm.

"Sorry. Sleep in if you want. I need to get going."

He groaned and rolled over. I got up, pulled on my robe, chose a burgundy velour dress with lace trim and headed for the shower. When I emerged, I smelled coffee. Tony, in t-shirt and little else, was standing in my kitchenette watching the coffeemaker's delicate stream slowly filling the carafe.

"Hi," I said. "Sleep OK?"

"Mmm." He slid an arm around my waist and pulled me close. I gave him a light kiss, then gently slid out of his grasp.

"Want some breakfast? I usually just have tea and toast, but I could make some eggs."

"Mm." He looked back at the coffee machine.

OK, not a morning person. I could understand.

I got out bread, butter, and jam, and fired up the toaster. Not knowing Tony's habits or metabolism, I decided to be safe and provide some protein. Scrambled eggs were easy.

Tony didn't speak until he'd consumed a plate of eggs, two pieces of toast, and two mugs of coffee. Then he said one word: "Thanks."

"You're welcome." I got up, rinsed my dishes, and put them in the dishwasher, then picked up the coffee carafe to give Tony a refill. "I need to get downstairs. Take your time."

"Mm."

I made sure I had both my keys and my phone, then stepped out into the upper hallway and gently closed the door to my suite. I poked my head into the office doorway, but Kris hadn't arrived yet, so I headed downstairs.

Julio, Hanh, and Ramon were all hard at work. They paused when I came in.

"Good morning," I said. "Everything under control?"

Julio gave me a two-second stare. "Yes, but we'll need more sugar for Monday," he said. "Delivery's on Tuesday."

I stepped over to where he was mixing cinnamon sugar in a big bowl. "I can pick some up tomorrow, unless you need it today," I said.

"We're good for today."

"OK. Let me know if we're low on anything else."

Julio nodded. I glanced at the other two, who both quickly became absorbed in their tasks.

Hmm.

Looking out the kitchen window, I saw Tony's bike beside my car, big and black and dusted with snow. Head high, I left and paused in the butler's pantry to put a kettle on. I'd had a little of Tony's coffee, but I actually preferred tea.

None of the servers had arrived; they would be in at ten. Nat, however, was in the gift shop, wearing a cheerful red and green plaid dress and humming "Let it Snow."

"Morning, dear," she said as I came in.

"Morning." I stepped behind the counter to bring up the reservations listing for the day. We were booked solid again.

Nat paused in the act of straightening the tea accessories, turned to look at me, and gave me a wide smile.

"You're smirking," I said.

"No I'm not. I'm just happy for you." She smiled again, then returned to her task.

The first giant blush of the day washed up my neck and into my face. I hoped there wouldn't be too many.

Retreating to the pantry, I made a pot of Irish Breakfast and carried it upstairs. The door to my suite was still closed, so I went into my office.

The stack of message slips in my in-box was so high it threatened to spill out of the box. I picked up a handful and glanced through them, then started sorting them into piles according to what type of person had left the message. The tallest pile was "friends and family"—mostly from Gina—followed by "people who want to sell me something." Next came "tearoom business" and "ask Kris," then "deal with it today," which included far too many messages for me to deal with in one day. That left a trio of monosyllabic messages from Tony, and one cryptic note: "Your ghost wants company."

I frowned at the lavender message slip. Was that a threat?

There was no name on it, nor phone number. Kris might be able to get the number off the caller ID, though. I wondered briefly if it could be from Willow, but that didn't feel right.

I did not like this message, especially since it had apparently arrived late yesterday, not long before my adventure with the stalker in the driveway. I wondered whether Tony would want to follow up on it. Problem was, though the message was weird, there wasn't much to connect it with the stalker. Just the timing, which could be coincidence.

Yes, yes, all right, Willow.

I set the slip aside and went to work on the "deal with it today" pile. I was on my third cup of tea when I heard Kris on the stairs. I went out to meet her.

"Good morning," I said as she hung her coat on the coat rack.

"Morning." She gave me an arch look over her shoulder. "Have a good night?"

"Lovely," I said, and turned before she could see Monster Blush #2. "Would you like tea?"

"Yes, please."

I poured her a cup, and took the time to fetch my own cup and the mystery message from my desk. By the time I carried it all into Kris's office, my blush had mostly receded.

"Do you remember who this was?" I asked, handing her the message.

She frowned at the slip. "No. And I've already deleted yesterday's messages, so I can't check it. Sorry."

"OK, thanks anyway," I said, standing to go. "Are we all set for tomorrow?"

Kris nodded. "El Vaquero will deliver the food at 5:00."

"So I should pick up the drinks well before then."

"Want me to get them on my way here?" Kris offered.

"Thanks, but I have to buy sugar for the kitchen anyway, so I'll do it. Do you have a list for me?"

"I'll write one up."

I picked up my teacup and headed for my office. As I passed the doorway to the hall I heard a quiet thump. Looking out, I saw Tony standing by my suite, shrugging into his jacket. I left my teacup on my credenza and went to meet him.

"Hi. Awake now?"

He nodded. "Sorry."

"Don't be." I kissed his cheek and smiled to reassure him. His arm slid around my waist and I leaned against him, closing my eyes and breathing in his Tony-ness.

"Gotta go," he murmured.

"Call about dinner?"

"Yeah."

He kissed me, then put a hand to my cheek and gave me a beautiful, soft-eyed smile. Better than words, which was good because words weren't his forte.

I went downstairs with him, figuring it would be better than having my staff watch him leave alone. Heat crept into my face with each downward step. Accompanying Tony out the back door, I saw various cars belonging to my staff taking up all the available spaces. Rosa's car, usually in the spot now occupied by Tony's bike, was parked behind the shed.

The sky was patched with clouds. It was warm enough that the snow was starting to melt, turning to slush. The cold air smelled of damp evergreens.

Tony stood looking around, especially at the ground near the back door. His eyes narrowed, cop mode setting in. He walked a few paces down the driveway, peering at the ground. Of course, my staff had muddled whatever marks he might have seen. I watched him, rubbing my arms. Despite my velour dress, I was starting to shiver.

Tony came back, shaking his head slightly as he met my gaze. "Nothing. Thought I'd check anyway."

"Thanks. I'd better go in," I said. "Talk to you later."

He nodded, then put on his helmet and climbed on the bike. I watched him ease it back, then start the engine. Fleeing the noise, I went inside and watched through the window until he turned out of the driveway.

Mick's pinto-splotched Mustang turned in almost at the same time. Not feeling up to another blush yet, I headed back upstairs.

My desk was still covered with stacks of message slips. I'd

neglected to mention my odd message to Tony. I set it aside, so I'd remember to bring it up the next time I saw him.

We'd spent quite a lot of time together the last few days. I didn't mind that at all, but as I retrieved my teacup and filled it from the pot on the credenza, I reminded myself that this probably wouldn't last. Even if Tony's present case was almost concluded, there would always be another one waiting.

Fortified by tea, I continued to sort the slips in my box until they were all in the stacks. The "deal with today" stack was now the tallest. I separated it into "do today" and "do tomorrow," which made it look less alarming but didn't really address the fundamental problem.

Too many ASAPs.

I divided the "today" pile again, and came up with a small stack that I might actually get through that day. I clipped the rest of the stacks together with labels and put them back in my box, then grabbed my desk phone and got to work.

By the time we opened and I went downstairs to help, nobody had the time to rib me about Tony's overnight visit. Holiday shopping had gone up a notch, starting to approach frenzy level. I spent the afternoon helping Nat in the gift shop, with periodic dashes to the kitchen for biscochitos or upstairs for more merchandise. By closing time, I was exhausted.

"Thank you! Merry Christmas," I said as I ushered the last customers out the front door at 6:15. My gratitude was sincere and multi-layered. When I locked the door after them and turned the sign around to "CLOSED," I heard Nat give a cheer behind me.

"It's the weekend!" she said. "Last chance to shop before Christmas!"

Shopping. Aargh. I had sugar and drinks to get tomorrow. And I wasn't done buying presents, but all I could think about at that moment was putting my aching feet up.

Kris was already at the register, cashing it out. Dee and Dale were tending to the fireplaces, and Rosa and Iz were stacking clean china in the pantry, while Mick worked his way through the last of the dishwashing. Julio, Ramon, and Hanh had all left at four.

"Mind if I go?" Nat asked, taking down her coat from a hook in the hall. "We're going to a party tonight."

"Go ahead. Give Manny a hug for me."

"Give it to me, and I'll pass it along."

I hugged her and walked her to the back door. "See you tomorrow night," I said.

"Sleep well," she said with a grin.

Despite how tired I was, apparently I could still blush.

I trudged upstairs to check my office. A few fresh messages slips had fallen in my in-box. I glanced through them: none from Tony.

He hadn't texted or called my cell, either. I sighed. If his day had been anything like mine, I couldn't blame him.

"I'm going," Kris said, stepping to the door and holding up the bank bag. "Dropping this by the bank."

"OK – be careful and I'll see you tomorrow," I said.

I couldn't bring myself to go downstairs and see the others out. My legs refused. I sat at my desk, listening to them leave one by one. At last, all I could hear was the distant thrumming of the kitchen's water heater.

I should go down and check that everything was locked up.

No, said my feet.

Raising my head, I let my gaze roam my office. It lit on my *chaise longue*, silently waiting beneath its fringed lamp, my current book lying on top of the neatly folded lap rug.

Oh, yes. That was what I wanted.

I turned off my computer, took the tea tray across the hall to my suite and made a pot of Wisteria White, then brought it back to the office and took up residence on the chaise. With my cell phone at hand in case Tony called, I snuggled down with a steaming cup of tea and opened my book.

It was dark when the phone woke me. Blinking, I worked an arm free of the lap rug, which I had twined around myself, and grabbed the phone.

"H'lo?"

"Babe. I'm so sorry."

"S'ok." I rubbed my eyes and peered at the wall clock across the room, but couldn't read it in the darkness outside the pool of light from the standing lamp beside me.

"You drunk?" Tony asked.

I cleared my throat. "No. I was asleep."

"Oh. Sorry."

"What time is it?"

"Eight thirty. I can't do dinner tonight."

"That's OK. Clearly, I need to go to bed."

There was a pause. I heard a voice in the background—sounded male.

"I have to go," Tony said. "See you tomorrow?"

"It's the staff party. You want to come?"

"I'll see. What time?"

"Six."

"Don't count on me."

"OK."

"Sleep well, babe. Wish I could tuck you in."

"Mmm. Night."

"Check all the locks."

Click.

I sighed and struggled out of the lap rug. He was right. Though I wanted to just curl back up again, I dragged myself downstairs to make the rounds.

Before I reached the foot of the staircase, I realized the hall light was on. Either someone had left it on, or the captain had turned it on for me. This inspired me to plan on collecting a fireplace poker from the dining parlor before going around to check the locks.

That, however, was unnecessary. As I reached the foot of the stairs, I saw two six-foot banquet tables set up against the north wall of the hall, the way we used them for big events. Someone—Julio, probably—had fetched them out of the shed and set them up. Calling down silent blessings on whoever had done it, I continued my rounds.

All was secure, all quiet. I checked the pastry case: empty. Nat had wiped it down. There was a take-out box on the shelf beneath it, which of course I had to check for monsters. It contained four biscochitos, which would certainly go stale by Tuesday.

It would have been wasteful to leave them there.

On Sunday I slept in, then went shopping and got my last few presents before picking up the groceries. The stores were all zoo-like with last-minute shopping and Deals! Deals! Deals! I escaped in time to curl up with tea and my book once again, and this time I didn't fall asleep. I read until it was time to get dressed for the staff party, engrossed by the hair-raising antics of the heroine, who had joined a circus to find a murderer, and was collecting bruises while learning to stand on a horse.

I would *never* do that. Nor, I was certain, would Tony. Nor was I convinced it was needful in order to catch the murderer, but it was certainly entertaining.

I put on jeans and a holiday sweater that my mom had given me —soft, cream-colored with blue snowflakes—before going downstairs to get ready for the party. I put away the lace tablecloth from the dining parlor and spread a plain cotton cloth there instead, and put two more on the serving tables in the hall. I set up the chafing dishes, and had just finished putting out paper plates and cups when the front doorbell rang.

Rick Garcia stood outside, snow dusting his dark hair, and a younger man behind him. Each had his arms full of a large insulated carrier. Parked at the curb was a white van with "El Vaquero" painted on the side.

"Hi, Rick! Come on in."

A gust of snow-chilled air accompanied them. I glanced out the door and saw tiny flakes coming down—not sticking yet, but the path was wet.

"We're set up here," I said, indicating the long tables, and picking up the lighter for the chafing dishes. "How's business?"

"Crazy," Rick said, laughing. "You're my third catering job today."

"Yikes. Well, thanks for taking us on."

"You kidding? My kids would never let me hear the end of it if I didn't."

Ramon had been working for his dad at El Vaquero when I'd first met him, but now he and his sister Rosa both worked for me. I watched Rick's assistant unpacking trays of food and decided that he was unrelated.

The two of them had everything transferred to the tables in just a few minutes. I saw them out and wished them a Merry Christmas, then fetched the sodas from the kitchen fridge and put them in two tubs. Just as I topped them off with the last bag of ice, I heard a car out back. I took the empty ice bag to the kitchen and looked out the window.

It was the Mercedes.

Drying my hands, I watched Julio and Owen get out of the car and head for the back hall door. Julio hesitated and they exchanged a glance before he pulled his keys out of his pocket. I slipped into the side hall and emerged into the main hall as I heard the back door close.

"Hello?" I called.

"It's me, Boss," Julio answered.

Donning a smile, I headed toward them. "Julio, did you bring in the tables? Oh, hello, Owen!"

"Hi," Owen said. He looked smashing (as usual) in a black satin shirt, black jeans, and a sandcast concho belt, with his hair loose over his shoulders and down his back.

I smiled at him, then turned an inquiring look to Julio, who was almost as striking in a high-collared linen shirt and jeans, hair curling free instead of confined by hairnet and cap.

"Yeah," Julio said. "Dale and I brought them in."

"Brilliant. Thank you."

"Um. Well…" Julio glanced at Owen.

Owen's eyes narrowed with mirth. "He thinks you should know that we're roommates," he told me.

"Oh! Well, that makes sense. I know Julio likes to bike to work, and places near here aren't cheap." I looked at Julio, whose cheeks were a little red, but perhaps that was from the cold. "I'm glad it worked out," I added, smiling.

"Thanks," Julio said.

"Would you mind if we set up your coffeemaker out here?" I asked. "We've got sodas, but it's snowing…"

"What, no gallons of tea?" Owen said.

I faced him, serious though I knew he was teasing. "Of course there can be gallons of tea. But some prefer coffee."

"I'll go get it," Julio said, and ducked into the side hall.

Owen met my gaze. "He was worried you'd disapprove," he said softly.

"It's none of my business," I said, turning to straighten a stack of red and green paper napkins. "But, honestly, I can't criticize his taste."

Glancing back at Owen, I saw his delighted smile a moment before he headed down the side hall. I smiled to myself.

It was beginning to feel like Christmas.

Within an hour, my staff—who that night were my guests—arrived and filled the house with joy and laughter. They had all brought friends or family, and I got to meet several new people, including Iz's mother, Grace; Hanh's very polite husband, Tam; and a serious-looking young man named Carlos Moya whom Rosa was apparently dating.

Rick's excellent enchiladas, tamales, and *rellenos* were swiftly consumed, as were sodas and coffee and a gallon or two of tea. I carried my plate from group to group and visited with them all, taking time to chat about their plans for the upcoming days off. Mick and Dee were going to drive to Los Angeles and visit their father; everyone else had plans closer to home. Rosa and Ramon were going on a skiing trip to Taos with their family. Dale and Kris and their Goth community were planning a black-and-white ball for New Year's Eve. Iz would be participating in the traditional dances at Tesuque Pueblo on Christmas Day, and shyly invited me to attend.

"Oh, I'd love to," I said, "but I'm already booked up for Christmas this year. Maybe next year? When is your feast day?"

"November twelfth," Iz said. "You could come then."

"Come and eat with us," Grace added, and I knew she was paying me a special honor. To be invited into a pueblo home on a feast day was to be treated as one of the family.

"I'll put it on my calendar," I said. "Thank you!"

"Hey, Ellen," Dee said, bouncing up in a sparkly red top that looked too light for the weather, over black tights, "Is it time for dessert yet?"

"It is," I said, standing and giving Iz a smile. "There's flan and whipped cream."

Dee helped me fetch these from the kitchen, and a line quickly formed at the serving table. I made more tea, then helped myself to some of the custard. Rick's chef had done it perfectly; creamy custard in a sugar sauce caramelized to a point just short of tasting burned. It was magnificent.

Someone opened my mother's piano and started playing Christmas carols. I filled my party cup with tea and continued visiting. When the last of the flan had been consumed, I asked everyone to gather in the main parlor. Kris and I had considered a gift exchange, and decided it was better just to let people handle that on their own. I stood by the tree in the center of the room and passed out my gifts, and while I had their attention I made a short speech:

"We're having a very busy holiday season, and I just want to thank you all for your patience and your willingness to put in the extra work. I also want to thank you for making our first year—or most of a year—a success. You are a fantastic team. In fact, you're more than a team. You're the Wisteria Tearoom family, and I couldn't be more proud of you. So to thank you, I'm adding a small bonus to your next paycheck."

An excited cheer broke out, and someone whooped. "Don't go buying cars or furniture," I warned. "It's not that big. Just a token of my esteem, as they say." I raised my cup of tea to them. "Thank you."

I stepped back, expecting conversation to begin again, but Rosa and Dee forestalled it. They came forward with a plush red velour Santa hat with tiny lights embedded all over it, which Dee insisted on putting on my head. Rosa handed me a card in a green envelope, while Mick and Dale brought in a small rectangular table and set a large box wrapped in holly-covered paper on it.

"If we're a family," Dee said, "then you're our matriarch. Merry Christmas from all of us, Mom!"

A second, much rowdier cheer went up. I was stunned, and felt a moment's guilt that they had interpreted the party as my wanting a present from them. I shook off that foolish thought and managed to smile.

"Wow," I said. "Th-thank you!"

"Open it, Mom!" a male voice called from the back of the room. I glanced up, but couldn't tell who it was. Feeling myself blush,

I opened the envelope and took out a Christmas card covered in handwritten messages from the staff. I would read them all later; the cry of "Open it, Mom!" had been taken up by others, so I handed the card to Dee and approached the box.

It was perhaps two and a half feet tall by two feet square. I had a sudden vision of a plush Holstein cow inside.

Praying I was wrong, I pulled the paper from the box amid encouraging cries of "Go, Mom!" and "Are we there yet?" The box was unmarked; I unfolded the top and pulled out a wad of brown paper, revealing more paper beneath and a gleam of metal.

I dug through the paper, throwing it all on the floor to the delight of my audience, who cheered and wooted as I lifted an exquisite, enameled samovar from the box and set it on the table. It was deep green, and painted all over with vines and clusters of wisteria blossoms. My throat tightened with tears.

"There's more," Kris said.

I reached back into the box and retrieved a teapot that exactly matched the samovar and nestled into its golden crown. I had spotted something else in the box, and fished it out. It was an electrical cord with a large, pronged plug.

"It's been converted to electricity," Kris explained.

"It's so you can make tea right in your office, and not have to go across the hall or come downstairs," Dee added.

"Oh!" I squeaked.

"The table is from me and Manny," Nat said, grinning from one of the wing chairs, holding hands with Manny in the chair beside her. "It'll fit in that little space at the entrance to your office. We measured."

I looked closer at the table. At first I had thought it was one of the many that belonged to the tearoom, but no. It was an antique, with lovely wood inlays of flowers and scrollwork and a satiny finish. Three shallow drawers offered space to store leaf tea and utensils.

I brushed at my face. "Thank you," I said in a choked voice, then cleared my throat, grabbed the teapot and hugged it to my chest, and addressed the whole room. "Thank you, everyone! It's absolutely perfect. I never dreamed of having such a splendid thing!"

Dee caught me in a hug, after which pretty much all the staff lined up for hugs, while their guests came to admire the samovar and table up close. After they'd all had a look, Kris picked up the samovar and Mick and Dale carried the table up the stairs, with me following anxiously, clutching the teapot, at the head of a parade that included Nat, Kris, Dee, Julio, and Rosa.

The two men placed the table in the space opposite the door into Kris's office and mine, creating a small, symbolic barrier that Kris would no doubt appreciate. Kris set the samovar on top of it and I carefully put the teapot in its place on top, then stepped back to admire the whole ensemble.

"Perfect," I said.

Nat caught me in a hug. "Merry Christmas, love!"

"Merry Christmas, Ellen!" Dee put in.

"Merry Christmas, Mom!" quipped one of the men.

I glanced up, but all the faces were innocent. Whoever that was, he was being careful not to let me catch him.

We all trooped downstairs again, to find that Hanh and Ramon had organized a lightning cleanup in our absence. Plates, cups, and all had been collected, the trash taken out, and the chafing dishes were already in the drying rack in the kitchen.

As the guests gradually began to take their leave, I stayed in the hall chatting. Candles flickered on the serving tables, and the piano struck up again, with a few voices joining in to sing "Deck the Halls."

"Lovely party, dear," Nat said as Manny helped her into her coat.

"Thank you so much for that gorgeous table," I said, still in awe.

She kissed my cheek. "You're welcome. Should we pick you up tomorrow, or do you want to meet us?"

I stared blankly at her.

"Dinner with Joe," Manny prompted. "The Compound."

"Oh! That's tomorrow? Oh, yes. Um, pick me up, please. The parking on Canyon Road is terrible."

"Will do."

"He's coming in around noon," Nat added. "I'm going to make him take a nap."

"Good luck with that. He always hated naps."

"Ah, but he's an adult now, and he'll be jet-lagged."

I kept my doubts to myself, hugged Nat and Manny again, and saw them out. Rosa and Ramon were on their way home as well, and we said good night at the door. A sudden thought struck me.

"Ramon, did I miss your concert?"

"No, it's Wednesday."

"Oh, good! I'll be there."

He smiled. "See you tomorrow."

"Yes. Good night."

I said goodbye to several others, then drifted into the parlor where Kris, Julio, Owen, and Dale were gathered around the piano. Dee was on the bench, playing "Jesu, Joy of Man's Desiring" with a skill I hadn't known she had.

"Miss Gallagher, you never cease to amaze me," I said when she concluded.

She tossed me a grin. "Thanks. I took lessons from fourth grade on. I even played in one of Mick's bands for a while."

"One of them?"

She shot a glance at her brother. "Yeah, well—they change every couple of months or so." She set her hands to the keys again, and began "The Holly and the Ivy."

I experienced a frisson of wonder and just a tiny pang of fear. Had Captain Dusenberry somehow suggested the song to Dee? As I marveled, Owen began to sing in a beautiful, resonant voice.

> *The holly and the ivy, when they are both full grown,*
>
> *Of all the trees that are in the wood, the holly bears the crown.*

Kris joined in, followed by Dale. I knew the song, too, so I joined the chorus.

It felt good to sing. Heaven knew how long it had been. I'd been so busy....

The past year spun around me in a kaleidoscope of memory. The more I recalled, the more grateful I became, and I gave silent thanks as we sang together, with firelight glowing and the tree twinkling and snow falling in the darkness outside.

13

Monday morning, the biscochito mill started up again, and ran all day. The serving tables that were still in the hall were soon covered with trays of cooling cookies. Though I didn't admit it out loud, I was beginning to get just a little tired of the smell of cinnamon and anise. I pitched in to help, wanting to assuage my guilt over demanding an extra six dozen cookies on Christmas Eve, though Julio assured me it would be a drop in the bucket.

"We're spending all day today on biscochitos," he said. "Everything else for the week is prepped, so we should be able to maximize production today."

I maximized as hard as I could, though inevitably, since I hadn't been making biscochitos all month, I was slow and wound up doing the simplest jobs, like boxing up finished cookies. At four o'clock I went upstairs to change for dinner with my family.

I chose a sleek, black crepe dress and a silver heishi necklace, and put my hair up in a French twist, secured with a silver sandcast barrette that my father had given me. That was about as chic as I could get, and I hoped it would be good enough for my New Yorker brother.

Odd, to be so anxious about what Joe thought. I'd never felt that way growing up, but now it had been a few years since we'd spent any appreciable time together, and I felt a little like I was dressing to meet a stranger.

My long wool coat and a black scarf were not as classy as the dress, but they'd have to suffice. I reached the downstairs just as the headlights of Nat's Subaru splashed across the back door lights.

The kitchen was still going. I looked in and found Julio and

Hanh packing up cookies while Ramon washed baking sheets. I bade them good night and reminded them to lock all the doors up, then went out the kitchen door.

Manny was getting out of the car, but when he saw me he hopped back into the driver's seat. Nat welcomed me into the back seat, and Joe and I exchanged greetings while Manny turned the car around.

"How was your flight?" I asked, leaning forward to address his profile, which was half-illuminated by the dashboard.

"The flight was fine," he said. "La Guardia was terrible, but that's nothing new."

This did nothing to diminish my sense of him as a stranger. I considered asking about his job but decided to wait until we could make eye contact over the dinner table.

Traffic was hectic. I watched in silence while Manny negotiated the narrow, winding course of Canyon Road. Tourists swarmed, and every Santa Fe driver knew to keep an eye on them, as they tended to step into the street without looking for traffic while they photographed a building, a wall, or a sculpture on display in the courtyard of a gallery.

Manny expertly piloted the Subaru down into the snow-packed parking lot by the Compound, downhill from the street. Glad that I'd decided against stiletto heels, I slid out of the back seat and gratefully accepted Manny's arm as we headed for the restaurant's trademark sign lit by spotlights that made the night seem darker.

I had not dined here since before Mom had died. The family had only come to the Compound on the rare special occasion. I was pretty sure the last time I'd been here was to celebrate my high school graduation. Joe had already been gone then; in his second year at Harvard.

The smell of piñon in the fireplaces made me feel at home. Our table was near enough to one to feel the warmth, for which I (in my stylish, sleeveless dress) was grateful. The lighting was subdued but bright enough for reading the menu. Candles flickered on the tables, and other guests conversed in low voices.

"Shall we have some wine?" Nat asked.

Joe picked up the wine list, scanned it intently, then handed it to Manny, apparently unimpressed. Manny chose a Cabernet from

Black Mesa Winery, one of the better New Mexico vineyards. While the waiter was fetching it, I turned to my brother with a smile.

"It's so great to see you again. I'm glad you could come out for a few days."

Now that I actually *could* see him, I noticed the stylish cut of his brown hair waving away from his temples. It was shorter than he'd worn it in high school, and the cut was very flattering to the long bones of his face. One or two thin lines had developed on his forehead, most notably between the eyebrows. Otherwise, he looked much like the brother I remembered, but rather more polished.

"Good to see you, too, El," he said. "How've you been?"

His old nickname for me raised echoes of childhood. He'd often liked to follow it with a tease: El Diablo, El Paso, El Camino Real.

"Fine," I said hastily. "Very busy, with the holiday season."

"That's right, you're a retailer now."

"A restaurateur," Nat corrected.

I glanced at her, then back at Joe. "I hope you'll have time to come and have tea while you're here."

That evoked a smile. "Still tea-crazy, eh?"

"Very much so," I said with dignity.

Nat gave me a skeptical look, and I knew she was thinking of our booked-solid reservations, but there was no reason I couldn't serve tea to Joe upstairs by the front window.

The waiter arrived with our wine, and poured Manny a meticulous sample. Joe watched the ritual with an air of resignation. Manny nodded, and the waiter filled our glasses, then took our orders for dinner. I decided on duck with cherry glaze.

Joe launched into a spirited discussion of blue-chip stocks with Nat. I stayed out of it; I'd never been interested in stocks, and all my worth was currently invested in the tearoom.

Manny listened for a while, sipping his wine, and eventually gave me a sidelong glance. "Your brother's changed some, no?"

"Yes. Had you met him before?"

"Not before today."

This reminded me that Joe had failed to come to the wedding. I drank some wine, telling myself to forgive and forget, but I knew Nat had been disappointed.

A female waiter brought the foie gras appetizer that Joe had ordered. She looked familiar; I watched her, trying to place her and not succeeding.

Joe and Nat had apparently found grounds for agreement, because they both picked up their wine. Joe's face lit with surprise after he sipped it, and he reached for the bottle.

"What is this again?"

"Black Mesa."

Joe examined the label, then set the bottle down. "Not bad," he said.

"Your father liked to picnic there," Nat told him. "Don't you remember?"

Joe, helping himself to foie gras, gave a noncommittal shrug. I thought back and dredged up some hazy memories of a sprawling compound with picnic tables on grassy areas and a fountain in the middle of a pond that attracted huge, blue dragonflies. Summer time. Eating peanut butter sandwiches in the heat, while Dad chatted with Mom and maybe a friend or two. Playing soccer on the grass while the grownups sampled wines under a vine-laden pergola.

"How's the skiing this year?" Joe asked.

"I haven't been up," Nat said.

Joe looked at me, and I shook my head. "Haven't had time."

Not to mention the expense. I no longer owned any skis or boots, and renting equipment on top of buying lift tickets made for an expensive day. I actually hadn't gone skiing in several years.

Not since Dad died.

Blinking, I picked up my wine and sipped. Memories of my father called to me and I followed them, letting the conversation flow over me without registering. Dad taught me to ski, took me hiking up in the mountains, rousted me out of bed early to see dances at the pueblos, and showed me many of the wonders of New Mexico. A big part of my love for the state was founded in the way my father had led me to explore it.

Mom and Joe had been along on many of those adventures, too. I wondered if Joe remembered them as fondly as I did.

A busser came and cleared the foie gras plate, and the familiar-looking waiter brought our entrees. I watched her, still trying to figure out why she was ringing a bell.

Her clothes were the standard unisex waiter outfit: white dress shirt, tie, black pants, small black apron, sensible black shoes. She had her black hair pulled back tightly and twisted into a taut, sleek knot.

That was it! I had seen that knot before. But where?

"Duck breast?" she said catching my eye to confirm as she laid the plate before me.

I nodded. The bells were ringing even louder. I had to make an effort not to stare at her as she served the others.

"Well, maybe we can take a day and hit the slopes," Joe said, smiling.

Gina's face came to my memory, bright with speculation as she proposed a skiing excursion to Taos.

I've had a crush on him ever since fifth grade. Don't tell me you didn't know.

Ay yi yi.

"You do have some days off coming, Ellen," Nat said.

"She's the boss, right?" Joe said. "She can take off any time she likes."

I shook my head. "No, I really can't. We're too busy right now."

"But after Christmas," Nat said. "You'll be closed for four days."

Joe tilted his head, looking at me. I shot Nat a perplexed glance.

"Maybe," I said, picking up my knife and focusing on slicing off a bite of duck.

"Do you ski, Manny?" Joe asked.

"Nah. Never had time to learn."

Or money, maybe. Manny was comfortable, but he'd built his business up himself, and his roots were blue-collar.

Why did everything keep coming back to money?

Maybe it was just on my mind right now. Money: who had it, who didn't, and why that mattered so much. Tony flitted around the edge of my thoughts, but I shied away from him, back to the more abstract concept of money.

That was something that might help unravel Debbie's murder: who had money, and who didn't. I hadn't really looked at it from that specific angle. Would money cause any of the suspects to kill? Debbie had money; she had an upper-level job at a bank.

Who inherited her estate? There wasn't an insurance policy, but she must have had savings, retirement....

"How's your duck?" Joe asked.

"Excellent," I said, cutting off another bite. "How's your tenderloin?"

"Not bad."

High praise. But then, he was probably accustomed to beef raised somewhere in upstate New York, or maybe Pennsylvania, with much sweeter grasses to graze on than our local cattle enjoyed. Back there, it would be "how many cows to the acre." Out here it was "how many acres to the cow."

Joe returned to the skiing idea, and with Nat's assistance put together a vague plan for Boxing Day. I refrained from commenting. I had been rather looking forward to sleeping for forty-eight hours or so after Christmas. Also, if I got dragged into the skiing excursion, I'd have to invite Gina or risk being strangled by her when she found out about it later.

I loved Gina, but I didn't want her for a sister-in-law. Mostly because the thought of Gina and Joe together was rather alarming.

They were finalizing the plan when our waiter returned and presented us with dessert menus. A tomatillo mince pie sounded exotic, and sticky toffee pudding was a contender, but my uncertain mood prompted me to choose the bittersweet ganache tart. Nat got the pudding and Joe ordered a cognac, while Manny stuck to coffee.

When our order was in, I excused myself to visit the ladies' room. As I reached it, the female waiter with the familiar hairstyle came out.

"Excuse me," I said. "Have we met? You look familiar."

She gave me a tight smile. "I came to tea at your tearoom."

"Oh! Were you with someone...?"

She nodded. "Erica Wegman."

Memory flashed back: Erica in a red cocktail dress and Parisian hat, her friend in black with a fascinator perched atop that perfect knot.

"Oh! Oh, Erica. I'm sorry," I said, flailing a little as my heart replayed emotions I'd thought I was done with.

The waiter smiled sadly. "You went to school with her. I remember."

"Yes. I'd like to talk with you about her, if you don't mind. May I give you my card?"

She looked mildly surprised, but nodded again. "OK."

I dug out a card for her. "Thanks. Please call when you have some free time in the next few days. I'm Ellen, by the way."

"Juana."

"Thank you, Juana."

She gave another brisk nod as she slid my card into her apron and headed back to the restaurant. I continued to the privacy of the ladies' room, musing.

If Juana had met Erica at work, then maybe they shared the same shifts. There was a chance that Juana had been around the night that Erica had seen Debbie and her mystery date.

Tony would have already talked to her, though. He had talked to all the staff here, he'd said. But maybe talking about Erica would bring a forgotten detail to Juana's mind.

Long shot. Still worth a try.

I returned to the table, preoccupied with Erica and Debbie. The desserts had arrived, along with petite cups of strong coffee. As I resumed my seat, Joe turned his attention to me.

"Nat tells me you recently lost a classmate," he said. "I'm sorry."

"Three classmates, actually," I said, adding a generous dollop of cream to my cup.

"Three?"

"You didn't tell me there were three!" Nat said.

"Didn't I? Well, it's been busy."

"Wow," Joe said, swirling his cognac in the snifter. "Was it a car wreck or something?"

"Nothing so easy," I said. "It's a bit of a story, and not really fit for the dinner table. I didn't know any of them that well, but it's disconcerting all the same. Thank you for the sympathy."

"Is Tony working on the case?" Nat asked.

I nodded.

Joe looked at her. "Tony's the cop?"

"Yes," Nat said.

Joe shot me a glance, but said no more. So they'd been gossiping about me and Tony in my absence. I drank some coffee, and tried to think of a way to redirect the conversation.

"Joe, was Heather Fisher in your class?" I asked.

"She was a year after me. I took her out a couple of times.

Why?"

"Her sister Debbie is one of the ones who died."

"Oh! Damn. Well...hm. Should I give her a call?"

"She'd probably be grateful," I said.

Condolence calls were almost always appropriate. Miss Manners said so.

For the first time that evening, Joe looked uncomfortable. He frowned at his cognac. "You know, she wasn't that fond of Debbie in high school."

"I know," I said. "Debbie wasn't that fond of her, either."

"Do you have Heather's number?"

"Yes, in my office. I'll text it to you, She's Heather Davis now—though that may change."

Nat gave me a look.

"I heard she's getting divorced," I said.

"After her sister was killed?" Nat said in astonished tones.

"Bad year," Manny remarked, picking up his coffee.

"Actually, she filed for divorce before Debbie died, or so I gather," I said. "Right after Thanksgiving."

I ate a bite of my tart. The bitter chocolate and the strong coffee complemented each other perfectly. I wondered belatedly if I'd be able to sleep that night, after consuming such a dessert.

"Who were the other two?" Nat asked.

"Other two?"

"Your other two classmates who passed."

"Oh. You know about one," I said. "Erica."

"Oh, yes. But the other?"

"Richard Hernandez. I don't think you ever met him."

Nat gazed at me with a slight frown. "Does Tony think they're...related?"

"Possibly. Don't worry, I'm being careful."

"Oh, Ellen! Sweetheart, do you want to come stay with us?"

I glanced at Joe, smiling. "Your guest room is occupied. And anyway, it wouldn't be convenient. I'm safer at home than driving around by myself."

"There's a safety issue?" Joe asked.

I traded a glance with Nat. "No, not really," I said.

"Do you have a gun?"

"Certainly not!"

Joe's face showed a hint of disdain, but he made no further comment. Instead he lifted his glass. I returned my attention to my dessert, even more glad that it was chocolate.

"So what's the skiing like in New York?" Manny asked.

Joe launched into a description that included lots of driving time, overcrowded resorts, and tame slopes that could never compare to those in the Rockies. I slid a grateful look toward Manny, which he acknowledged with a small smile.

Looking down at my dessert, I felt a faint blush. My brother and I had been apart since he'd graduated from high school, and now we were both adults, and he had become sort of a stranger.

Not that we'd been best buddies. I was the pesky, tag-along little sister he was obliged to tolerate, though he'd never been mean. But we'd lived in the same house, and had grown up together. At the time, we'd belonged together. Now, not so much.

A wave of sadness swept through me. The family I had known in my childhood was largely gone.

There was Nat, of course, and now Manny. And I had Gina, and all my wonderful tearoom staff. They were family, in a way. A different family, but real.

You have no reason to feel sorry for yourself, Ellen Rosings.

I drank some more coffee. I'd had enough chocolate, I decided, and pushed the plate away.

"You not going to eat that?" Manny said.

I shook my head and nudged it toward him. I felt weary now.

The waiter brought our check, and Joe insisted on paying it. I would have resisted more strongly if I hadn't been so tired. As it was, I gave in and urged him to come to tea. He returned a noncommittal answer.

As we gathered our coats to return home, Nat gave me a keen look. "Straight to bed for you, youngling."

I nodded. "No argument here."

"I might be in a little late tomorrow."

"Take your time."

She slid her arm through mine as we walked to the car. "This was nice," she said cheerfully. "The whole family together again."

What was left of it.

I smiled, content to leave the ghosts in the shadows.

We were now in the final few days before Christmas. Last-minute shoppers joined the tourists in my gift shop, while locals who were done with their preparations relaxed with tea in my parlors. Reservations were booked solid, with a long waiting list, until after New Year's. We could see light at the end of the tunnel, and that gave all of my staff the energy to persevere through the holiday craziness.

Tuesday went by in a blur. Tony and I exchanged a couple of texts, but neither of us had time for more.

On the 23rd, Christmas Eve Eve as I'd called it in my teens, Ramon would be leaving early to prepare for his concert that evening. Tony had declined to accompany me to the performance, so I'd invited Gina. Meanwhile, I would be short-staffed in the last three hours of the day, so I spent the morning catching up on messages and paperwork in order to be free to help downstairs. The whole staff was on deck for that day and the next, Christmas Eve.

Shortly after noon, I stepped into Kris's office, smiling at the samovar as I passed it. Kris was putting the payroll together early so we could hand out checks Thursday, since we'd be closed on Friday. She looked up at me, one hand over the number pad on her keyboard.

"When is Mrs. Olavssen's reservation?" I asked. "Is it four o'clock?"

Kris nodded and entered another number, fingers flashing over the keypad.

"In the dining parlor, right?"

"No, she changed that a week ago. She's got the main parlor."

"Iris?"

"No, the whole parlor."

I goggled. The main parlor's four alcoves could seat up to two dozen—more if the furniture was rearranged.

"Holy—how many people?"

"Twenty-three," Kris said.

A shiver went through me, leaving me a little faint. "I need tea,"

I said, and headed for the samovar.

Kris had made lapsang souchong. I poured a bracing cup of the strong, smoky tea, and swallowed it black. Visions of the main parlor filled with jumping cows and snowflake ballerinas made me feel slightly ill, but I fought back and straightened my shoulders.

"Right. Do you need me for anything else right now?"

Kris shook her head, still busy with numbers. I went downstairs and plunged into assisting Nat and Rosa in the gift shop. Due to demand, we'd set up a gift-wrapping station in the hall, and I manned that for a while, trying not to imagine what the Bird Woman was about to do to my parlor.

Hers was the last reservation of the day, I reminded myself. We could clean up whatever happened after closing. And there would only be a few other customers, in the south side and the dining parlor, to witness whatever havoc she created.

Ay yi yi.

At 3:30 I checked on the kitchen. Julio was putting a tray of scones in the oven, and Ramon was putting on his coat. Hanh had already left for the day. Boxes and covered trays of biscochitos sat stacked on the counter.

Julio glanced up at me as he closed the oven door. "Heading home as soon as the four o'clock food is done. I'll be in early tomorrow."

"Me, too," said Ramon, pulling on gloves over his long fingers.

"OK," I told him. "I'm looking forward to the concert!"

Ramon gave me a slightly nervous smile and took off. I headed upstairs to check with Kris before the Bird Woman arrived.

Kris had closed out the registers early and was making up a deposit. I promised to balance the registers again after we closed, then slid into my office to check messages. I had found that sorting them was saving me time, as the low-priority stuff could just stay at the bottom, so I dealt out the new message slips into piles.

No Tony. One from Gina confirming the concert that evening. Three for "deal with today," which would be dealt with tomorrow, and the rest low priority. I was about to get up when the intercom buzzed.

"It's a Juana Duranes," Kris said. "She said you asked her to call."

"Yes, put her through, please."

I picked up the phone. "Juana? Thank you for calling me."

"Sure," said Juana in the voice I remembered, low and firm. "You wanted to talk about Erica?"

"Yes." I glanced at the time: 3:42. "You probably know that another classmate of ours died earlier this year."

"Debbie Fisher. The one that was murdered."

"Yes. Erica told me that Debbie came to the Compound on a date not long before she died. I wondered if you happened to be working that night, or if Erica mentioned it to you."

"I was there. Erica told me she was waiting on an old classmate, and pointed her out to me. I didn't talk to Debbie, but I had tables in the same room."

That sounded promising. "Do you remember anything about Debbie's date that night?" I asked.

"Tall guy, kinda thin, brown hair."

I frowned. This did not sound like Dickie.

"Receding hairline?"

"No. The hair was good. A little long, maybe."

Definitely not Dickie.

"Did you tell the police about this?" I asked.

"I haven't talked to the police."

My heart skipped. "Why not?"

"I've been out of town. Got back last weekend."

"I see. Well, thanks—that's helpful. Thanks for returning my call."

"You're welcome. Are you helping the cops?"

"Um, sort of. I have a friend who's working on the investigation, and he knows I knew Erica and Debbie."

"Tell him to find the bastard."

Her anger came through clearly. Through the phone...through the ether?

"He will," I assured her. "He'll probably want to talk to you, now that you're back."

I thanked her and said goodbye, then looked at the time. Almost 4:00. I took out my cell phone and wrote Tony a hasty text:

Call Juana Duranes — saw Debbie at Compound.

The front door banged below-stairs. I heard a distant voice shouting, "Ho, ho, ho!" I copied Juana's number from the caller ID and added it to the text, then scurried downstairs.

More "Ho, ho, ho!" I arrived in the hall in time to see a diminutive Santa Claus go into the main parlor, followed by two "elves" who must have been recruited from a local high school but looked like they belonged in Middle Earth. They were slender and ethereally beautiful young men, both dressed in green tunics, with holly wreaths around their brows and long, gorgeous hair spilling loose over their shoulders. I had to look hard at the darker of the two to be sure it wasn't Owen Hughes.

Each elf carried a giant, lumpy sack of presents. Behind them came a troop of women in Santa hats—red and green, with bells jingling—all of them grinning like kids at…well, Christmas.

Like the snowflakes—and probably the milkmaids, come to think of it—they were all strangers to me: I recognized none of them as the Bird Women's regular friends, and all were much younger than she. A mixed bag of women in their twenties, thirties, and even forties: Anglos, Hispanics, a few Pueblos, a couple of Asians, one African American, and a few I wasn't sure about. They whispered shyly to each other and gazed around the hall with wide eyes.

"Ho, ho, ho! Me-e-e-e-r-ry Christmas," boomed a voice from the parlor.

Dale, sporting a dark red brocade vest and a candy-cane-striped bow tie, stood by the door to the main parlor, welcoming the ladies with his best smile, collecting their coats, and speaking to them with a deference I was beginning to suspect they rarely heard. I relieved him of an armful of coats and began hanging them up on the hooks in the hall.

"Where's Mrs. Olavssen?" I asked Dale *sotto voce*.

"She's already in."

"I didn't see her."

"She's the one in the Santa suit."

"Oh."

Of course.

I was about to roll my eyes, then it occurred to me that the Bird Woman must be playing Santa in more than a figurative sense. I seriously doubted that any of her guests could afford the cost of our hand-made, gourmet tea cuisine.

This gave me pause. I looked at the remaining coats in my hands. Parkas, mostly. Not a designer label among them, nor the light weight and subtle tailoring of fancy ski gear. They were strictly practical, warm and inexpensive.

"Ho, ho, ho! Hurry up and sit down, girls! Time's a wastin'!"

"Do you need help managing the group?" I asked Dale as I hung the last coat.

"Maybe with the food trays? Dee's going to help me with the teapots. She just has the dining parlor to cover."

"All right. I'll look in on you shortly."

I made a beeline for the stairs. Kris was just finishing the deposit.

"Payroll's on your desk," she said as I stepped through the door-way.

"I'll finish it, thanks. Kris, do you happen to remember how Mrs. Olavssen's party paid the last time she was here?"

"She put it all on her credit card, just like today."

"Today?"

Kris nodded. "Parties over ten pay half in advance. Don't you remember when we set the group policies last summer?"

"Yes, yes. Thank you."

"I'm taking this to the bank," Kris said, hefting the bank bag as she stood. "Need me to come back? We're having our Yule potluck tonight..."

I glanced at the time. After four, and Kris had been putting in extra hours. "No, go on home. Enjoy your party. Say hi to Gwyneth and Cherie."

She stepped past me and took her coat off the rack. I held the bank bag while she put it on and wrapped her scarf around her neck.

"Thanks," she said. "Night."

"Good night."

Standing by the samovar table, I frowned in thought as I listened to Kris descend the stairs. *What* the Bird Woman was doing was becoming clearer to me. *Why* she was doing it still eluded me, and I had questions about the *how*.

I was a little embarrassed that I hadn't paid attention to Mrs.

Olavssen's financial status. She was a frequent visitor, one of my best customers, so she was plainly comfortably well-off, but beyond that I hadn't thought much about it. This month, though, she wasn't just coming to tea with her besties.

I went down to the butler's pantry, where I met Dee and Dale coming out with teapots in hand. More pots were steeping on the counters, and Iz was busy putting hot scones onto tiered trays already loaded with food. I helped her finish this task, then carried one of the trays as part of a small procession of my staff to the main parlor.

The guests were all seated, looking around in wonder at their surroundings, some seeming afraid to move for fear of breaking something. While the major furniture hadn't been changed, the chairs and sofas had been adjusted so that everyone had at least a partial view of the Bird Woman, who had set herself up beside the big Christmas tree in the center of the room. She made rather a diminutive Santa, and I thought for a moment that she might have done better to dress as Mrs. Claus, but I swiftly realized that role wouldn't have suited her. She was loud and jolly and blunt, far more appropriate to the Santa role. Dale had set a small table before her with a teapot all her own, keeping warm under a cozy while she conferred with the two beautiful elves.

Those elves raised a question in my mind. After I delivered my food tray to a group of delighted women in Rose, I retreated to the hall doorway to watch the proceedings, and to muse about the elves.

Based on my limited knowledge of the Bird Woman's taste, I would have expected her to recruit handsome, probably burly young men to assist her. Football players. Instead, her elves, while definitely male, were about as unimposing as healthy young men could get.

Non-threatening, I concluded. That had to have been a deliberate choice, and I pondered why the Bird Woman had made it as I watched her wave her arms to attract the attention of her guests.

"Ho, ho, ho! OK, everybody," she bellowed, her improbably white beard bouncing up and down, "fill up your cups and settle down a minute. I got a few things to say. First of all, this is Dale."

She pointed to Dale, who was handing out postcard-sized copies of the afternoon tea menu to all of the guests. Someone must have grabbed it off the tearoom's website and printed it out. The ladies accepted the menus with delight. A simple thing, but for them, it might be a treasured keepsake.

Mental note: print copies of the menu for guests who want them.

"Dale's gonna take care of us," continued the Bird Woman. "If you need any more lemon curd or anything, he's the guy to ask."

Dale gave a cheery salute to the room, and continued giving out menus.

"Hey, Dale," called a tanned woman with straw blonde hair and a red sweater, in the husky voice of a long-time smoker. "What's lemon curd?"

Everyone laughed.

"Lemon curd," said the Bird Woman in a voice of authority, "is that yellow goo in the little cup with the scones. You smear it on them. But first you gotta eat your savories."

"Hey, Dale, what's a scone?"

The Bird Woman frowned at the straw blonde while the rest laughed again. "Don't get ahead of me," she said. "Now, second, this is Nicholas and Zachary. Be nice to them, or you won't get any presents."

She swept an arm toward the elves, who had set their bags before them on the carpet. They waved and grinned. A smattering of polite applause followed.

"Third, that nice lady over there by the door is Miss Ellen Rosings. She owns the place. Without her, none of us would be here, so be nice."

I cringed, but it was too late to hide. A rather heartier round of applause followed, to my consternation. I smiled and waved, feeling a blush rise up my neck. As soon as the Bird Woman started talking again, I ducked out into the hall.

"Now, this here's afternoon tea," her voice continued as I fled toward the pantry. "It's not High Tea. That's something miners in England have for supper. You start with the savories—that's those little sandwiches and stuff on the top tray…"

One lone teapot remained on the counter in the butler's pantry, sitting under a cozy. I almost filched a cup of tea from it, but resisted and put the kettle on instead, taking deep breaths to settle myself. Iz came in and smiled.

"Everything going smoothly?" I asked her.

"Yes. My groups all have their food now." She gave me an impish smile. "They're quiet."

I swallowed. "Good. Is this tea for them?" I indicated the cozy-covered pot.

Iz shook her head. "Maybe it's Dee's."

To check on that, I went back to the hall and crossed to the dining parlor. Three youngish couples, nicely dressed, sat around the table. Dee was pouring tea for them as I looked in.

A spare pot, then. I could have had some, but not knowing what kind of tea it was, I preferred to continue making my own. I chose robust Irish Breakfast, and while it was steeping I looked in on the kitchen.

All quiet. Not a creature was stirring. The stack of biscochito boxes was lower, but still enough to get us through closing...unless the Bird Woman decided to buy us out.

I wouldn't put it past her.

Back in the pantry, I hovered until my tea was ready, chugged one cup black, then poured a second cup and added milk and sugar. Dale came in as I was stirring.

"Oh, Ellen—could you start two more pots for me?" he asked. "They're going through it fast."

"Sure. What are they drinking?"

"The holiday blend."

"Is that what this is?" I gestured to the cozy-covered pot.

"Yeah," Dale said. "That was supposed to be for the elves, but the guests are thirsty."

"I'll start four more pots."

"Thanks! Bless you."

"Do the elves have food coming?"

"Just some scones. They're keeping warm in the kitchen until after they hand out the presents."

"What about Mrs. Olavssen?"

"Scones for her, too—if she has time for them. Might not happen; she's doing a lot of mingling."

"Do you happen to know who her guests are?"

"They're from Esperanza."

Dale plucked the cozy off the teapot and left it on the counter while he took the pot away. Musing, I filled both kettles and set them heating, then set up four teapots with leaf tea.

Esperanza was a shelter for victims of domestic abuse.

14

THE BIRD WOMAN HAD BROUGHT ALMOST TWO DOZEN STRANGERS to my tearoom, at Christmas time. Strangers who had left their homes, who had fled situations of pain and fear at a time when most people were celebrating.

Hence the non-threatening elves.

She had brought these women away for a couple of hours of comfort and luxury at a level that some of them, if not all, had never experienced.

I leaned back against the counter, listening to the kettles rumble, sipping tea, and remembering every moment of exasperation with the Bird Woman I had felt over the past few months. They were nothing—less than nothing. I forgave them all.

I thought about the snowflake ballerinas and the milkmaids with their jumping cows. I wouldn't be surprised if they had come from Esperanza as well. I boggled at what the Bird Woman must have spent on all of it, but the money was the least of it. She had used her imagination and her boundless, cheerful energy to create fun outings for all of those women. All of those broken strangers.

Feeling humbled, I set the tea to steeping as the kettles boiled, stood watch over them until the timers rang, and snugged a cozy down over each pot. Then I went upstairs to the storage room at the back of Kris's office.

The tiny room had been crammed full at the beginning of the month. Now it was less than half full. A few boxes, emptied in haste while restocking the gift shop, lay at random. I carefully stacked these near the door, then looked over the inventory that remained.

Kris was efficient; she had kept us supplied with just enough of everything we needed. Leaf tea and other standard items were on the right; seasonal merchandise on the left. With one more day before Christmas, we'd probably sell out of most of it.

My brain wanted to calculate profit margins as I looked at the contents of each box. I told my brain to shut up. Dollars were not what mattered right now.

For myself, I had enough. That was the highest of blessings. A fleeting thought of my mortgage arose; I brushed it away. For now, for today, I had enough, so I could afford to be generous in my turn.

I had never expected the Bird Woman to be setting me an example.

I knew which box I wanted, but the problem was, it was only half full. A dozen items were insufficient. I picked up the box, and as I did so I noticed its twin tucked behind a neighboring stack. With a little crow of delight, I put down the first box and unearthed the second, grabbing Kris's utility knife to cut through the packing tape.

Two dozen, I confirmed. More than enough fairy ornaments for each of the Bird Woman's guests to have one.

Smiling, I stacked both boxes for good measure and carried them downstairs.

The elves were now sitting in the old Marigold wing chairs in the hall, relaxing with their tea and scones. They hopped to their feet as I reached the foot of the stairs.

"Can we help?" said the fairer one.

"Let me take that," said the darker, coming forward.

"Thank you...Nicholas?"

"I'm Zach," he said, favoring me with a movie-star smile as he relieved me of my burden.

"Thank you, Zach. By the door here is fine." I indicated a short bench just outside the gift shop. Zach set the boxes down, then returned to his chair. To set him and Nicholas at ease, I stepped into the gift shop.

Nat looked up from loading biscochitos into the pastry case. "Any damage?" she asked.

"No, no," I said hastily. "They haven't been too noisy, have they?"

"A couple of bursts of laughter. Nothing horrible."

I nodded. "Thank you."

Crossing the hall to the main parlor, I saw that the guests all had their presents and were busy opening them, making a splendid mess of torn gift wrap and discarded bows. One woman showed off a slender box with a picture of a fancy curling iron on the side; another had a colorful floral scarf that had to be silk draped around her neck.

The Bird Woman was in her chair by the tree, her Santa beard pulled down to her neck while she ate a scone, the two empty gift sacks at her feet. I joined her.

"No, please don't get up," I said. "I just want to ask if you'd mind my giving your guests a little present. Just an ornament for each of them."

The Bird Woman stared at me for a full three seconds, her mouth working at her scone. I told myself she did not, either, look like a cow chewing its cud.

At last she swallowed. "That's really swell. Should I make an announcement?"

"No, no. Enjoy your tea. I'd like to say hello to each of them."

"OK," she said in a tone of bewilderment. Suddenly she grinned. "Have at it!"

I fetched the full box and set it on the floor by the tree, then took out half a dozen ornaments and went to the group in Lily. "Hello, ladies," I said. "I have a little gift for you from the tearoom."

"Oh!" cried the nearest woman, a Latina in her mid-twenties, pretty except for the perpetually knit forehead. She cupped the fairy ornament I gave her in both hands as though it would break if she breathed on it. "Thank you, Miss Ellen!"

"You're welcome—will you tell me your name?"

"Anna," she said.

"You're welcome, Anna. Merry Christmas!"

I gave ornaments to the others sitting with her, asking each of their names and repeating them with good wishes. Returning to my box for more fairies, I did the same with the women in the other alcoves. I would never remember all of their names, of course, but that didn't matter. It was acknowledging them that mattered.

As I handed out the last round of ornaments, I saw Dale and the Bird Woman with their heads together, talking intently. Negotiating, it looked like. I told myself not to worry. What harm could be done?

The Bird Woman had never done any *harm*, really.

I handed a fairy ornament to the straw blonde woman, who surprised me by brushing away a tear as she muttered a gruff "Thanks."

"You're welcome...?"

"Her name's Betty," said her neighbor, a plump thirty-something with mouse brown hair cut too short.

"Betty," I said, gazing at the straw-blonde. She looked up at me, eyes gleaming a little wetly.

"Thanks," she said more clearly. "Nicest Christmas I've had in a while."

I finished giving out the fairies, then returned to the tree and picked up my box, which held four remaining ornaments. The Bird Woman and Dale appeared to have reach an agreement; he had left the room. I took a fairy out of the box and handed it to the Bird Woman.

"This one's for you."

"Aw, you don't have to do that!" she said, pulling up her beard. It landed crookedly. I set down the box and straightened it for her.

"I want to. Dale tells me your guests are from Esperanza. It's lovely of you to give them a treat like this."

"Aw, heck," she said, her cheeks above the beard turning as rosy as any Santa's should be as she gazed at the fairy ornament in her hands. "He ratted on me."

"No, I asked him."

Dale returned, accompanied by Dee, who smiled at the guests as she seated herself at the piano. The house music was no longer playing, I realized. Dale and I left as Dee struck up "Jingle Bells" and the women began to gather around the piano.

"I hope it's OK," Dale said as we reached the hall. "She wanted me to put this on the stereo. I thought the piano would be better."

He showed me a CD entitled "Christmas Rappings." I repressed a shudder.

"Good thinking," I told him as I set my box next to its twin on the bench. "Live music is always better."

I gave ornaments to the two elves and stayed chatting with them while Dale went back to the pantry for yet more tea. I learned that they were theater students at Santa Fe High School, my alma mater.

As we talked, the party in the dining parlor emerged and put on their coats, then headed for the gift shop, pausing before they went in to listen to the music. The singing was far from operatic, but otherwise surprisingly good. It helped that the song of the moment was "Silent Night," easy and gentle.

I gave each of the elves a cream tea card and thanked them, then went back to the dining parlor to help Dee clear. Her brother, Mick, had gone out for an hour of "errands" (I suspected last-minute shopping), but had promised to return by six to finish the dishwashing. As Dee and I carried china into the kitchen, I heard his car pulling up out back.

Leaving brother and sister to deal with the china, I returned to the gift shop, where a party of three well-dressed women (mother and two daughters, was my guess), was just paying for a dozen biscochitos. I saw them out, and noticed two white vans parked at the curb, engines idling.

"OK, girls," I heard the Bird Woman bellow in the main parlor. "Ride's here. Go get your coats. Make sure you got your presents."

Dale was already at the parlor door with an armful of coats. I collected as many as I could carry and joined him, holding out coats one by one. As their owners claimed them, they all thanked me and Dale. "Miss Ellen" had stuck, and I heard "Thank you, Miss Ellen" so many times I lost count.

The Bird Woman followed them outside, herding them like ducklings into the vans. When they had driven away, she returned, pulling off her Santa beard and wig.

"That beard really itches," she remarked. "OK, let's see here."

She dug in her ample Santa pockets, and came up with two crumpled envelopes. She smoothed them out against the wall, then handed one to each of the waiting elves.

"Thanks a million, boys. You were great. Merry Christmas!"

They returned the greeting, and Nicholas gave her a hug. As they donned their own coats and headed for the door, the Bird Woman turned to me.

"I think that Natasha gal has my bill ready," she said, digging in her pockets again and producing a much-worn, bright yellow billfold.

An idea struck me. My heart gave a little flutter and I took a deep gulp of air, then spoke before I could chicken out.

"Never mind that," I said. "You've already paid."

"I paid a deposit," she said.

"Yes, and that's enough," I said. "Merry Christmas, and thank you for being such a loyal customer."

She stared at me in open-mouthed astonishment. I smiled and gestured toward the Marigold chairs.

"Come and sit with me for a minute, if you have time."

She followed me over to the wing chairs, still staring at me like I'd grown a second head. I took a seat and watched her slowly lower herself into the other.

"It's been such a busy year, and I've never really had the chance to chat with you," I said. "You're one of our best customers, and I wanted to thank you, and also to support your kind gift to the women from Esperanza. Were the other groups you brought here this month from there as well?"

She nodded slowly. "Yeah. I got a niece that works there, that's what gave me the idea."

"Well, it's a wonderful gift to our community."

"Eh, pssh," she said, waiving a dismissive hand. "Least I can do. Santa Fe's been good to me, I wanted to be good to it."

"Have you lived here long?" I asked.

She smiled, the corners of her eyes crinkling. "Old George and I came here in the eighties. He had a job with TWA and he traveled all over the country. He decided he wanted to live here."

"Is he still in the airline industry?"

"Oh, he's been gone ten years now. Left me a bunch of dough, though, along with the house. So I always try and give some back to the town, since it's been so good to us."

"I see."

She tilted her head and peered at me in the birdlike gesture I'd come to know so well. Her bright eyes above the red Santa suit made me think of a cardinal, if cardinals had white, curly hair.

"*You're* a Santa Fe native," she said, aiming a somewhat gnarled finger at me. "I remember from the articles when you opened this place. I got them all in a scrapbook. I clip out every story about the Wisteria Tearoom."

"Oh! My," I said, hoping that didn't include the various stories about murder investigations.

"See, Old George took me to England for our fiftieth," she continued, "and I had a ball in London having tea at all the fancy hotels. I really loved going to tea, 'cause you get little bites of all different foods. So when you opened this place—" She gestured around at the walls. "—I was in seventh heaven."

"You're an Anglophile," I said wonderingly.

"I dunno about that—those English can be pretty weird—but I'm for sure a tea-o-phile."

I swallowed a chuckle and smiled.

"And I know from those articles that you went to England and fell in love with tea the same way. So we're birds of a feather!" she said triumphantly.

I felt as if a bell had rung in my heart. A thought of Willow fleeted past.

"Yes," I said slowly. "Indeed we are."

She grinned. "Well, I gotta get going. Taking the niece out to dinner. Boy, December's sure busy! I got something to do every night, seems like."

I nodded, reminded that the day was far from over. Gina would be arriving soon to pick me up for the concert.

"Very true," I said, standing. "Will you bring your niece to tea some time? I'd like to meet her."

She gave me another bird-like gaze. "OK. It'll have to be next year, though. I'm booked solid through New Year's, and a body's got to rest some time!"

She planted her feet on the floor, stretched her arms before her with the Santa beard dangling from one hand, and rocked back and forth a couple of times before heaving herself to her feet. I hopped up to help her up, but she did it on her own.

As we passed the gift shop on the way to the front door, Nat stepped out and handed the Bird Woman a candy cane. "Merry Christmas, Mrs. Olavssen," she said, smiling.

"You too, pumpkin! Thanks!" She reached the front door and paused to put on her beard and Santa hat again. Turning to us, she grinned. "You girls be good, now! Don't make me put coal in your stockings! Ho, ho, ho!"

"Merry Christmas," I called after her as she tromped down the path to the street in her big, black, Santa boots. She went through the gate and got into a massive Cadillac parked at the curb. I watched her slowly drive away, then closed the door.

"Are there any others?" I asked Nat.

"No, she's the last," Nat said. "I overheard your conversation. I hope you don't mind my giving her the candy."

"Of course not! Thank you for thinking of it."

"She's such a dear." Nat smiled softly. "And so are you. What a lovely gift you gave her, waiving the bill."

"Now I just have to figure out how to tell Kris," I said as we walked back toward the kitchen. "I'm afraid she'll throttle me."

"No, she won't." Nat threw her arm around my shoulders and hugged. "You did it in the spirit of Christmas."

"Or Yule, or whatever," I said, remembering that Kris and her friends looked at holidays a bit differently. "It's the darkest time of year. Good to shed some light."

"Very true!" Nat said, putting on her coat.

I didn't have time to change, but the green dress I had on was nice enough, and I had managed to avoid decorating it with tea or food during the day. I brushed my hair and touched up my makeup, then grabbed purse, phone, coat, hat, and scarf, and headed downstairs. The headlights of Gina's Camaro shone through the lights around the back door as I reached the hall.

"We've got a table at Luminaria," she said as I climbed into the car. "I figured that would be fastest since they're right next door to Loretto Chapel. They have a prix fixe tonight."

"Sounds perfect!"

"Got the tickets?"

"In my purse."

I kept silent as Gina navigated heavy traffic on the short but complicated drive to Loretto, which was basically kitty-corner across the middle of town from my house. We could have walked, had there been time, but that was a commodity in short supply lately. Also, it was cold. She pulled into the Inn at Loretto's parking lot, turned the car over to a valet, and marched me down the long hall to Luminaria.

The last time we'd been here, early in the month, we'd been alone. Now there was a line of people waiting to be seated, and the bustle and chatter of the restaurant reached us halfway down the hall. I was glad Gina'd had the foresight to make a reservation; it hadn't even occurred to me, though it should have. This week was like an extended weekend: everyone wanted to dine out.

Which, upon reflection, was fortunate for me.

"How's Joe?" Gina asked when we were tucked into a small table and had glasses of wine in front of us.

"He's fine," I said with a small shrug. "We've gone different ways, really."

"Oh? Remind me what he does."

"He's an investment banker."

"Is he? Successful, I presume?"

"Very."

I sipped my wine, hoping she wouldn't mention skiing. Fortunately, the waiter returned at that moment with an *amuse-bouche*, which distracted her. When he left, I launched into a description of the Bird Woman's Christmas party that day. Gina laughed out loud a couple of times, and at the end of the story she beamed.

"That's *great!* What a wonderful old lady! I want to be her when I grow up."

I started to say "Perish the thought," then changed my mind.

"You be *you*," I told her. "I'm sure you'll make a splendid old lady someday, but that day's a long way off."

"Yeah, but I'm already in training. Nonna keeps me in line."

"How is Nonna?"

"Terrifying. She reminds me of Admiral Whathisname. 'Damn the torpedoes, full steam ahead!'"

"Farragut, I think."

"Hm?" Gina threw me a long-lashed glance over her wine glass, and I felt my own flash of terror at the thought of how Joe might react to a look like that.

"Admiral Farragut," I said.

"Oh. Yeah, him. Nonna'd flatten him like a steam roller if she had the chance, I swear."

I laughed, and it felt good, so I did it again. "What's she up to?"

"The family party's getting too big, so she wants to move it to a rented hall, but it's two days away! Everything's booked solid. The church is out—they're going to be busy 'til New Year's. Hotels, forget it! And she doesn't want catering anyway. She still wants it to be a giant potluck."

"Yikes."

"Yeah." Gina took a big swallow of wine. "I swear if I didn't love her so much, I'd throttle her."

"Your current guy is in real estate, right? Does he have any places listed that you could rent from the owners? Pay them a fee, like you would a hotel, for the use of their space?"

Gina gave me a wide-eyed stare. "That. Is. Brilliant." She dug in her purse and found a pen and a small memo book, into which she scribbled furiously, then she sent out a couple of texts.

Our dinner arrived, and we ate it with an eye to the time. With customers waiting, the service was less leisurely than usual, which suited us perfectly. We finished our dessert—piñon crème brûlée, quite good—and paid the bill with just five minutes to spare.

Donning our coats, we went out through the restaurant's back door and crossed the now-empty courtyard. In warmer weather, Luminaria had outdoor seating there, but now it was deserted and dusted with snow, both the fountain and the fireplace empty.

Loretto Chapel stood nearby, its high and narrow Gothic Revival form a contrast to the pueblo-like piles of the Inn at Loretto behind us and La Fonda across the street. Light glowed softly through jewel-colored stained glass windows. We walked around to the front, where we were welcomed by two young women in velvet dresses.

The chapel was commissioned by Bishop Lamy in the late 19th century, for the nuns of the Sisters of Loretto who had come to Santa Fe to found the Loretto Academy. I'd always thought of it as a diminutive cousin of Lamy's greater church, the San Francisco Cathedral (now a basilica), nearby. The chapel had ceased to be a Catholic church when the Academy closed in the 1960s, and was now privately owned and mostly used for weddings and concerts, though Sunday services were still conducted there.

Its most famous feature was the Miraculous Staircase, a gorgeous spiral stair from the floor to the choir loft, built entirely of wood without any nails. Rumors and legends about its "miraculous" construction had largely been debunked, but it remained a beautiful object, and of habit I glanced at it as we passed on our way to our seats. The wood gleamed warmly, and a sign hanging from a cord across its base sternly forbade visitors from setting foot on the stairs. I smiled, as if at an old friend. I remembered scrambling up those stairs as a kid, and peering down at the chapel's interior in triumphant awe.

The pale stone of the chapel walls glowed softly in the light of lamps hanging on chains from the high ceiling. The pews were already half filled. Gina and I found seats and settled in, glancing at the programs given to us by the women at the door. Half a dozen chairs sat in a semicircle before the altar, with instruments waiting before them. I saw two guitars and a harp, plus an eclectic collection of small percussion instruments.

The audience's chatter diminished a bit as the bells of the nearby cathedral rang out the half hour. A rush to fill the remaining seats followed, and soon the musicians came in from a side door.

The three men and two women all wore white shirts with full sleeves over black trousers. One man and one woman carried flutes, and the other woman—a stunning, slightly plump redhead—seated herself before the harp. Ramon was next to her, and as he picked up his guitar I felt an odd little swell of pride. He'd had a number of gigs since I'd first asked him to play at the tearoom in the summer. He had come a long way since the night I'd met him, when he and a couple of friends were trespassing on my property, hoping for a glimpse of Captain Dusenberry.

Was that what it felt like to be a parent, I wondered? To see a person, and marvel at how much they'd changed and grown in a short few months?

The other guitar player was taller, older, and omigod it was Justin Davis! What was he doing here?

Paying the bills.

My mind flitted back to Del Charro and Tony. I wondered if I should text him to let him know Justin was here.

Text! Phone! I needed to silence it.

The male flute player stepped forward to introduce the performers. I took my phone out and checked for messages. To my dismay, I saw that the text I'd composed to Tony that morning, advising him to call Juana Duranes, had failed to go out.

"Damn!" I whispered, and tried sending it again.

"What?" Gina whispered beside me.

"Nothing."

There wasn't really any reason to inform Tony that I was listening to Justin play again, and I didn't want to bury him in texts. I silenced the phone and put it away, giving my attention to the musicians.

The flute player concluded his introductions, and the ensemble launched into their first piece with little delay. Delicious music filled the small chapel, rich with the sound of strings and flutes, ringing back from the stone walls with just enough echo to add a tone of mystique. The piece was a Renaissance work that I hadn't heard before. It was lovely, if a little stilted. The program was a mix of ancient music and more recent, traditional Christmas music. All of the musicians were also singers, and I found myself singing softly along with familiar carols.

Before I knew it, an hour and a half had gone by. I'd melted into my seat, blissfully absorbed in the music, by the time the flute player announced their last piece of the evening, "an older carol that some of you may know."

The short introductory measures were enough to raise the hair on my forearms. Three notes in, I recognized the descending scale. The opening verse followed, then the female flute player lowered her instrument and sang:

The holly bears a blossom, as white as lily flower—

I sat listening, appreciating the rich chords of harp and guitar while the two flute players alternated singing the verses. My mind refused to be still, though, and recalled Willow's declaration: *There are no coincidences.*

Did it mean something, the fact that I kept encountering this song? If so, what?

I was not clever enough to deduce a mysterious message, so I thought about how the song made me feel. The verses were sensory descriptions—evoking color, texture, aroma—always as some aspect of holly. The second half of each verse was always, "and Mary bore sweet Jesus Christ," with something to make a rhyme. Mary must represent the ivy, I decided, but there were no evocative descriptions of ivy's qualities. The message there, over and over again, was that Mary had borne Jesus.

If the holly represented Jesus, then he was clearly more important as far as this song was concerned. Mary's only importance was in bringing him into the world. I had not realized it before, but this carol rang loudly of patriarchy.

The chorus appealed more to me:

> *The rising of the sun*
>
> *And the running of the deer,*
>
> *The playing of the merry organ,*
>
> *Sweet singing in the choir.*

These were all images I could appreciate and enjoy. No judgment here, no reminders to keep women in their place.

When the final verse came, all the musicians sang it together:

> *The holly and the ivy,*
>
> *When they are both full grown,*
>
> *Of all the trees that are in the wood,*
>
> *The holly bears the crown.*

Again, the implication seemed patriarchal. If the holly represented man, and the ivy woman, here again was the statement, "man is dominant."

As beautiful as the song was, I wasn't so sure I liked that message.

The musicians put down their instruments, rose, and took a bow together. I applauded, musing. As the audience began to leave, I remained seated, still sorting my feelings.

Male dominance was a huge part of mankind's history. That didn't mean I had to like it, or accept it. I had shaped my own life. I was not dependent on any man. I *liked* men, but that didn't mean I was willing to play second fiddle to one.

Even Tony. *Especially* Tony.

Shying away from that train of thought, I stood and gathered my coat and purse. The musicians had stayed in the chapel, and a few audience members had gone up to chat with them.

"I'd like to congratulate Ramon," I told Gina.

"Sure," she said, gazing at her phone. More texting happening; I assumed about Nonna's Christmas party.

We made our way to the front, and waited while others chatted with the musicians. At last a party moved away, making room for us to go up and greet Ramon. Justin, standing next to him, was talking to two women in fur coats and cowboy boots.

"Beautiful concert," I told Ramon, offering a hand. "You all sounded glorious!"

He grinned, pleased, and shook hands. "Thanks. It's partly the space."

"The space is wonderful, but that by no means diminishes your performance. Will you be playing together more?"

As if recognizing my voice, Justin turned his head to look at me. His expression was of consternation rather than pleasure.

"I'm not sure," Ramon said. "We've talked a little about it. We'll know more after this."

"Well, if you do, let me know," I said, smiling. I let my glance drift to Justin, who was still staring at me, and gave him a nod. "Loved the concert."

Frowning, Justin nodded in response, then looked away. Gina and I said goodbye to Ramon and threaded our way through the thinning crowd to the exit. Outside, a sharp breeze made me hug my coat closer.

"That was great," Gina said, as we sheltered in the hotel doorway while we waited for the valet to bring Gina's car. "Thanks for taking me."

"Thanks for giving me a ride. May I tip the valet?"

She waved a hand. "You bought the tickets."

Once we were in the car, Gina cranked the heater up and drove down Alameda Street. "Ed thinks he has a place we can use for the party!" she said. "He's waiting to hear back from the owner. If this works, I owe you a bottle of champagne."

I chuckled. "Not necessary."

"Champagne is always necessary."

She'd stopped at a four-way stop, and was starting forward

when a white SUV came blasting down the street to our right without pausing.

15

"GINA!" I CRIED, FLINCHING FROM THE CAR barreling toward me.

Gina floored the accelerator, and the Camaro roared through the intersection, squeaking ahead of the SUV with inches to spare and probably leaving a patch of rubber on the pavement. Gina rolled down her window and flung a burst of Italian into the night after the vehicle as it continued speeding away.

"Testa di cazzo!"

I gulped a breath, my heart pounding. Had that been deliberate, or was it just someone who'd partied too hard and missed the stop sign?

Memory presented Justin Davis's face to me, after the concert. He had not been pleased to see me.

Gina rolled the window up and turned to look at me, eyes wide and concerned. "You OK?"

"Yes, but that was so close! I don't suppose you caught the plate."

"No, but it was a local."

She drove on, twining through the area west of the Plaza to the street that ran behind my house. As she turned up it, a pair of headlights approached us. I watched them warily, and when Gina started to turn left into my driveway, they accelerated.

Gina had been watching, too. She floored it again, clearing the street as the vehicle swept past. I stared after it while Gina cussed some more.

It was the white SUV, or another very like it. The plate was the hard-to-read, yellow-on-turquoise New Mexico plate. I was able to make out the first three letters.

"HLV," I said. "I didn't catch the numbers."

"*Porca vacca!* I'm calling the cops," Gina said, parking next to my car.

I put my hands over my face and took a deep breath. No coincidences. That car had come at us twice, both times at my side of Gina's Camaro.

Gina poked angrily at her phone. "You should call Tony, too."

I shook my head. If I called Tony, he'd come rushing over.

Oh, wait. I *liked* that idea.

Pulling out my phone, I saw that I had a text from Tony.

> Who is she, and what should I
> ask her?

Staring blankly at the screen, I finally figured out he was talking about Juana Duranes. I punched the "call" icon.

I was less collected than I'd thought, because after a couple of disjointed sentences, Tony interrupted me.

"I'll be right over. Is Gina still there?"

"We're in her car."

"Go inside and make sure all the doors are locked."

"OK."

"A white SUV, New Mexico plate," Gina said into her phone. "The first three letters were HLV."

We went inside. Gina was fuming, and came with me as I checked all the doors and windows on the ground floor. Anticipating a long evening, I put a kettle on in the butler's pantry.

"Want me to make you some coffee?" I said, reaching for calm.

"No, thanks. Got any gin?"

I hesitated. "There's some brandy ...."

"It's for you, not for me. Don't worry, I'm going to be *completely* sober when I drive home, *gratzi!*"

Her tone was fierce, which I found oddly comforting. I went upstairs and poured myself a brandy, then brought it back to the pantry just as the kettle boiled.

"What kind of tea would you like?" I asked Gina, who was investigating the brandy aroma captured by my snifter.

"That caramel-chocolate-flavored one," she said, putting down the glass.

I nodded and reached for a teapot. Scented blacks aren't my favorite; I partake of them sparingly. However, caramel and chocolate flavors sounded like a wonderful idea just then. I set the tea to steeping, then lifted the snifter and inhaled from a short distance. The richness of the brandy's flavors brushed my palate, and the tease of alcohol in the bouquet tickled my throat. I took a tiny sip and relaxed a little as its fragrant fire swept across my tongue.

By the time the tea was ready, Tony was at the back door. I pulled out the infuser and tossed a cozy over the teapot, then hurried to let him in. The first thing he did was catch me in ferocious hug.

"You all right?" he said into my ear.

"Yes."

He leaned back to look at me, brows drawing together. "You been drinking?"

"I just poured a brandy."

"Other than that," Gina said, emerging from the pantry, "we each had a glass of wine with dinner—" She checked her watch. "—three hours ago."

"Did you recognize the car?" Tony asked us both.

I shook my head, and Gina softly scoffed. "There are a zillion white SUVs in town."

Red and blue lights came flashing up the driveway. Gina had kept her coat on; now she pulled it closed. "I called them, I'll talk to them," she said, and went out the back door.

Tony had shoved his hands into his pockets. He looked at me, and his face softened as he gathered me into his arms.

"The killer's still out there," I said into his shoulder. "It wasn't Dickie."

"Or this is someone else."

"Justin Davis was at the concert Gina and I went to tonight."

Tony's hand, which had been rubbing my shoulders, paused. "OK."

"He wasn't happy to see me. Didn't smile. Could it have been him in the SUV?"

"Why would Justin try to kill you?"

"I don't *know* why. If I knew why it would be easier to understand! Three of my classmates are dead. The killer's after me, isn't he?"

"Could be after Gina," Tony said.

I gave a little gasp and raised my head, affronted. Tony smoothed my hair.

"Don't worry," he said. "We'll get him. Meanwhile—"

"Keep everything locked and don't go out alone." I sighed.

Tony nodded. His worried eyes searched my face, then he kissed my forehead. "We'll get him," he said again.

"I need to deal with a teapot. Do you want some tea?"

"Sure. It's a cold night."

I got milk out of the small fridge in the pantry and took a sugar bowl down from the shelf. Stopping short of cups and saucers, I got out two mugs instead, and poured tea into one of them for Tony. He tasted the tea, blinked, and added some milk.

"Sugar brings out the caramel flavor," I suggested.

He took a swig, apparently uninterested in caramel. "Who's this Juana you wanted me to call?"

"Oh! She works at the Compound. She was there the night Erica waited on Debbie and her date, but she went out of town right afterward and just got back, so I think you didn't get a chance to interview her?"

Tony shook his head and glanced at his phone. "Too late now. I'll call her in the morning."

"Why, Tony! Do I detect a glimmer of civility?"

He shot me a look over his mug. "I'm beat. Spent the day going over Dickie's apartment again. The manager wants to get in there and clean it up."

I picked up my brandy and leaned back against the counter. "Anything new?"

"No. I did take a picture of this for you."

He turned on his phone and scrolled through some photos, then handed it to me. The phone displayed a handwritten note on a piece of paper torn from a memo pad; the top edge was rough. I peered at the photo.

> *I'm sorry I killed them. Deborah and Erica. They were bitches. But I shouldn't have killed them. I'm sorry.*

Richard Hernandez

I frowned. Something was off.

"The handwriting looks shaky. Is it really Dickie's?"

"Analyst says yes," Tony said.

I tried to picture Dickie writing such a note, but just couldn't imagine it. He might have said something like it, conspiratorially, in an unguarded moment. But I couldn't see him actually feeling regret.

"He wouldn't be sorry," I said slowly, "even if he did it. He might be sorry if he got caught, but only because he'd been caught."

Tony watched me with an impatient frown. "Why'd he kill himself, then?"

The photo of the note seemed to draw me in. The words blurred, then a memory of Dickie's sardonic grin came to me along with his voice:

Only her family calls her that.

My mouth dropped open as I inhaled sharply.

"He didn't."

I looked at Tony. "He was forced to write this! He wouldn't have called Debbie 'Deborah.' He told me only her family called her that!"

Tony's eyes widened. "Her sister."

I nodded. "Yes. Heather always called her Deborah. And they hated each other!"

"Enough to kill?"

"I didn't think so, but—"

Tony reached for his phone, and I surrendered it. He gave me his mug and started poking at the screen.

The back door opened, then slammed. I turned to see Gina, every line of her body expressing outrage.

"He said he'd file a report, but unless we can find a witness there's nothing they can do. *Bastardo* tried to *kill* us, and there's nothing they can do! Tony, you gotta—"

I gestured to her to wait; Tony was on the phone already, pacing up the hall as he talked to a colleague. I beckoned Gina into the pantry.

"Tea's ready," I said. "There's milk and sugar here."

Gina pressed her lips together and put two heaping spoonfuls of sugar into the mug I gave her. "Tony's gotta do something about this."

"Don't worry, he will. He's working on something more important right now."

"More important?"

"Yes. I think we just figured out who killed Dickie. And probably Debbie and Erica. Only thing I'm not sure of is why."

Gina swallowed a mouthful of tea and stared.

"OK, girlfriend. Spill!"

I couldn't spill much, having given my word to Tony, but I gave her a couple of juicy details and dropped some hints about the rest. She seemed satisfied, and by the time she went home her thoughts had turned to the more immediate problem of managing Nonna's Christmas party.

Christmas Eve was a bit surreal, or maybe it just seemed that way because I was distracted. I drifted through the day, helping the servers and Nat, exchanging pleasantries with customers, all while wondering what progress Tony was making, and turning the problem over in my mind: *why?*

It didn't help that Gina texted me repeatedly asking about the murder case. I finally just left my phone on my desk.

The afternoon brought a rush on biscochitos. Fortunately, I had stashed my gift for Mrs. Aragón up in my suite before then. Julio and Ramon stayed late, baking cookies until 4:30, when I finally told them to stop and go home.

"There are still three sheets in the oven," Julio said.

"I'll take care of them. You go home and have a wonderful Christmas. I'll see you on Monday. Oh—are the orders in for next week?"

Julio nodded as he took off his apron. "I called them in earlier."

"Perfect."

I gave the two of them their paychecks and saw them out, and with Mick and my own thoughts for company, waited for the timer to go off. Mick, as usual, had his earbuds in place and was gently bopping while he washed dishes, so I had time for quiet contemplation. Inevitably, my thoughts went to Dickie, who had, in his last moments, cried out with a clue to the cause of his death. If I was right, it meant Heather had killed him. Why?

And she had killed Erica and her own sister, Debbie. *Why?* None of the reasons I knew about seemed enough.

I was still in the kitchen, musing and boxing biscochitos, when Rosa looked in. "Ellen, you're wanted up front."

I picked up the finished boxes and followed her to the gift shop. Nat and Dee were waiting on a line of customers, but it was the familiar figure by the front door—in a floor-length fake mink coat, matching hat adorned with a giant spray of holly, and bright red gloves—who had summoned me.

"I won't hold you up," said the Bird Woman. "Just wanted to drop this by for you."

She proffered an unmarked business envelope. I set the cookies on the bench by the gift shop door, and accepted it.

"Boy, those smell great!" she added, eyeing the biscochito boxes. "Can't get enough of the darned things!"

Inside the envelope was a receipt from Esperanza for a tax-deductible donation, in the exact amount of the second half of the Bird Woman's bill from the previous day. I looked up at her, truly grateful. This would help me break the news of my spontaneous donation to Kris, which I hadn't yet had the courage to do.

"Thank you!" I said, returning the receipt to the envelope.

She grinned. "Merry Christmas! Toodle-oo!"

"Wait—take this." I handed her a box of biscochitos.

She gave me an impish glance. "I'd say no, but you got me addicted. Thanks! See you next year!"

We sold every biscochito in the house, apart from my stash. The last few dozen went out the door as soon as I boxed them, still warm.

At four o'clock, I asked Dale and Ramon to help me set out the four dozen *farolitos* I had bought from my high school's marching band. I had originally planned to make them myself, but realized about midway through the month that I wouldn't have time. Fortunately, they were a popular fundraiser. The paper bags had been delivered that morning, already filled with an inch of sand and a votive candle, the top inch of the bag neatly folded down on the outside.

We set them along the front *portal* and on both sides of the path up from the gate, each bag a long step apart from its neighbor. I took great pleasure—and amused my employees—by using my marching band training to pace them out. With long butane lighters, we lit the candles, a less romantic but safer and more efficient method than the matches I remembered using as a kid, when the whole family would make *farolitos* for our house and set them out together.

Standing by the front door, I gazed at the lines of glowing paper bags, warmth filling my heart. This was Christmas. The candles would glow brighter as the evening deepened, and last a good five or six hours before they finally burned out. Fortunately, it wasn't windy, so the bags shouldn't catch fire. I stepped inside to turn out the front light. Our last group of reservations had already been seated; they would see this on their way out, after enjoying their tea.

Gradually, the tearoom wound down not only for the day, but for the holiday. Four days! I hoped to spend at least one of them in bed.

I helped the staff finish their tasks and saw them off, giving them their checks and wishing them well. Nat reminded me to be at her house with Tony by 10:30 the next morning for brunch. Christmas Day, I realized. It was Christmas! I'd been saying "Merry Christmas" for months, it felt like, but now it was actually here.

Kris, who had stayed late to make up the final deposit, only frowned a little when I explained my donation to Esperanza and presented the receipt to her. She shot me one skeptical look, then said, "Well, it's a deduction. That'll look good on the taxes."

She departed with a bulging bank bag discreetly hidden inside her coat. Everyone else was gone except Mick, still finishing the last of the dishes, and Dee, who had stayed to keep him company. I joined them in the kitchen, after making sure the front door was locked and the notice that we were closed until Tuesday was prominently displayed.

Dee grinned at me. "We made it!"

"Yes," I said, and felt relief wash through me. Now all I had to do was spend the evening with Tony's family, and tomorrow morning with mine.

I turned off the house stereo, thinking gratefully of the different music it would play next week. Dee and I grabbed clean towels and wiped down the china as Mick finished washing it. When the last piece was put away, I gave the Gallaghers their checks and saw them off, then locked up.

Peace. I made the rounds, not because anything needed doing, but because I wanted to visit the silent parlors. Enjoying the aroma of the piñon coals gently fading in the fireplaces, I turned off the lights on the trees for safety, but left the ones in the windows on, because it was Christmas Eve.

In my childhood, I had been enchanted by the Christmas tree. One year my parents let me spend the night under the tree in a sleeping bag, as my brother had done a few years before. I had lain awake, looking at the colored lights, hoping to witness Santa's arrival, finally succumbing to sleep. It was magical. The morning swept away the magic, replacing it with family love and the child's joy of presents. I didn't remember now what the presents were; what I remembered was peering up through the needles of the tree at the colors gleaming off of beloved family ornaments, some of which now hung on the tree in the center of my main parlor.

Checking the clock, I saw that I had half an hour before Tony was supposed to arrive. We'd agreed that he would ride with me to his mother's place for Christmas dinner, then we'd go for a walk along Canyon Road before meeting his family at the cathedral for the midnight mass. I went upstairs to change out of my fancy lace and into a simpler and warmer knit dress.

A small shopping bag stood waiting on my table along with the biscochitos. In defiance of Tony's orders, I had wrapped some very small gifts for Angela (a fairy ornament) and Tony's *abuela* (piñon fudge), because I felt certain in my soul that they would have gifts for me. It was Christmas.

My gift for Tony, the motorcycle gloves, would be given later, when he came home with me to get his bike.

Or possibly in the morning.

Smiling, I brushed my hair and made sure my face was presentable, then collected gifts, hat, coat, and purse, and went downstairs to wait in the dining parlor by the last warmth of the fireplace. I left the lights off, the glow of the back porch light softly illuminating the room through the sheers. The centerpiece of holly and ivy lay dark against the lace tablecloth. A gentle creak or two, of the staircase settling after my descent, might have frightened me months ago but was now familiar.

A little more than a year since I'd moved in. On a bright, cold day in mid-December I had arrived with a suitcase, a cooler full of miscellaneous perishables, and my favorite teapot, to take possession of my suite above the then-empty and still mostly imaginary tearoom.

Smiling, I gazed up at the chandelier gleaming softly above the table. Captain Dusenberry and I had been roommates for a while now. He'd been quiet this week, but that was normal. When the tearoom was at its most hectic, he was least likely to make himself known.

I had not had time or energy to follow up on the note I had found in Maria's diary. Maybe over the long weekend. I watched the crystals overhead, silently apologetic, hoping the captain under-stood. After so many years, he probably knew how to be patient.

The chandelier remained motionless.

I closed my eyes, enjoying my silent house. Old wood and old adobe surrounded me, gently radiating the warmth of their years along with the heat of the day's fires and sunlight. I breathed it all in gratefully, until the distant sound of a motorcycle roused me.

I met Tony at the door and demanded a hug. He gave it willingly, but briefly.

"We're late," he said.

"Let me get my things."

He followed me into the dining parlor and frowned at my packages as I put on my coat. I handed him the cookie boxes.

"Biscochitos for your mom."

I put on my hat and gloves, picked up purse and shopping bag, and led the way out the back door, locking it behind us. The sky was overcast, a soft, dark, windless gray. I turned the car's heater on and left the radio off. I'd had enough of Christmas music for now. After emerging rather warily from the driveway, I headed for Cerrillos Road.

"Any progress?" I asked.

"Yeah," Tony said. "We're waiting on a warrant. Heather Davis drives a white SUV, license HLV 229."

I nearly stomped on the brakes. Gripping the steering wheel, I took a deep breath.

"Oh, man."

"And I talked to Juana Duranes," Tony went on. "She picked Debbie's date out of my photo lineup."

"Not Dickie?"

"Nope. Justin Davis."

"Justin? *Justin* was dating Debbie?"

"Yep. Juana said they were pretty hot and heavy, too. She and Erica talked about it."

"That's right—Gina said Justin was cheating on Heather. But I never thought it would be with her sister!"

Well, *that* might be enough to make Heather want to murder somebody.

"So, not only was Debbie dating her sister's husband, but Erica knew about it," Tony said.

"And so did Dickie!" I said. "He dated Debbie in November—he went to their family Thanksgiving."

"Which is probably when Heather decided she'd had enough," Tony said grimly. "She went to Debbie's apartment to confront her."

"And Debbie, being Debbie, probably told Heather she was pregnant," I said.

With Justin's child.

"And Heather went ballistic," Tony said, nodding. "It wasn't premeditated. She used a knife from Debbie's kitchen. The others—Erica and Dickie—were premeditated. Damage control."

A wave of horrified pity for their unhappiness went through me. Debbie using her sister's husband to torment her, Dickie adding his own twist to the family's pain. Erica must have said something to Heather about it, and Heather decided she had to be silenced as well.

The violence had expanded wider and wider. Would it eventually have taken me? Possibly. I'd been asking questions, talking to Dickie and other classmates, and Heather had obviously been watching me. She must have followed me and Gina to the concert, and afterward, in her white SUV. Maybe she really *had* been trying to kill us!

I shivered, and silently obeyed Tony's directions the rest of the way to his mother's apartment, which was in a modest, two-story complex a block off the noisy, traffic-laden main drag that was Cerrillos Road. Tony led me to a door on the ground floor, next to a window whose curtains were open to display the top half of a Christmas tree covered with multicolored lights, ornaments, and tinsel.

Angela opened the door, welcoming us into the small apartment filled with warmth and the aromas of red chile, corn *masa*, and cinnamon-scented candles. Mrs. Aragón embraced me when I gave her the biscochitos, and from then on the evening was pure pleasure.

The only exception was that occasionally I remembered Debbie's tragic mess. Whenever this happened I glanced at Tony, and marveled at his ability to leave it behind and immerse himself in his family's celebration.

The Aragón women looked to him as the traditional head of their family. Angela was the possible exception—I saw a certain look in her eye now and then—but she neither said nor did anything to contradict her elders. I looked forward to spending a couple of hours with her over tea in January.

Dinner was a feast of tamales, *posole, refritos*, a *calabacitas* casserole (Angela's contribution) and rice, followed by biscochitos and hot cocoa. Presents were exchanged and enjoyed. I was right; I received a pair of white pillar candles (the perfect size for the candlesticks Tony had given me), a hat crocheted by Mrs. Aragón in shades of lavender and purple which I instantly tried on, and a carefully handwritten copy of *Abuela*'s recipe for tamales. I knew the value of these gifts—the time and care and thoughtfulness that went into them—and I was deeply grateful.

After a couple of hours, *Abuela* withdrew for a nap to recruit herself for the midnight mass. Tony and I made our farewells, promising to meet the family at the cathedral.

"Get there early," Mrs. Aragón warned. "It fills up by eleven thirty."

"We'll be there, Mama," Tony said.

"You be careful," she said, kissing his cheek. "All those crazy drivers."

Tony glanced at me over her shoulder. "We will."

She turned to me and paused just a second before pulling me into a hug. I felt her lips softly brush my cheek. "You keep my boy in line, *hija*. Don't let him push you around."

Surprised into a cough of laughter, I nodded. "Yes, ma'am."

Driving back into the heart of town, I was quiet. Debbie's murder, that whole mess, kept invading my thoughts, and I didn't want to talk about it.

"They like you," Tony said after a while. Meaning his family, I surmised.

"Well, I like them, too. And *Abuela* didn't say anything nasty about me in Spanish."

"I never said she'd be nasty. She just likes to gossip about Anglos in front of them and watch their faces. She cut it out the minute she realized you understood what she was saying."

I parked across the street from the entrance to Canyon Road, in a big parking lot near Kakawa Chocolate House. Since the windows of that most excellent establishment revealed a jam-packed crowd inside, I was glad that we'd already had cocoa with Tony's family. We walked past Kakawa and waited for a gap in traffic to cross the busy street.

Canyon Road had been blocked off to vehicle traffic for the evening, and was a pleasant contrast to the brightly lit boulevard we left behind. Streetlights and bright porch lights were turned off: *farolitos* lined the street and the walls, and even the roofs of many of the old adobe buildings, the candles inside the paper bags glowing with a golden warmth that took me back to childhood. The evening had remained calm, fortunately, so none had been blown over or caught fire.

Clusters of people bundled in warm coats strolled up and down the street, dark silhouettes against the glow of the *farolitos*. Several galleries were still open, serving hot cider and coffee to catch the tourists who were up late and looking for amusement. Tony and I walked on, farther up the street, where the crowds were thinner.

"I want to thank you," Tony said as we passed the Compound. "This case broke because of you."

I hunched my shoulders, pleased. "Glad I could help."

"Gotta admit, it was frustrating. There's stuff I just can't tell you, and to be honest I'm not supposed to discuss investigations with you at all."

I pressed my lips together and took a breath before answering. "Except when I'm a suspect."

"You were eliminated early."

"This time."

"Well," he said with an ironic laugh, "you can't be a suspect in every investigation."

"I sincerely hope not."

"It's a small town, but it's not *that* small."

We paused at a driveway where a *luminaria* was burning. A couple of people sat beside it in lawn chairs, enjoying the warmth of the tiny bonfire.

"*Feliz Navidad*," one of them said to us after a moment.

"Merry Christmas," Tony replied, moving on.

This part of the road was steeper and narrower, and not many people were walking up this high. The *farolitos* became patchy; some were dark, their candles burned out. I could see my breath as we slowly climbed. It was all houses now; we'd left the galleries behind on the lower road. Tony took out a flashlight and switched it on, lighting our way. Its beam revealed tiny snowflakes swirling. Now that I saw them, I was aware of their cold, damp caress on my face.

We came to another *luminaria*, this one unattended and burning low. It was just inside the end of a driveway, in a space well-cleared and sheltered on one side by an adobe wall. Against that wall, out of range of any sparks, a small stack of split piñon logs stood ready. Tony took a couple of sticks from it and added them to the fire. I inhaled the fragrant smoke that arose as they caught, and stood enjoying the warmth from the new bright flames.

Only in New Mexico would you find a law enforcement officer adding fuel to an unattended fire. But it was important: the *luminarias* were there to guide the Christ Child.

"So anyway," Tony said, holding his hands out to the heat, "I really appreciate your help, and I really can't keep doing it this way."

A flicker of sadness went through me. Had his superiors warned him off?

"It's just…"

I turned toward him, saw frustration in his face. "I understand," I said.

He swallowed. "I'm not good at this."

"It's OK."

"No, I mean…I mean, I want to change it."

I waited, lost now, but I knew he needed space to sort his thoughts.

"Aw, hell," he muttered.

"We can still see each other," I said. "We don't have to talk about your work."

"But I want to talk about it. I *need* to."

"Well…"

"See the only way it'll work is if we're married," he said in a rush. "Then I could talk to you more. Do you—do you want to marry me?"

I stared, astonished.

"Ay, I did it wrong!" He moved away, took a step out of the firelight.

"Tony—wait—"

Slowly he came back, his face pinched with anxiety, dark eyes afraid of my answer. My heart was trying to do gymnastics in my chest.

"I—I think I do," I said.

"You think?"

"Well I hadn't—I mean, I wasn't expecting…"

"I asked too soon."

I shook my head slowly. "Not necessarily."

"But you're not sure. You need to be sure."

His gaze in the flickering firelight was intent, silently demanding. I knew that look. He needed reassurance, because uncertainty was painful.

I took a breath. "Well, that's what engagements are for."

His lips parted. "Is that a yes?"

Something blossomed in my chest. Relief? Joy? I smiled.

"That's a yes."

Biscochitos

This traditional treat, the official state cookie of New Mexico, is a holiday favorite.

Ingredients:

6 c flour
3 t baking powder
1 t salt

1 lb lard*
1½ c sugar
2 t whole anise seed

2 eggs, beaten
½ c+ brandy (or whiskey, or juice)

Coating:

1 c sugar   4 T cinnamon

*Lard is traditional, but coconut oil or shortening may be substituted.
Butter contains water and will produce a less flaky texture.*

Preparation: Preheat oven to 350°F. In medium bowl, mix flour, baking powder, and salt. Set aside.

In large mixing bowl, cream lard, sugar, and anise. Blend in eggs. Alternate adding dry ingredients and brandy. If dough is crumbly, add more liquid a little at a time until it pulls together. Dough will be stiff.

Knead a little, then roll out to ¼ inch and cut. (Fleur-de-lis is reportedly the traditional shape, but I never saw one. A friend suspects Bishop Lamy of starting the rumor. Rounds, crescents, and round flowers are more common, but any shape will do.) Bake on ungreased cookie sheet for 10-12 minutes or until lightly browned.

While cookies are baking, mix sugar and cinnamon in small bowl. Cool cookies slightly, then gently coat in cinnamon sugar. I like to lay one on the mixture, cover it over and press gently, then lift the cookie out with a fork, letting excess sugar fall. Set on plate or rack to cool completely. Makes about five dozen.

Wisteria Tearoom
upper floor

Kris's Office

Master Bath

Kitchenette

Sitting Area

Ellen's Office

Sitting
Area

Bedroom

Ellen's Suite

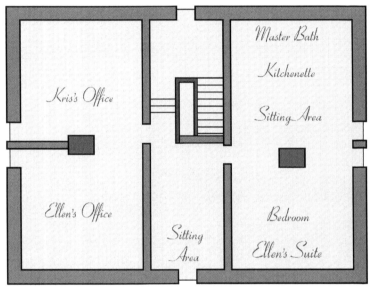

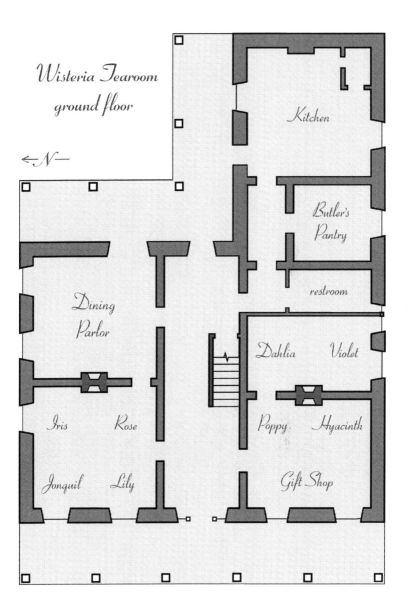

Wisteria Tearoom
ground floor

← N —

Kitchen

Butler's
Pantry

restroom

Dining
Parlor

Dahlia   Violet

Iris   Rose

Poppy   Hyacinth

Jonquil   Lily

Gift Shop

Wisteria Tearoom Staff

Ellen Rosings	Owner
Kris Overland	Office Manager
Julio Delgado	Chef
Mai Hanh	Assistant Chef
Ramon Garcia	Assistant
Mick Gallagher	Dish Washer
Dee Gallagher	Server
Rosa Garcia	Server
Iz Naranjo	Server
Dale Whittier	Server

Ellen's Family

Joe Rosings	Brother
Nat Salazar	Aunt
Manny Salazar	Uncle

⚜ Ellen's Friends & Associates

Gina Fiorello	Bestie
Tony Aragón	Beau
Willow Lane	Spirit Tour Guide

Tony's Family

Angela Aragón	Sister
Dolores Aragón	Mother
"Abuela" Aragón	Grandmother

About the Author

photo by Chris Krohn

PATRICE GREENWOOD was born and raised in New Mexico, and remembers when the Santa Fe Plaza was home to more dusty dogs than trendy art galleries. She has been writing fiction longer than she cares to admit, perpetrating over twenty published novels in various genres. She uses a different name for each genre, thus enabling her to pretend she is a Secret Agent.

She loves afternoon tea, old buildings, gourmet tailgating at the opera, ghost stories, costumes, and solving puzzles. Her popular Wisteria Tearoom Mysteries are colored by many of these interests. She is presently collapsed on her chaise longue, sipping Wisteria White tea and planning the next book in the series.

Made in the USA
San Bernardino, CA
27 June 2018